10ᵀᴴ ANNIVERSARY

Special thanks to our well-wishers, who have contributed their congratulations and support.

"The best historicals, the best romances. Simply the best!"
—Dallas Schulze

"Bronwyn Williams was born and raised at Harlequin Historicals. We couldn't have asked for a better home or a more supportive family."
—Dixie Browning and Mary Williams, w/a Bronwyn Williams

"I can't believe it's been ten years since *Private Treaty*, my first historical novel, helped launch the Harlequin Historicals line. What a thrill that was! And the beat goes on...with timeless stories about men and women in love."
—Kathleen Eagle

"Nothing satisfies me as much as writing or reading a Harlequin Historical novel. For me, Harlequin Historicals are the ultimate escape from the problems of everyday life."
—Ruth Ryan Langan

"As a writer and reader, I feel that the Harlequin Historicals line always celebrates a perfect blend of history and romance, adventure and passion, humor and sheer magic."
—Theresa Michaels

"Thank you, Harlequin Historicals, for opening up a 'window into the past' for so many happy readers."
—Suzanne Barclay

"As a one-time 'slush pile' foundling at Harlequin Historicals, I'll be forever grateful for having been rescued and published as one of the first 'March Madness' authors. Harlequin Historicals has always been *the* place for special stories, ones that blend the magic of the past with the rare miracle of love for books that readers never forget."
—Miranda Jarrett

"A rainy evening. A cup of hot chocolate. A stack of Harlequin Historicals. Absolute bliss! Happy tenth Anniversary and continued success."
—Cheryl Reavis

"Happy birthday, Harlequin Historicals! I'm proud to have been a part of your ten years of exciting historical romance."
—Elaine Barbieri

"Harlequin Historicals novel are charming or disarming with dashes and clashes. These past times are fast times, the gems of romances!"
—Karen Harper

FLINT HILLS BRIDE

CASSANDRA AUSTIN

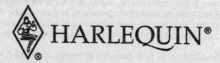

HARLEQUIN®

TORONTO • NEW YORK • LONDON
AMSTERDAM • PARIS • SYDNEY • HAMBURG
STOCKHOLM • ATHENS • TOKYO • MILAN • MADRID
PRAGUE • WARSAW • BUDAPEST • AUCKLAND

For Megan,
our family's most recent bride

ISBN 0-373-29030-6

FLINT HILLS BRIDE

Copyright © 1998 by Sandra Detrixhe

Jake felt too damn good to even consider apologizing.

He glanced Emily's way and discovered her scowl had deepened. "What?" she demanded. "Why are you grinning?"

"You first," he said, making an effort to be serious. "Why are you frowning?"

"You're impossible," she said. "I should hate you!"

"Why?" He truly was bewildered now. "Because I left you? Or because I kissed you?"

"Yes. Yes. And for other reasons. I should hate you. But I can't!" She slammed her gloved hand down on the saddle horn, and it made the softest of thuds.

He laughed. He knew he shouldn't. He should take her unhappiness seriously, no matter how little sense it made. "You're angry because you can't hate me? Of course you can't hate me. We've been friends forever. That's what friends do. They get angry, and then they forgive each other."

"I don't *want* to forgive you," she muttered....

Chapter One

Kansas, 1881

"Am I to understand I'm under arrest?" Emily's gaze went from the deputy's badge to the serious green eyes.

"Well, I'm not sure, ma'am. You say you're Emily Prescott, but you don't fit the description. I was expecting a tomboy in braids."

"Very funny, Jake."

His flash of a smile faded as she glared at him.

Noisy activity surrounded them on the train depot's platform. Emily barely noticed. She wrapped her cloak more tightly around her and regarded Jake Rawlins with growing irritation. "My parents sent you, didn't they? I can just hear them. 'Take her to her brother's ranch, and see that she stays there.' 'Telegraph immediately if she doesn't get off the train.' It amounts to house arrest, Jake!"

She brushed past him to find her trunk. He followed, of course. She hadn't expected to get away from him, merely to be out from under his scrutiny long enough to get her temper under control. None of this was Jake's fault.

"I'm not your guard," he said softly. "I'm just your ride to the ranch."

"And that explains why they sent you, Deputy?" She found her trunk. A sudden wave of exhaustion made her turn and sit on it, clasping her gloved hands on her lap.

He moved to stand in front of her. "I volunteered, Emily. I'm headed the same way you are. Remember, my parents live on your brother's ranch."

She sighed, regretting her short temper as she always did. "I remember, Jake. But I visit the ranch regularly, and I've hardly seen you the last three years."

A somber nod acknowledged the truth of the statement. "I'm trying to correct that," he said. "I heard you were coming early for Christmas, and it seemed like a perfect excuse to take a vacation and spend time with…my family."

Emily noticed the hesitation. Perhaps there was a rift between him and Martha or Perry that she had not been aware of. Perhaps he would be more understanding than she had expected. She cocked her head to one side as she looked up at him. "So that's all they told you? That I would be coming in today?"

After a long moment, he slowly shook his head.

The anger swept over her again, and she came to her feet. She didn't know if she wanted to scream or run. Before she could do either, he placed his hands on her shoulders. She was momentarily surprised by how gentle the touch was, then wondered why. Jake had never been anything but kind to her.

"We've known each other since we were babies, Emily. I thought we were friends. Have things changed so much?"

His soft voice dissolved her anger, leaving only defeat in its wake. "Everything's changed, Jake. Look around you. When my parents were separated, I came here once or twice a year to be with my father. This was a little place called Cottonwood Station. Now it's a town called Strong."

He was eyeing her quizzically, and she had to laugh at herself. "Which has nothing to do with anything, I suppose, except that all the way here I kept wishing I was still the little girl you remember. I wanted to get off the train and find everything as it was, for life to be simple again."

The deep worry that was always with her rose to the surface. She turned away to keep from revealing it to Jake. She had grown accustomed to hiding it with anger until she didn't like herself anymore. "I'm ready to go now," she said. "And, Jake—" she turned back to face him "—it's good to see you again."

Jake made Emily wait inside the depot near the stove while he loaded her trunk into the boot at the back of the buggy. He had ridden out to the ranch the day before to bring the buggy into town. Emily's brother, Christian, had suggested he use the wagon since Emily might have more than one trunk, but Jake had declined. The buggy offered more protection from the cold wind than the wagon. He would make two trips if he had to, but Emily would be as comfortable as he could make her.

He hadn't really been too busy to come home for

holidays the past three years. He had avoided the ranch when he knew Emily would be there. His hopeless attraction for her would fade, he had reasoned, if he didn't have to look at her. The irony was it had almost worked. Then he had heard she was in trouble, and reason had gone out the window.

In three years she had only grown more beautiful. At eighteen, her face had lost a little of its plumpness making her dark brown eyes more striking. They sparkled when she teased, as they always had, and her expressive lips that smiled and pursed and pouted looked as kissable as they did in his fantasies.

He shook himself and hurried into the depot. Emily was chatting with another patron, and he let her finish as he collected the blanket he had hung over a chair near the stove. "Are you ready to go?" he asked when she turned toward him.

She moved to walk outside with him. "Do you need anything in town?" he asked, handing her up into the buggy. "Are you hungry?"

She shook her head. "Mama sent a lunch with me," she said. "But thanks."

It was foolish to cherish the smile she gave him, but he would readily admit to being a fool where Emily Prescott was concerned. At least her anger of a few minutes before seemed to be forgotten. He climbed up beside her and unfolded the warm blanket, tucking it across her lap.

"That was sweet of you, Jake," she said. She sounded more amused than grateful.

"Easy enough to do," he said, shaking the lines and starting the horse forward. Now he was feeling foolish to the point of embarrassment. She had an annoying knack for doing that.

She laughed, and he risked a glance at her. The teasing grin took him back so quickly he could have sworn he was seventeen and she twelve.

"You better be careful or you'll spoil me," she said.

"Oh, no, not me. Somebody—everybody—else took care of that long ago."

She laughed, wrapping herself around his upper arm. "Didn't you help them at all, Jake?"

The face that turned up to him was so appealing he wanted to kiss it. Or at least throw off his glove and run his fingers down her soft, pale cheeks. He gripped the reins more tightly. "I guess I did my share," he admitted softly.

The teasing light went out of her eyes, and she turned her face away. He was being too serious, and their relationship had never had much room for that. But he couldn't pretend he wasn't worried about her.

He took a deep breath, letting the bite of the cold air clear his head. His voice was even when he began. "Emily, your parents sent you here because of some young man." She let go of his arm and moved away from him, and he was sorry. "Tell me your side."

"My side! Did they write to you? Tell me what they said!"

Jake kept his voice quiet. "I talked to Christian. He said the fella's unemployed, reckless, wild—"

"What!"

"And in jail for tearing up a neighbor's yard."

She kept her face turned away from him, hiding

even her profile behind the hood of her cloak. He waited patiently for her to speak.

"It was an accident," she murmured. "It's all a big misunderstanding."

"He accidentally rode through their rose garden on horseback? He accidentally pulled up a fence? He—"

"Enough!"

Jake waited for her to decide what, if anything, she would tell him. It was a long ride to the ranch, and he had hoped she would confide in him. He couldn't imagine why he had thought she would. What was he to her anyway? A childhood playmate? Something less than a brother? Certainly not what he wanted to be.

The team clopped along the road, creating a monotonous rhythm. A rabbit darted across their path and disappeared in the tall grass. The buggy creaked and rattled softly. Jake heard his back teeth grind together and made an effort to relax. After several minutes he gave up hope of hearing any more from Emily.

"I don't believe it happened the way they say," she said, startling him.

"What do you believe?"

He heard her take a deep breath. He didn't dare look at her for fear she would read the pain on his face. He kept his eyes on the track and waited.

"Anson is a good man," she began. "He isn't reckless and wild. He just believes in having fun. Old people can't understand that. He's going to work in his father's flour mill, but there isn't any room for him yet."

Jake cast her a skeptical glance, but she was turned away.

"The neighbor that accused him of tearing up his garden is a grouchy old man who doesn't get along with anyone. Even Papa doesn't like him."

Jake resisted the urge to turn toward her, hoping she would continue, afraid she wouldn't if she knew what he was feeling. He turned his gaze toward the sky. It was blue, he thought irrelevantly. Blue in December. It should be gray, damned gray.

When she had remained silent for several minutes he tried to prompt her into more details. "Your parents objected to Anson Berkeley before this incident."

"They want to keep me a baby and would have objected to anyone. His parents have at least as much money as mine do. There's no reason to treat him the way they do."

Jake schooled his features and turned to watch her. He was rewarded a moment later when she glanced at him. He hoped she read the honest concern in his face; he read indecision in hers. "Emily," he said softly, "I'm your friend. Tell me about him."

She wrapped her arm around his and rested her head on his biceps, sighing deeply. "I know you're my friend, Jake. In fact, you may be my only friend. Everyone else is ready to judge both Anson and me."

"Not me," he lied. "You're both innocent till proven guilty." He had to swallow hard before he could ask, "Are you in love with him?"

Her sigh sounded different this time. "Yes, I love him. And he loves me. We've promised to love each other forever."

Jake didn't want to think about the implications of that statement. His pulse quickened. From her touch? From anger?

Unmindful of his pain, she continued, "He's so handsome, and exciting. I've never known anyone like him."

Jake heard his back teeth crunch together again. He spoke to the team, urging them to increase their infuriating pace.

"He takes me places," she went on, "that I'd never get to go if my parents had their way."

"Places?" He hoped his voice didn't sound as furious as he felt. Where the hell had this bastard taken his Emily?

"Clubs. Where there's music and dancing and laughter."

"And drinking? That's illegal now. They voted in prohibition last year, Emily."

She pulled away from him again. "You're no different than the rest."

"Well, maybe all of us are right!" He regretted it immediately.

They rode for miles without either of them saying a word. The sound of the plodding hooves and creaking buggy was broken only by the brief chirp of a robin too stupid to have flown south. Jake watched it fly off into the ridiculously blue sky.

Jake knew he should have just listened, but his own feelings kept getting in the way. He told himself that if Emily loved this man he couldn't be all bad. Her happiness was what was important. His jealousy was jeopardizing their friendship, and they needed to stay friends if he was going to help her.

"I'm sorry," he said finally. "You're right. I have no call to judge. If Anson Berkeley is the man you want, then I hope things work out for you."

She murmured her thanks, but didn't move back toward him. He wanted to wrap his arm around her and pull her against his side, but he knew she would resist.

After many minutes he cleared his throat. "Ma packed some lemonade if you're thirsty."

"I don't want any."

"Well, Ma's not going to buy that. She's going to think I forgot to offer it to you."

She turned and glared. "Tell her you ruined my appetite."

At least she was looking at him. "I guess I can accept the blame there. But I did apologize." He pulled the basket out from under the seat. "If you don't want any, I'll have to drink all the evidence. If it's a choice between a bellyache and being in trouble with Ma, well…"

She hadn't smiled, but she was having to work to hold it back. "You could just pour it on the ground."

"You would let me do that? With lemonade? You *are* mad at me!"

She finally laughed, and he felt relief that was clearly more than the situation warranted. He handed her one of the small jars from its straw nest in the basket.

She took it and drank a little before screwing the lid back on and placing the jar between her feet. She didn't seem quite as tense as she had earlier, and he hoped that meant she had forgiven him. Still, as he waited for her to talk to him again, he tried to think of something to say, something neutral that would prove he was her friend. Finally he accepted the silence, though he didn't enjoy it. The ride to the ranch seemed to take longer than it ever had before.

Emily wished she hadn't told Jake anything. He was as closed minded as the rest. For a moment she had thought she detected some jealousy in his reactions. But surely she had imagined it. He was just being stupid and brotherly like Arlen had and Christian, no doubt, would.

Go where we say! See who we say! Do as we say! She was sick of it. Anson had come at just the right time to rescue her from the boring life they all had planned for her.

And she would be with Anson again. There was no question about that. One way or another, they would be together.

She let her mind drift back to the first time they had met, reliving the excitement of his eyes on her, the adventure of being included in his close little group, the wonder at being singled out as his favorite, then his love. She tried to push away the apprehension that prickled the back of her mind.

She was so lost in thought that when she felt the buggy turn off the road she looked up in surprise. The huge rock house with its many balconies filled her with sudden nostalgia. They rode up the hill and around the house to the second-level entrance. Before Jake had even pulled the buggy to a stop, Christian was there to greet her. He lifted her out, hugging her to his chest and spinning her around as he had done since she was a child.

He set her back on the ground but waited a moment to let her go, giving her his familiar dimpled smile. "Get inside where it's warm, muffin," he said, guiding her toward the door, with his arm around her shoulder. "Jake and I'll get the trunk."

She spared Jake one last glance and, though his father had joined him, his eyes were on her. She wondered what he was thinking then decided she would just as soon not know.

Christian's pretty wife, Lynnette, opened the back door and welcomed her inside with a kiss on her cheek. Two little children peeked from behind her skirts as she helped Emily out of her cloak, scarf and gloves.

"Hello, Willa. Hello, Trevor." Emily crouched down and tried to coax them out. "Do you remember me?"

Trevor grinned and buried his face in a fistful of his mother's skirt, but Willa stepped forward. "I 'member you. You're Aunt Emily. Trevor's just a dumb ol' baby and doesn't 'member nothin'."

Lynnette pried her skirt free and lifted the boy, positioning him around her protruding belly. Another child was due in three months. "Let's get inside by the fire," she said. "You must be freezing."

Willa took Emily's hand. "Mama said it was too cold to go outside and meet you, but it wasn't, was it?"

"It's pretty cold," Emily said. "I think I'll ask Martha for some tea."

"I'll take care of it," Lynnette said. "You go on in and make yourself at home."

"It's not too cold for Papa to go outside and meet

you,'' Willa observed, dragging Emily into the living room.

"Papa's doing chores," Emily said, laughing at Willa's pout. She was a perfect combination of her parents, with her mother's fine features and her father's blond hair. Trevor was the opposite, a dark-haired version of Christian, dimples and all.

"I can do the chores," the little girl insisted.

"I bet you can," Emily said, moving to stand before the fire. "Though why you would want to is beyond me."

"I'm almost five," Willa said, explaining everything.

Christian and Lynnette hadn't changed the living room much in the five years they had been married. Her father's books and artifacts had gone with him to Topeka and had been replaced by some of their own. The room bore traces of little children, but the furniture and its arrangement was essentially as it had always been, making her feel for just a moment as if she had stepped back in time.

Lynnette, with Trevor on her hip, joined them. "Martha will have the tea ready in a few minutes." She sat down and swung Trevor onto her lap. He grinned shyly at Emily.

Emily was trying to get him to say "Emily" when Jake and Christian brought her trunk through the room and up the stairs. She tried not to watch them. They had shed their coats at the door, and it was disconcerting to realize that Jake was a full-grown man. Though why this troubled her she wasn't sure.

"I'll help," yelled Willa, running to catch up with the men. She pushed her little hands against the trunk.

"Run around in front, biscuit, and get the door," Christian suggested.

Emily laughed. "She's his biscuit and I'm his muffin."

"All his favorite females he nicknames after food."

Emily grinned at her sister-in-law. "And you are…?"

Lynnette grimaced and adjusted her snug dress. "Right now I'm his dumpling."

Emily laughed. She hadn't realized her gaze had gone back to the men working their way up the open stairway until Lynnette spoke again.

"Jake's taking two weeks off to visit his parents. He tries to visit often, but he doesn't usually stay long. They've really looked forward to this."

Emily nodded. She hoped that meant his parents would keep him so busy she wouldn't see much of him.

Emily made a face at Trevor, trying to coax another smile out of him. She didn't want to talk about Jake. But she didn't want to talk about herself, either. She wondered what her parents had said about her and Anson in the letter that preceded her. She would probably find out soon enough.

Trevor mimicked Emily's wrinkled nose and scrunched lips, making Emily laugh. Willa's high-pitched giggle and the sound of footsteps on the stairs caught her attention. Christian, with Willa on his shoulders, turned in their direction at the bottom of the stairs. Jake, without a glance at her, went the other way toward the kitchen.

"We're glad to have you here, muffin," Christian

said, joining them. He set Willa on the floor, then kissed Emily's cheek. "I'll finish the chores then we can talk."

As Christian left the room, Emily sighed and slumped into a chair. "Another lecture?" she asked her sister-in-law.

"From Christian? I doubt it," Lynnette replied. "But you know your brother. He feels responsible for everyone, and he's very worried about you. He wants to hear your side."

"Where have I heard that before?" she muttered.

"Emily, I'm the first one to say a woman should be allowed to make up her own mind, but you're young and the things we hear about this young man are not good. We want to be sure it's you making the decisions, not this young man."

Martha, with a tray of tea and teacups, saved her from having to make a response. Willa declared it a tea party and kept the women busy moving tables and chairs to accommodate the younger guests. By the time the tea was gone Emily could honestly claim fatigue and retire to her room.

She sat down on the bed, her mind in too much turmoil to try to rest. She eyed the trunk that she knew she should unpack, but even thinking about it seemed to take too much energy. She let her eyes roam the room. The holidays she had spent here the past few years seemed to blend together in her memory, but the summers when she was a child were as distinct as separate photographs.

She sat and recalled when the quilt, the picture on the wall, the little writing desk had each been bought and added to the room. Her eyes fell on a doll propped beside a row of books on the shelf above the desk. She had been six when her father had bought it. She had taken it back and forth between the ranch and Topeka for several years. Then when she was twelve, she had left it here.

She lifted the doll from the shelf, unconscious of having moved toward it. She smoothed aside the mangled hair and smiled down at the painted face. This had been her baby. In a display of vanity she had named it Emily.

She felt tears forming in her eyes and tried to blink them away. It was too early to know, too early yet to worry. And besides, Anson loved her. It would all work out. They would convince their families somehow and be married before the baby came.

She put the doll back on the shelf, determined not to think about it, and resolutely turned her attention to her trunk. She was nearly unpacked when she heard a knock on the door.

"Can I come in, muffin?"

She slid the drawer closed as she answered, turned and waited for her brother to enter. He closed the door behind him and opened his arms to her.

She ran to him, accepting his offer of comfort. He stroked her hair and rocked her gently. "I've been worried since I got Pa's letter." She heard the rumble of his voice in his chest under her ear. "I guess I wish you'd stay a little girl forever."

She drew away so she could see his face. "I can't," she stated. "I'm grown, and I'm in love. Why make things hard for me?"

"The man's in jail." He cut off her protest with a

finger on her lips. "We don't want to see anyone break your heart."

"Let me go back to him."

He shook his head. "It's hard for me to deny you anything, but our parents have forbidden you to contact him, and I have to say I agree with them."

She pulled out of his arms and crossed the room, moving aside the curtain that hung in front of the glass balcony door and looked down on the brown valley below.

"Emily, they'll be here in two weeks. We can talk it all out then. If you still feel the same, I'll take your side."

"I don't want to wait," she said.

"If it's love, it'll survive two weeks."

She swung around to face him. "But he needs me now!"

Christian seemed only saddened by her outburst. "I'm sorry, Emily," he said.

She scowled at him as he left her room. Two weeks wouldn't make any difference to her parents. Christian's arguments probably wouldn't, either. Even her pregnancy—if there was a pregnancy—might not make them see reason. One of her friends from school had confided in her parents and had been sent to a maternity sanitarium. She had come home after the baby was born—a baby she was never even given a chance to see.

No, she couldn't count on her parents. Or Christian. If she was going to be with Anson, she would have to do something herself.

Emily had hoped to spend the rest of the afternoon alone, but only minutes after Christian left, there was another knock followed by a loud whisper. "Are you sleeping?"

Emily opened the door and Willa flounced in. "Mama put Trevor down for a nap, and now she's writing."

Emily smiled at the girl's sour face. Lynnette wrote love stories under the name Silver Nightingale. It had created quite a sensation when the family had first heard about it, though they were used to it now.

"I know!" Willa declared, trying to snap her fingers. "I'll go make cookies."

"You will?" Emily was always surprised at the girl's self-confidence. "Have you made them by yourself before?"

"No, but I can. I'll show you how, if you want."

Emily laughed and took the child's hand. While they went down the stairs, one step at a time, Willa related all the times she had helped make cookies, cakes and pies. By the time they rounded the bottom of the stairs and went through the dining room, Emily was almost convinced that the girl could make the treat herself.

She pushed through the kitchen door with a chattering Willa behind her and came face-to-face with Jake. The little girl skipped around her and headed toward Martha at the other end of the room. Emily stood staring at Jake.

After a moment she realized that he was actually several feet away and the plank table separated them. Somehow their eyes had locked in such a way as to minimize the distance. It was disconcerting, and she made an effort to shake it off.

She tore her eyes from his face and only then did she realize what he was doing. On the table were several piles of Martha's dried flowers and a half-filled vase.

She grinned at him. "Here's a talent I wasn't aware of. Is this how you keep yourself busy between chasing desperados?"

He looked down at the flowers as if surprised to find them there. "I'm afraid you've caught me," he said. "I'm arranging flowers without the first idea of what I'm doing."

She laughed and joined him on his side of the table. "Are these for the dining table?"

He nodded.

"And what are these for?" She slid a pair of scissors out from under a few dry stems.

"Trimming my nails?"

She chewed the inside of her cheek. It wouldn't do for him to think he had actually made her laugh. She was still mad at him. "Dear little Jake," she said, looking up into his face a good eight inches above hers. "Flowers on the table can't be so tall as to block people's view of one another. These must be trimmed."

She lifted the flowers out of the vase and prepared to start over. "You can run along now," she said, uncertain whether she really wanted him to go or not.

"Oh, no. If I leave this to you, Ma'll find me another job, and you might not come help."

Had she imagined his emphasis on *you*? She was suddenly warm. Did he really have to stand so close? She was starting to feel slightly light-headed. It was the faint scent of the flowers, surely. She trimmed two of the brittle stems to the appropriate length and handed him the scissors, forcing him with her elbow to move a step away. "Trim all of those," she said, indicating a pile of flowers, "the same length as these."

She watched him take four of the flowers, line their heads up and carefully measure them against one of her trimmed flowers. *Snap.* He handed her the newly trimmed bouquet, giving her a courtly bow.

The pleased look on his face made her want to laugh. He was acting more inept than he actually was. She dropped the flowers into the vase and waited for his next offering. It came quickly. He was having fun now, trying five and six at a time. Soon the vase was full, and she called a halt to his trimming.

He snapped the scissors in the air twice, as if unsatisfied. "Now what?" he asked.

"Now, nothing. We put it on the table."

"We're done? That wasn't so hard."

Emily lifted the bowl as Martha stopped beside the table. "That's lovely, children. I think the two of you should make the Christmas wreaths, you work so well together. Why don't you go set the table while I clean up here?"

Emily nodded and headed for the door. Jake went around her quickly and held it open. "See what you did," he whispered as she passed. He followed her into the dining room adding, "Now we have to make the wreaths. You should have let me do it wrong, and we'd never be asked again."

She laughed as she set the vase on the sideboard and bent to find a tablecloth inside. "What kind of attitude is that for a lawman?"

She rose and turned before he answered. She thought for an instant that the gleam in his eye was something other than teasing, but it was gone before she could determine what it was.

"Lawman," he said. "There's the key. One wrong move, and I was ready to arrest those flowers." He took an end of the cloth as she unfolded it and helped her spread it smoothly over the table. "But gussy up a wreath with pine cones and ribbons? I don't know."

"Come on, it'll be fun." Emily retrieved the vase of flowers and set it in the middle of the table. She realized she was looking forward to working on decorations with Jake. For the past few minutes, while they had made up the bouquet, she had been able to forget her worries.

She looked up to find him watching her again, that strange light back in his eyes. He turned quickly and headed for the sideboard. In a moment he was back with a handful of silverware. He didn't look at her, and she didn't speak, afraid of what she would see if she forced him to turn in her direction.

She went to gather the plates and napkins, aware of Jake in a way totally different from a few moments before. She felt almost an attraction. But that was absurd. She was merely missing Anson. Or responding to Jake's attraction to her.

How could this have happened, this sudden change in perspective? And she knew she wasn't imagining it.

Chapter Two

That night Jake lay on his bed in his parents' frame house not far from the Prescotts' stone mansion and studied the window-shaped moonlight on the ceiling. Why was he in love with Emily? Of course he had asked himself the same question many times over the years. There had never been a satisfactory answer.

Why *shouldn't* he be in love with her? Now there was a question with plenty of answers. His family worked for hers, for one. Her family was rich, and he was a two-dollars-a-day deputy. She was a city girl who played at being a rancher in the summer and on holidays. He was a country boy who would be lost in the city and make a fool of himself at any fancy social event.

And it wasn't as if she were perfect. She was more than a little spoiled, moderately lazy and very mouthy. Of course her sharp tongue had always been witty enough to be entertaining. He had usually felt he held his own in their verbal sparring.

Maybe she wasn't really lazy. He only saw her when she was on vacation. Her family had bragged about her high marks in school, and he assumed she worked for the grades. She was actually quite an accomplished horsewoman, and, according to his mother, wonderful with Christian's lively children.

Jake groaned and rolled to his side. Soon he would be convincing himself that she wasn't really spoiled, that she simply deserved all the attention and advantages she had gotten all her life.

The whys and why-nots of his feelings didn't change them. He wanted her. She made his pulse race simply by entering the room. She made him feel like a king when she smiled up at him. She filled his dreams.

God knows he had tried to feel the same way about other, more accessible, women. It never worked. He had compared them all to Emily, and they had all fallen short.

And now she was in love with someone else, someone totally unacceptable. God forgive him, but he had been thrilled to learn her family didn't approve. He could feel less guilty for hating the bastard.

It was going to be hell being with her every day, knowing she was thinking about Berkeley, but it was something he had to do. He had to protect her. He told himself he wasn't going to try to win her. He wasn't acceptable, either. Someday he would have to watch her marry someone else.

But not now. And not Berkeley.

Emily woke early the next morning. It was Sunday, and both families would be attending a little country church. Martha would have been up early preparing a box dinner to eat at the church. She wasn't sure if she was looking forward to seeing all her old neighbors or not.

She lay in bed listening to the soft voices coming from the other room. Lynnette was trying to keep Willa quiet, but it was impossible. The girl chattered nearly every waking moment.

Emily smiled as a few of the child's words reached her. "But Aunt Emily…" and "…almost Christmas!" Not the kind of things to encourage an excitable little girl to additional sleep.

She heard doors open and close and guessed Lynnette had gone into the nursery to get Trevor. After a few minutes of Willa's hushed chatter the little group went downstairs.

Emily considered getting up and joining them for breakfast, but she hated breakfast. In fact, just thinking about it made her feel queazy. And sharing the table with the two little ones last night didn't make her eager to repeat the experience. Oh, they were lovely children; in fact, they were adorable. But they were more than she could handle this early in the morning.

"What I have to look forward to," she muttered, then wished she hadn't. She wasn't sure yet.

She sat up in bed and fought back a wave of dizziness. "It's too early to get up," she muttered, holding her head. But the spell passed quickly.

After slipping into her robe, she crossed the room in her bare feet. She would write to Anson. She would address it in care of his family; they would see that he got it. Somehow she would figure out how to get the letter to the post office.

With pen and paper she told him how much she

loved him and missed him. She tried to relate how much she wanted them to be together, how she would be there with him if it were possible.

She didn't tell him about the baby. She needed to be sure then tell him in person. She didn't know how he would react. He had never mentioned marriage, though it had seemed to be understood between them. Still, it wasn't something she should tell him in a letter.

She did tell him, however, that she was confident he would soon be released, and, if not for her family's obstinacy, they would be together.

She wrote that she was staying with her brother, where the ranch was located, and how, from a certain direction, it was almost hidden by a hill. She described a spot where a trail behind the barn curved around the hillside. She promised to walk there every morning and think of him.

An hour later the carefully worded letter was finished. She left it on the desk and dressed and fixed her hair. When she was ready to go downstairs, she reread the letter, hoping it said what she needed it to, and folded and sealed it.

How was she to get it to town? Christian had said she was forbidden to contact Anson. Lynnette wasn't likely to defy her husband. Besides, she was so burdened with children she was next to no help. Martha or her husband, Perry? Too loyal to Christian.

Jake. His connection with her family was certainly less than his parents'. Would he sneak it into town for her? Did she dare ask him? He had made it clear, in spite of his apology, what he thought of Anson. Still he was her best hope.

She slipped the letter into the bodice of her dress, checking herself in the mirror to make sure it didn't show. Before she turned away she caught a glimpse of her face and stopped. Her eyes looked almost haunted. She forced a smile to her lips and blinked away the fear. If not for the constant worry, she could believe that being in love was good for her complexion. She almost glowed.

She started to turn toward the door, laughing off the silly thought when something else occurred to her. She hadn't imagined the look on Jake's face last night. He had feelings for her. Could she use them? She stared at her reflection. It seemed so dishonest, so...cruel. Yet.

She pictured herself on her wedding day, walking down the aisle while the guests snickered at her rounded belly. She couldn't wait until her family came to their senses. With a seductive wink at her reflection, she turned away.

The open stairway was situated in the center of the house, and Emily could look down on both the living room and dining room as she descended. Lynnette was in the living room retying a bow at the back of Willa's dress while the girl chattered an explanation of how it had come undone. Trevor sat on Martha's lap watching his sister with devoted attention.

Lynnette had just turned the little girl around and kissed her on the cheek when Emily entered the room. "Emily, dear," she said, moving to greet her. "We were going to let you sleep. Of course, we'd love to have you join us."

"Thanks," she said as Willa came to take her hand.

"I'll go along and keep my niece occupied. I'll see if I can make her giggle aloud in church."

"No. Not me. I'll make you giggle."

Their tickling match was interrupted by Christian's announcement that the buggy was ready. Wrapped in coats and hats, the women and children crowded into the seat while the men mounted horses to ride alongside.

Emily caught a glimpse of Jake as she settled Trevor on her lap, but he rode enough behind that she didn't see him again until they arrived. He helped his mother out of the buggy and, with his father, escorted her into the little stone church.

Through the service and the lunch that followed, she was never successful at catching his eye. She was conscious always of the stiff letter tucked inside her bodice.

Finally the families began to repack their dishes, gather up their children and start for home. Both Willa and Trevor were asleep by the time they reached the ranch. Lynnette carried Trevor up to his bed while Christian carried Willa inside. She awoke as soon as the warm air hit her. Christian left her in Emily's care and went out to take care of the horses.

"Let's play checkers," Willa suggested.

Emily agreed. There was little else she could do. Jake was no doubt helping with the horses, but if she went out to find him now, she would also find Christian. Jake would probably spend the rest of the day close to his family. Her chances of delivering the letter were almost nonexistent.

By the time Willa had the game board set up, Lynnette joined them in the living room. She offered to play the winner, giving Emily an excuse to beg off. Willa didn't seem to mind, and Emily, pleading a headache, escaped to her room.

Upstairs Emily pulled the letter from the bodice of her dress. How was she going to get it to Jake? Of course, even if she found a way, there was no guarantee he would agree to take it to the post office.

Feeling depressed, she dropped the letter onto her desk and removed her dress and shoes. She hadn't intended to sleep, but now that she was alone she found herself feeling increasingly tired. In a very short time she was asleep and didn't awaken until nearly supper time.

Martha was given the afternoon off on Sundays, and Emily found Lynnette in the kitchen preparing the evening meal. Both children were there offering their own brands of help. Emily gathered Trevor into her arms, but he decided to be shy and cried for his mother. Emily handed him to Lynnette and took over the cooking instead.

In short order the simple meal was ready, and they moved into the dining room to set the table and wait for Christian.

"I'm glad you came with us this morning, Emily," Lynnette said as they laid out plates and forks. "It went a long way to relieving Christian's mind."

"Was he afraid I'd run away while you were gone?"

Lynnette laughed, startling her. "No, I don't know as that occurred to him. He just imagined you moping around here all day. He doesn't think that would be good for you."

Emily straightened the place setting in front of her,

avoiding Lynnette's eyes. "I decided that time would pass more quickly if I was busy. Anson and I may not be together any sooner, but it'll seem like it."

Lynnette didn't respond and in a few minutes Christian joined them. The children required considerable attention during the meal, and Emily was left in peace. Later, she volunteered to do the dishes, shooing the family into the other room. Once the dining room and the kitchen were put back in order, she returned to her room, using an exciting novel as an excuse.

In her room, she found herself too keyed up to read. Instead she paced until she was tired enough to sleep.

The children woke Emily again the next morning. She listened to them go down the stairs and fought off a queazy feeling she was beginning to associate with the thought of breakfast. People weren't intended to get up this early, she decided. She lay in bed for a long time, plotting how she was going to talk to Jake alone. She would do it today if she had to help with chores herself, she decided.

Then she went over just what she might say to him, and what his response might be. She hoped to prepare herself with a convincing plea against any possible argument.

Finally she realized her planning had become an excuse to put off the doing and rose. Still she found herself taking her time getting dressed, wishing for some sudden flash of insight that would lead her to just the right words to convince Jake.

Before she left her room, she slipped the letter into the bodice of her dress as she had the day before. She had a brief picture of her doing that every morning from now till Christmas. No. She would get the letter to Jake today.

As she descended the stairs she noticed that both rooms below her were empty. She walked through the dining room to the kitchen, expecting to find Lynnette and the children there. Martha was alone.

"Where is everyone?" she asked, peering over Martha's shoulder at the bread she was kneading. She watched for a chance to grab a pinch of the yeasty dough. It was now late morning, and she was hungry.

"They're downstairs."

"Downstairs? You mean down-downstairs?" She brought her prize to her mouth and sucked her fingers. "You mean in the ballroom?"

"It's more like a playroom, now," Martha said.

Emily wanted to groan. The house had been built on a hillside with the middle floor at ground level in back. That and the top floor were the only parts of the house that were used regularly. The lowest level, with its bay windows overlooking the valley had been intended for entertaining. It had been built to please her mother, who hadn't stayed very long.

She considered going down but knew she had a much better chance of seeing Jake right here in the kitchen, since this was where he would come when his chores were done. Martha gratefully accepted her offer of help. Besides dinner preparations, Martha was starting the stew for supper. Emily spent the next hour cleaning and cutting vegetables saved from the fall garden.

She had discovered a few years back that she enjoyed cooking. The warmth of the kitchen and the pleasant smells were very relaxing. She found herself humming as she chopped.

She stopped midphrase when the door opened to admit Christian, Jake and Perry. A cold breeze came in with them, and she shivered. After she and Martha had greeted them all, she discovered Jake's eyes on her and felt herself warm too quickly. No, it was just the heat from the stove dispelling the chill.

Jake, his eyes still on her, grabbed Christian's arm. "What's she doing in the kitchen?" he whispered in awe.

Christian chuckled. "Strange sight, I know."

"I'm cutting up vegetables for tonight's stew." She managed to sound irritated even though they made her want to laugh. "What does it look like I'm doing?"

He removed his hat and came slowly toward her. "You're in the kitchen, Emily. Working."

She glared at him, aware of an audience. "And?"

He stopped near her, bringing cool air with him. Emily felt it caress her warm cheeks. She hadn't realized how much heat the stove was putting out until the past few moments.

"Are you feeling all right?" he asked.

She wondered if her face was flushed then realized he was still teasing her about working. "I'll have you know," she began, pointing at him with the tip of her knife, "I've become quite handy in the kitchen."

"I'm impressed." He grinned at her as he shed his coat. Instead of taking it and his hat to the hooks in the back hall, he leaned against the counter beside her. "You even kind of enjoy it, don't you?"

She returned her attention to the chopping board,

giving him a brief nod. When he didn't move away, she looked up to find him watching her. Christian had left, presumably to hang up his coat, and Perry was helping Martha set the kitchen table for the Rawlins's meal. She asked softly, "Can I talk to you after dinner?"

"Of course."

"I'll take a walk—" She had almost told him the path beyond the barn. That was where she hoped to meet Anson when he came for her. It wouldn't do for Jake to think of it as her usual place to walk. She suggested the opposite direction. "How about meeting me past your parents' house?"

"Fine," he said, and moved away.

She found herself breathing easier when he was gone. She didn't like deceiving her family, and she didn't like using Jake. That was why she had felt breathless when he was so close. That and the knowledge that he was attracted to her.

After dinner, Emily donned her cloak and gloves and left the house. Willa had wanted to go with her, and she felt guilty about leaving her, even though it would have been impossible to take her along.

She had tried at first to dissuade the child by telling her it was too cold, but Willa had said she had a warm coat and hat. Next she said she would be walking too far for a little girl, but Willa claimed to have walked miles without getting tired. Finally Lynnette had stepped in, telling her that sometimes grown-ups needed time alone.

She knew the path she followed well enough to walk without much attention to her surroundings and quickly sank deep in thought. Guilt for disappointing the child added to what she already felt and made her miserable. She couldn't lose courage now. Her family was giving her no choice.

She had to see Anson and tell him what she suspected. To do that, she had to mail his letter. And for that, she needed Jake.

A figure suddenly appeared in the path before her, and she stumbled back, losing her balance. A hand caught her arm, righting her before she fell. "I didn't mean to scare you."

"Jake." She sighed with relief. "I didn't realize I had come so far."

"You looked pretty distracted."

His breath made little white clouds in the cold air. He still held her arm; in fact, he had stepped closer. She had been this close to him before, but couldn't remember ever being quite so aware of him. Her stomach shivered, from the cold, she tried to tell herself, or from recently being startled. She should step away, pull herself together.

Instead she looked up into his eyes. It was a mistake. They burned into her, seared her to the core with their heat. She gasped as her body reacted.

His eyes softened immediately. "Are you all right?"

She nodded, stepping away. Of course she wasn't all right. Nothing was all right. She wanted to scream at him for making her feel this way, but that would hardly suit her purpose.

She gave him a smile that she hoped looked shy— she didn't dare try seductive—and said, "I have a favor to ask."

"Then ask." His voice was so kind she felt a new rush of guilt. She had a fleeting thought that she had never heard Anson's voice sound like that, and quickly brushed it away.

"I have a letter I need you to post for me."

Suspicion was easy to read in his narrowed eyes. "Why ask me? Why not your brother or whoever's going into town?"

"Please, Jake, none of them will do it." Quickly, before he said no, she turned around, opened her cloak and retrieved the letter from her bodice. "Here." She heard the uncertainty and pleading in her own voice.

"Emily." There was a plea in his voice, as well. "Don't ask me to do this." He closed her cloak, re-buttoning it against the cold she had barely been aware of. "Your family doesn't want you to contact him. *I* don't want you to contact him."

"You said you wouldn't judge him." She thrust the letter toward him, hoping once he took it in his hand he would give in.

"I tried not to. I want the best for you, Emily. I just can't believe he's the best."

"How is it your place to decide what's best for me?" She was failing. He was too stubborn. She felt tears sting her eyes and tried to blink them away. He would think she was using them as a weapon.

"You're right." He lifted the letter from her fingers. "Friends need to trust each other. And count on each other. I'll mail your letter."

"Jake." She threw her arms around him, pressing her cheek against his chest. "I knew I could count on you," she murmured.

His arms encircled her, holding her closer. The tears she had held back earlier trickled down her cheek. She was warm and safe in his arms and reluctant to leave them.

Finally he drew her away. She quickly brushed the tears from her cheeks and smiled up at him. "Thanks, Jake," she whispered.

He nodded solemnly. She thought for a moment that he would say something, but he slipped the letter into his coat pocket, stepped around her and walked away.

Jake walked into his parents' home, knowing it was empty. His mother would be busy at the Prescotts' until well after supper. If his father finished whatever Christian needed him to do this afternoon, he would be more likely to spend his free time with his wife in the big house than to come back here. No, he would be alone, and that suited him.

The house was dim, but he didn't light a lamp. He stood across the room from the front window and watched for Emily to walk past. He should have taken her arm and seen her safely to her door. He should still do it.

But he couldn't. He didn't trust himself to be that close to her. He was liable to take her into his arms and tell her he loved her. He had come too damn close already.

He saw her pass on the path, her head down, walking fast. She would be safe and warm in no time. He didn't have to feel guilty. He took a step closer to the window, then another, to watch her until she was out of sight.

Why did he let her do this to him? He should thoroughly dislike her for falling for that jailbird, for defying her parents, for using him.

For not wanting the love he was so willing to give her.

He was a fool. It was that simple and too late to change.

He unbuttoned his coat but didn't take it off. The room was cold, and he didn't want to light a fire. He wouldn't stay here long. He pulled the letter from his pocket and studied the clear, even lettering. Anson Berkeley. He wanted to destroy it, not mail it! He wanted to light that fire after all and watch the letter turn to ashes!

The violence of his reaction horrified him. He didn't trust himself to hold on to the letter for long. He shoved it back into his pocket and rebuttoned his coat. If he left now he could make it back before dark.

Half an hour later he was riding toward town. It hadn't been hard to convince his father that he needed to check in with his boss in Cottonwood Falls. It was an excuse he had used many times to avoid being on the ranch when Emily was expected. His mother might have been more difficult to convince, but he had left her to his father.

The cold crisp air in his face as he rode cleared his mind. He had started to harbor hopes about Emily again. The letter was a reminder that she would never be his. His purpose wasn't to win her away from Berkeley but to protect her from him. He couldn't do that if his mind was clouded with fantasies.

Of course, mailing this letter wasn't a particularly good way of protecting her, either. He should never have agreed to do it. But perhaps Berkeley would get the letter and not respond. Perhaps he had already forgotten her.

Perhaps. But it wasn't likely. This letter would probably encourage him. It might be the one thing he needed to send him out after Emily. Thank heaven, the man was in jail.

It was midafternoon when Jake rode into Strong. He posted the letter first, afraid that any delay might cause him to accidentally lose the letter. Then, still convinced he had done the wrong thing, he rode on to the river bridge and into Cottonwood Falls.

The courthouse, situated at the end of the main street, dominated the town. He rode toward it, taking in the activity on either side of him out of habit. He watered his horse at the trough before tying him and going inside.

Sheriff Tom Chaffee was in his office in the basement. He looked up from his cluttered desk when Jake walked in. "Afternoon, son. I didn't expect to see you again so soon."

"I know," Jake said, taking a seat across from his boss. "I was in town and thought I'd see if you have any word from Topeka." Tom would know what particular news he was after.

Tom winced. "You're not going to like this."

Jake tried to keep his face from showing his alarm. "What?"

The spring in Tom's chair squeaked as he rocked back. "The boy's out. Seems his folks paid for all the damages, and the old fella agreed to drop the charges."

"When did this happen?"

Tom took a moment before he answered. "I got word last night."

Jake felt his temper rise and knew it was unreasonable. He hoped his boss couldn't sense how he felt.

Tom's next words made him think he could. "I'm a little shorthanded here to be sending someone out to the ranch with messages. Besides, you're supposed to be on vacation, and this case is way out of our jurisdiction."

"The police will let us know if anything else happens, won't they?"

Tom brought his chair back to an upright position and bent over his desk. "I'm sure the Prescotts will let their son know if anything else happens." He found his place on the form and resumed writing.

Jake had been dismissed. He rose slowly and turned toward the door.

"Oh, and Jake?"

Jake turned back. "Yes, sir?"

Tom didn't look up. "Maybe you should concentrate on winning the little gal's affection and forget about the competition."

Jake paused, looking at his boss's bent head for the space of four heartbeats. "Yes, sir," he said, and left the office. He took the stairs two at a time, imagining his boss having a good chuckle at his expense once he was out of earshot. He shouldn't be surprised that Tom had guessed his real interest in the case. Loyalty to the Prescott family wouldn't be enough to make him quite so eager to see Berkeley punished.

He walked into the fresh, cold air, trying to will his frustration away. He shouldn't expect the sheriff to send someone all the way out to the ranch at the slightest word on the case. Emily probably wasn't in any immediate danger from Berkeley, anyway.

At least not until he got her letter.

''Damn,'' he muttered under his breath. He strode to his horse and mounted. All the way back through Cottonwood Falls, and across the bridge, he argued with himself. Should he try to get the letter back from the postmaster? If he did, what would he tell Emily? In the end, Emily's trust won, and he rode past the post office and out of Strong.

Chapter Three

Jake found Christian alone in the barn when he returned to the ranch. As he rubbed down his horse, he told his former boss what the sheriff had reported.

Christian stood silently for a long time. Jake was careful to keep his face turned away. The older man had been alternately big brother, mentor and boss to him. He was afraid his feelings for Emily would be at least as easy for her brother to read as they had been for the sheriff.

"I guess I'm not surprised," Christian finally said, "considering everything my folks have said about his family. I just hope he doesn't find Emily."

Jake closed his eyes, trying to block the pain. He ought to warn Christian about the letter, but that would betray Emily's trust. Or was he simply unwilling to accept the blame for his part in sending it. He hoped it was the former.

"I'm betting he'll come for her," Jake said.

"Why?" The question was sharp with speculation.

Jake's hand stilled on the horse's flank. "Because I would."

Christian laughed. "Don't use your own sense of honor to guess this fella's behavior. Chances are he was out celebrating with someone else the first night he was out of jail."

"The first night who was out of jail?"

At the sound of Emily's voice, Jake spun around. The movement momentarily startled the horse. By the time he had him calmed again, Christian had moved to his sister's side. Jake joined him slowly, waiting for the older man to speak.

"What are you doing out in the cold, muffin?"

Emily ignored the question and turned instead to Jake. "Was he talking about Anson?" she asked.

The dark brown eyes glaring at him made it impossible to lie. He cast Christian a glance before he nodded.

She turned to her brother. "When would you have told me?" There was enough accusation in the tone for Jake to guess she was asking "if" rather than "when."

"Tonight," Christian said quietly. "As soon as I got in."

"Then it's fine," Emily said. "He's out because he's innocent of the charges."

Christian shook his head. "His parents paid off the victim."

"That's ridiculous. Even if his parents paid the damages they wouldn't drop the charges unless he was innocent."

"You're not being reasonable, Em," Christian said.

"You're not being fair!"

Jake watched the exchange from a distance. After

the initial question she seemed unaware of his presence. She tried to stare her brother down, but Christian was too confident. After a long moment she spun on her heel and left the barn.

He watched after her, wishing he could offer her something—comfort, understanding, anything. The problem was he completely agreed with her brother, and she knew it.

He finally remembered the grooming brush in his hand. He turned back to the horse only to discover Christian's appraising eyes on him.

"You really think he'll come for her?" Christian asked.

"Yes, sir. Or she'll go to him."

"Why is she so stubborn? Why can't she see what he's really like?"

Jake didn't think Christian expected answers, but he responded anyway. "She's stubborn because she's who she is. We wouldn't want her any other way. And maybe we're the ones who don't know what he's really like."

"You're taking her side?"

Jake shook his head. "I said maybe. But why should she listen to us when we've never met him? He's the only one who's going to convince her, and he'll hurt her in the process."

Christian was silent, and Jake finished caring for his horse. When he left the stall, he found Christian still waiting. "Help me watch her," Christian said. "She trusts you more than me, right now. Don't let him take her away where I'll never see her again."

Jake considered just how much he should tell his

friend. Finally he answered softly. "That's why I'm here."

Emily knew it was panic that made her so sharp with her brother and shame that kept her from looking Jake in the eye. Neither of them were to blame for her predicament, and Jake had even tried to help.

She sat on her bed in her room, staring at the moonlight that filtered through the curtains. It was funny how quickly she went from irritated to furious these days. Or from disappointed to fighting tears. She had heard that expectant mothers were emotional; she had witnessed it to a small degree in Lynnette. But it wasn't proof, she told herself. The strain of worry could have the same effect. And worry could make her feel sick to her stomach.

She lowered her head to her hands. By the time she knew for certain, it would be too late to marry discreetly. Anyone who could count would know that she had fallen.

She sat up straight again, taking a deep breath. Anson would come for her. He loved her. She refused to believe anything else. Her hands shook and she clutched them in her lap. She needed sleep, for herself and for her baby if there was one. All she needed was a good night's sleep, and she would be fine.

After a light breakfast the next morning, Emily bundled up to take a walk. She knew it was too early for Anson to have gotten her letter and come to meet her, but she decided it would be good to establish a habit of walking every day to avoid arousing anyone's suspicion.

Martha had been alone in the kitchen when she had

gotten a slice of toast, and she assumed Lynnette and the children were downstairs. She was happy to slip out the back door without having to tell Willa she couldn't go along.

She headed toward the trail on the far side of the barn and suddenly found Jake walking beside her.

"Good morning," he said, as if there hadn't been a sharp word uttered the night before. "Mind if I join you?"

"Well, actually—"

"It's a pretty day for a stroll. Cold but sunny. Are you warm enough?"

"I'm fine. But I really—"

"Good. We wouldn't want you getting chilled. Don't you miss these wide-open spaces when you're in town? I know I do."

Emily gritted her teeth. He had taken her arm and was walking slowly beside her as if he were her escort. "No," she said. "What I miss is the solitude."

"Really? I'm surprised. I never figured you for someone who wanted to be alone a lot. But the country's good for that, too."

He was being deliberately obtuse. The only way to get rid of him would be to flat tell him to leave. Of course with Jake, even that might not work.

"I'd like to be alone now, if you don't mind," she said. His fingers tightened on her arm when she tried to pull it free.

"We are alone, sweetheart." His voice was low, almost a seductive whisper.

"Very funny. You know what I mean."

"Yeah," he said, continuing to walk beside her. "I know. But you might get lost..."

Emily pointed ahead at the path that wrapped around the hill. It was white where the thin soil had worn away from the limestone and stood out in sharp contrast to the brown and gold grass. "I'm not going to get lost!"

"Or fall and turn your ankle," he went on as if she hadn't spoken. "I wouldn't get anything done for worrying so I might as well come along."

Emily had to laugh. She wasn't sure if it was at him or at herself. Well, he could come today, since there was no chance that Anson was waiting. She would have to figure out some way to elude him in the future. Or perhaps he would get used to seeing her walking every day and stop playing the big brother.

"There's another thing I've missed," he said. "Your laugh."

"Don't go getting serious on me, Jake. I get enough of that from everybody else. Little lost Emily who needs to be straightened out."

"You've got a deal. I promise never to be serious."

If she had hurt his feelings, she couldn't hear it in his voice. He walked on at the same slow pace, his hand lightly holding her arm. She was about to venture a look at his face when she heard him chuckle. "What?"

"I was just remembering when you were little and came for the summer. Your pa and brothers in the mansion, me and my pa in the little house with Ma the only woman on the place. You turned everybody on his ear. The first time, you were a little bitty thing, about like Willa. Ma wanted you to stay with us. She was sure you'd miss your ma in the night and none of the men up here would know what to do for you. She had Arlen convinced right away, almost convinced your pa. But Christian wouldn't hear of it. He barely let you out of his sight."

Emily watched the prairie grasses nod in the light breeze. "You were what, about nine? What did you think of the idea?"

"Oh, I was against it. I figured you were a baby, and I didn't want some baby crying in the night, waking me up. I kept my mouth shut though, and let Christian do the arguing. After it was settled, and it was safe, I told Ma it had been a fine idea, and I was real sorry you wouldn't be with us."

Emily laughed. "You always knew how to get around your ma."

"Not as well as you could get around Christian. I swear! You would talk me into something, and I'd be in trouble. Do you remember the boat we were going to sail down that stream down there?" He pointed to the valley below where a narrow creek reflected the blue of the sky.

"Oh, Lord. I almost drowned."

"You didn't almost drown." He stopped and turned to face her, his hands on his hips. She choked back a giggle. "You convinced Christian that you had almost drowned so he'd let you off the hook. You know, I missed a trip to town because of your hare-brained scheme."

"If it was so harebrained," she asked with mock exasperation, "how come you went along with it?"

"Well," he said, turning to walk at her side again. "I didn't know it was harebrained until the boat sank.

I really thought I could build a boat. I didn't see how it could be so hard.''

Emily, still smiling, rested her head against his shoulder as she walked. "Dear Jake. You took the blame for other things, too, didn't you? Like the Indian-war-paint incident and riding the sled down the icehouse roof?"

"Now that one scared me."

"And then there was the great wilderness adventure."

Jake groaned. "I'd forgotten that one. We thought if we walked west for a couple days we'd be in the California goldfields. Never mind that we were about twenty years late."

"I pictured great cornfields growing gold. That's why I stole Christian's knife, so I could cut it."

"Telling Christian that you said you knew the way didn't seem to keep me out of trouble."

"Jake, you must have been twelve or thirteen. You should have known better."

He turned toward her again, all but taking her in his arms. No, it was just her imagination. He was only resting his hands lightly on her shoulders. "That's just it, Emily," he said. "I did know better. I always knew better—or usually, anyway. But you could convince me of anything. Emily—"

She took a step away. "You promised not to get serious."

He smiled then, more tender than teasing. "You're right. Are you ready to go back?"

"Yes, I think so," she said.

He was quiet all the way home. Emily found herself lost in memories of their shared childhood. There had always been a gentleness about Jake she hadn't truly appreciated as a girl. She was lucky to have such a friend.

He took her to the kitchen door instead of the back door where the coats were hung. "It's warmer in here," he said. Once inside, he took her cloak and gloves and turned her over to his mother, who recommended a cup of hot tea.

Emily warmed herself near the kitchen stove while she waited for the water to boil. She found herself wishing Jake would hang up the coats and return to share the tea with her, but he didn't. He must have gone back outside to resume whatever chores he had interrupted for their walk. It was difficult to explain her disappointment. Perhaps he distracted her, kept her from dwelling on her worries, kept her from missing Anson.

Dinner was a quiet affair. Christian made no more reference to Anson than Jake had. Trevor was still shy of Emily, though he let her hold him and feed him for a little while. Willa declared the noodles Martha had fixed her favorite and was so busy eating she was noticeably less talkative. Christian and Lynnette talked and teased each other, making Emily feel even more lonely.

Escaping before dessert, she sat on her bed and stared across the room without seeing it. This place, with its memories and its laughter conspired to confuse her. Things had been so much clearer in town. There she knew she loved Anson and he loved her. They were meant to be together. Her parents were the enemy, keeping her from happiness.

Here, so far from Anson, her love—and his—were less certain. Their chances of having a future like Christian and Lynnette seemed remote. Anson wasn't much like Christian. But then, she wasn't just like Lynnette, either. They would find their own way, their own life.

Somehow, even to herself, the argument seemed weak. She felt tears spring to her eyes and brushed them away. Tears, there always seemed to be tears! And often at the oddest times. Holding Trevor did it the fastest.

Things *had* to work out with Anson. What would become of her if they didn't? She rested a hand on her belly and swallowed the lump in her throat. If Anson didn't come for her, she would have to go away alone. She would be too ashamed to face her family and too afraid they might make her give the baby away.

She wished there was someone she could talk to, someone who wouldn't condemn her. She had come close to confiding in Rose who had been her best friend for so long. But Rose was married to Arlen, and he was worse than her mother when it came to propriety. He would have her packed off to a maternity home and spread the lie that she was on some European tour. A sister with a bastard could hurt his political career.

Lynnette was her next choice. She would be understanding at least. And so would Christian, maybe. But what help could she really expect from them? They couldn't tell her how to magically make the baby go away, how to magically undo the past.

You've made your bed and now you have to sleep

in it, had a whole new meaning now. She felt another
tear threaten and brushed at it angrily. She hated feeling sorry for herself! She had no patience for it in
other people. She would survive. She would be a
good mother to her child, with or without its father.

But, she told herself sternly, there wasn't any danger of that. Anson would come for her. They would
be married. When her family saw how happy they
were, they would relent and welcome her back. She
tried to picture her family gathered at Christmas, her
parents, her brothers and their wives, Christian's children, her own baby toddling around. It was easy.

But putting Anson in the picture proved difficult.
She couldn't imagine him sitting with her brothers
and finding anything to say to them. She couldn't
imagine him helping with the decorations, singing
carols, playing with the children.

She shook her head to dispel the thoughts. She was
setting limits on him, and it wasn't fair. More than
likely he would fit right in. She would just know a
more exciting side of him that her family would only
guess at. She smiled to herself and wondered if it was
forced.

A tap on the door startled her. "Are you sleeping?"

Emily had never been so glad to hear Willa's loud
whisper. She ran to the door and opened it.

Willa flounced in and threw herself across the bed,
her short full skirt billowing for a second to reveal a
tear in her stocking. "I can't stand another minute in
the nursery!" she exclaimed.

Emily held back a laugh. "What's so awful about
the nursery?"

"Everything! Trevor's such a baby. I don't have any place for just me. Sometimes girls need time alone, you know. Can I stay here with you?"

Emily watched the little girl throw her arm across her forehead dramatically, a gesture she had probably learned from her Aunt Rose. Willa was just what she needed to distract her from her worries.

But only for one night. Sometime soon she would be running away with Anson. She couldn't afford to lose her privacy.

She cleared her throat. "Willa, dear, how about being my sleepover friend tonight?" At the little girl's eager reaction she added, "Just tonight, mind you. We'll make a party of it."

Willa sat up quickly. "Honest? Shall I run and ask Mama?"

"No. Let her write while your brother's asleep. We can ask her later. I'm sure she won't mind." Emily sat down on the bed, and Willa scooted over next to her. "What do you want to do when you sleep over?"

Emily was trying to think of what games a five-year-old might like to play when Willa came up with a suggestion. "We can write love letters to our boyfriends." She quickly stifled a giggle behind her cupped hands.

"Boyfriends? Do you have a boyfriend?"

"We can make one up," she suggested with another giggle. "Or I could write mine to Jake."

"Jake!" Emily eyed the child. "Isn't he a little old for you?"

Willa shrugged. "Papa's older than Mama."

"Not twenty years older!"

Willa shrugged her shoulders until they touched her

ears. "But he's so-o-o-o handsome. And so-o-o-o strong. He can lift me onto a horse like that." She tried to snap her fingers.

"Anybody can lift you onto a horse," Emily argued. "You're a little girl."

Willa thrust out her chin. "But Jake does it better than anybody else. Even Papa."

Emily eyed the little girl sternly, but she felt her lips twitch with a smile. In a moment they were laughing in each other's arms. "All right," Emily said finally. "We'll write love letters tonight. What do you want to do now? Shall we see about making those cookies we never got around to the other day?"

"Cookies!" Willa cried, jumping off the bed. She quickly covered her mouth then whispered loudly, "Trevor's sleeping."

Willa remembered to whisper all the way down the stairs. In the kitchen, she tugged Emily's hand and pointed. Jake was cleaning the ashes out of the stove.

He looked up at the little girl's giggle. "Good afternoon, ladies," he said.

Willa ran to Martha but gave Jake a sidelong glance before asking permission to make cookies. Emily intended to follow Willa but found herself walking toward Jake instead.

"Don't come too close," he said. "You'll get ashes on your dress." She stopped a few feet away. She couldn't help thinking of Willa's description as she watched him work.

"What were you two giggling about?" he asked.

"I wasn't giggling."

"I thought I heard two distinct giggles."

"No. Only one. And it's girl stuff. Secret." The last she said in Willa's exaggerated whisper.

"Oh," he whispered back.

Willa joined them with her lower lip sticking out a good half inch. "Martha says we can't bake cookies 'cause she's gonna make Christmas stuff."

"Maybe we can help her with the Christmas baking," Emily suggested.

Willa shook her head sadly. "She says it's candy, and it's too hot for me to help. What are we going to do?"

Emily couldn't help but smile at the girl's sense of tragedy. "I don't know," she lamented.

"How about going riding with me?" Jake asked.

"Can we, Aunt Emily? Can we, can we?"

Emily bobbed her head, following the bouncing girl's movements.

"She says yes," Willa told Jake, tugging on Emily's hand. "Let's go change."

"I didn't say yes," Emily corrected, allowing herself to be dragged from the room.

"You nodded."

A few minutes later, Emily stepped from her room, dressed in a divided skirt, and found Willa in homemade pants waiting for her. They went quickly down the stairs and headed for the back hall to get their coats.

Jake met them there. "You won't need more than jackets," he said. "It's warmed up some since this morning."

Willa found what she wanted to wear, and Emily helped her into it and her gloves. "All I have is my cloak," she said. "Perhaps I could borrow something." She studied the row of coats, trying to pick something the right weight.

"This one's mine," Jake said, grabbing a flannel-lined jacket. "I left it here last fall."

For some unknown reason, Emily wanted to refuse it. But she could think of no reason, and Willa was obviously in a hurry. She drew on the jacket as she followed the others outside.

Jake was right, it was surprisingly warm for December. Christian and Perry had saddled the horses, and her brother helped her mount as Jake lifted Willa into the saddle. The little girl tossed her a smug grin as Jake mounted.

"Watch her close," Christian said to Jake before they started off. He was referring, of course, to his little daughter.

Jake led them down the path they had followed that morning. He stayed so close to Willa that Emily soon fell back to watch them. Jake took Christian's admonition very seriously. When Willa leaned down to scratch her ankle, his hand shot out to steady her.

Emily had to smile. Her talkative little niece was unusually shy. Yet she wanted to compose a pretend love letter to him that evening. At least Emily thought it was pretend. Of course, if the little girl actually delivered the letter, Jake would be nice about it. She couldn't imagine him ever doing anything that would hurt anybody.

She felt the most peculiar stab of jealousy, which she quickly shrugged off. She took a deep breath of the crisp cool air. It had been months since she had ridden. It had always been a favorite activity on the ranch in the summer. She leaned forward to pat the gelding's neck.

Ahead, Jake pointed something out to Willa, who nodded when she saw it. It was odd, Emily thought. When she wanted to be alone, Jake or Willa interrupted. When she wanted a diversion, like now, she found herself alone. Or nearly so. Her companions seemed to have forgotten she was along.

She was now quite certain she was increasing. Her flow was two weeks late, and she had always been regular. The bouts of stomach upset and moments of fatigue were more frequent.

She needed Anson. She needed to be married to Anson. Disloyal as it was, she wanted him less and less. If it wasn't for the baby, she wouldn't be particularly disappointed if she never heard from him again.

If it wasn't for the baby. That seemed to preface all her confused thoughts. If it wasn't for the baby, she could pretend this was a happy visit instead of a banishment. She could comfort her little nephew without tears coming to her eyes. She could write her parents that she knew she had been wrong and ask their forgiveness.

She could flirt with Jake.

She shook her head to clear it. Where had that thought come from? Willa, probably. She had been watching her ride beside her strong and handsome Jake, noting how the girl's shy smiles were an innocent form of flirting.

Maybe the baby affected her mind as well as her stomach. She had no interest in Jake except as a friend. She decided she couldn't trust herself to be alone with her thoughts. That bit of illogical whimsy made her want to laugh aloud. That would convince her companions that she had gone crazy. She imagined them looking at her pityingly and wanted to laugh even more.

She kicked her mount to ride closer behind the other two, hoping to get in on their conversation. Before she really did drive herself crazy.

After the ride, Willa ran to tell her mother that she was going to spend the night with Emily. She was restless all through supper, wanting to get started with what she was calling her party. She insisted that her mother help her wash and get ready for bed as soon as the meal was over.

Emily went to her room to prepare for bed herself and get the pen and paper ready. She was starting to look forward to hearing Willa's idea of a love letter. An invitation to help her look for frogs, maybe. Or a promise to make him a special heart-shaped cookie.

It wasn't long before she heard a knock on the door and the little girl bounded in, her hair flying around her shoulders.

"Don't you want your daddy to braid your hair before bed?" Emily asked, smiling at the eager face.

"I want you to do it," she said, climbing up on the bed to sit cross-legged in the center.

Emily grabbed a brush and a ribbon and crawled up behind her. "Did you know your daddy used to braid my hair every night?"

Willa shook her head. "Why didn't your own daddy?"

Emily laughed. She pulled the brush through the fine blond hair. "Most daddies don't braid little girl's hair. Usually it's mama's job. But when I was little and came to stay on the ranch, my mama wasn't here, so your daddy braided my hair.''

"But at sleep-over parties, we do each other's. And yours is already done."

"Sorry, I should have waited," she said, making short work of the girl's shoulder-length hair and tying it with the ribbon.

"That's all right. I don't know how anyway. When do we write our letters?" Willa asked.

"Let's do it right away," Emily said eagerly. "You want to write yours first, or shall I?"

"Me, me!" she cried bouncing on the bed. "You write just what I say."

"All right." Emily slid off the bed and took a seat at the desk. Willa crawled around on the bed, a childish version of pacing. "Shall I start with 'Dear Jake'?"

"No," Willa responded, stopping to stand on her knees and press her hands over her heart. "'My darling Jake.' No wait, 'My own darling Jake.' Write that."

Emily dipped the pen in ink and bent over the page. "Does your mother read her stories to you?"

"No," responded Willa, missing Emily's grin. "Tell him I think he's the most handsome man in the world."

Emily smiled. "'Most handsome man in the world.' What else?"

"'The bravest and the strongest.'" Willa said the words slowly, allowing Emily time to write. "And I want him to kiss me." The instant she said it, she threw both hands over her mouth, gulping back a giggle.

"Do you really?" Emily teased.

She shook her head vigorously. "Don't write that. What if he really did?" She grimaced.

"Are we going to send this letter?"

Willa thought for a moment. "No. That way I can tell him everything." She took a deep breath. "'Your eyes are like the sky.'"

"His eyes are green," Emily corrected.

"They are? All right. 'Your eyes are like the…grass. Your smile is like sunshine. Your kiss is like honey.'"

"Now, how would you know?"

Willa giggled. "Put it down. 'Your strong arms could carry me away.'" She threw herself backward onto the bed.

"Where did you get this stuff?" Emily quickly scratched down what the little girl had said.

"I spent a week with Aunt Rose. She writes poetry out loud when she thinks she's alone."

"Writes it out loud, huh?"

"Yeah. Some of it's real romantic."

"And she's married to Arlen."

Both girls giggled at that.

Emily drew Willa's attention back to the letter. "How do you want to end it?"

Willa thought for a moment. "How about, 'Your only love, Willa.'"

"Great," Emily said. When she was finished, she closed the ink bottle and wiped the pen.

"Aren't you going to write one now?" Willa sounded disappointed.

"I don't think so. How about I tell you a story, instead."

"I wanted to know what you would write to a boyfriend." She stuck her lower lip out and squinted her eyes.

Emily rose from the chair and put out the lamp. "How about we curl up in bed, and I'll tell you what I would write."

"Pretend like you're writing to Jake," Willa said, crawling under the quilt.

"Jake?"

"Yeah. Tell me what you would write about Jake."

Emily climbed into bed beside Willa. She tried to go along with the child's game, but the images of Jake that it conjured up made her somehow more lonely. She worked to turn the discussion to other things.

When she finally succeeded, the little girl fell asleep. Emily lay awake, unable to get the images out of her mind. Jake's eyes, voice, lips, height and muscles had all been discussed. Though they had left out his gentleness, kindness, and sense of humor.

She groaned and rolled to her side. Typical, she thought. Now would be the perfect time for the little girl to chatter endlessly about nothing in particular. But now she was asleep.

The next day Emily noticed a repeat of what she came to think of as her predicament. Always when she sought solitude, Jake or Willa or even Trevor intruded. When she needed company to dispel her somber thoughts, everyone else was occupied. She began to wonder if she really knew which she wanted or if she simply longed for one whenever she had the other. The paradox, she decided, completely described the confused state of her mind.

And the silly letter sat on her desk. She kept forgetting to ask Willa what she wanted her to do with it. And she couldn't quite bring herself to throw it away.

Jake leaned against the barn door, waiting for Emily to make her appearance. The past two days she had gone for a walk as soon as the sun was high in the sky, and he had joined her, though it was beginning to feel like torture. He had watched her grow more and more melancholy, pining for her love. Every time she got that faraway look in her eyes, he felt a pain acute enough that it nearly buckled his knees.

She left the shelter of the house, her cloak so securely wrapped around her she might have been hard for someone else to recognize. But he knew that step, that particular sway of her body as she closed the door, the tilt of her head, even under the hood, as she set off toward the path.

As she approached, he stepped from the shadow of the barn. "Good morning, Emily," he said.

She stopped dead in her tracks. "I don't want company this morning," she said.

"How unusual," he quipped. She never wanted his company. "Do we take the high road or the low road today?"

"Why don't you go that way," she said, motioning toward her left. "I'll go this way. We can meet back here before dinner."

He grinned at her, but it only made her grit her teeth. "Come on. I'm not that bad company, am I?"

She took a deep breath as if fighting her temper. "It's not you, Jake. I simply want to be alone. Please respect that."

There was a bite to her words that sobered him. "Emily, we walk together every morning. Why make a fuss about it?"

"Because I don't want you along. I've never wanted you along." The hood slipped from her head as she stomped a small foot on the hard-packed ground. "I don't need another shadow!"

Jake stood stunned as she whirled past him. For a moment, he considered following her. Then he turned and walked slowly toward the barn. His pa would appreciate his help with the chores. And he would keep an eye out for Emily's return.

Chapter Four

Emily headed out for a walk for the second time without Jake. She felt guilty about screaming at him the day before, but it couldn't be helped. There didn't seem to be any other way for him to get the message, and she couldn't let him continue to walk with her. What if Anson was waiting for her but unable to show himself because Jake was along?

She hadn't seen Jake since the fight, and, though she couldn't apologize without running the risk of him expecting to walk with her again, she found herself missing him. The thought made her smile. How could she miss someone so annoying?

She was caught up in thoughts of Jake and neared the bend in the path with some surprise that she had come so far. Perhaps when she got back she should seek Jake out, suggest something else for them to do during the afternoon.

A tall figure stepped from cover into the path in front of her. She took a startled step backward. For one instant she thought Jake had gone ahead of her to avoid any argument about coming along.

But the thought fled. "Anson?" He was thinner than she remembered him. And paler. She stood rooted to the spot staring at him.

"You're surprised to see me," he said, coming toward her, his blue-gray eyes hard. "Were you expecting someone else?"

"Of course not," she said, recovering. "I just didn't know if you would really come."

His eyes softened, and he enfolded her in his arms. "Oh, sweet child. Did you think I would abandon you? After you sent such a loving letter, how could I? I came as soon as I could."

His arms around her seemed familiar and strange at the same time. This was Anson, her baby's father. Everything would be all right.

"Are we leaving together?" she asked. She found herself afraid of the answer, whichever it might be.

"Tonight," he said, drawing her away. "Can you sneak back out here with some food? We can make our plans then."

"I don't know. I'll try but—" She had almost said Jake! "They watch me pretty close."

"All right," he said, leading her to a rock where they could sit. "I'll tell you the plan now, just in case. As soon as it's dark, and everyone else is asleep, meet me here. You'll need a horse, one bag of clothes, some food and some money."

"One bag?" She had waited so long for this, but now that it was happening she felt a need to stall.

"One bag. We're going to take the train back as far as Emporia. There we can change to the Missouri, Kansas and Texas. We might not have much time to change trains. At Junction City we'll get on the Kansas Pacific, and it'll take us all the way to Denver.''

"Denver?'' What were they going to do there?

"We'll need money,'' he said. "Get as much as you can.''

"You mean steal from Christian?''

"Emily,'' he said gently, drawing her closer to his side. "They've forced us to this. It isn't the way either of us want it, but it's the only way we can be together.'' He gave her shoulder a squeeze before letting it go. "Besides, they wouldn't want you to go hungry, would they?''

Emily shook her head. It was happening too fast. Yet a day ago she had thought it couldn't happen soon enough. She looked up at the handsome face, and he smiled down at her. There was no glint of mischief in his eyes; they looked…secretive. He had his doubts about running away, as well. But, as he had said, it was the only way they could be together. She loved him more, knowing he was as uncertain as she.

He bent and kissed her quickly. "Go back now, before they miss you. Come back with food if you can.''

Jake saddled his horse in preparation for riding into town. It was midafternoon, and he planned to spend the night at home and ride back to the ranch early in the morning.

He hated to leave Emily, though he had long since realized he was no real comfort to her. Still, the mornings when he had joined her for her walk, he imagined his presence gave her courage. Yesterday, however, had ended that pretense. She didn't need another shadow.

This morning he had watched for her to leave the house and waited impatiently while she was gone. She hadn't once looked toward the barn where he waited.

Shadow, he thought as he swung into the saddle. That pretty well described what he was to her. Something present but barely noticed, insignificant. Useless.

Well, he would make himself useful elsewhere. He would ask his boss for any word from Topeka. And, though he would leave her alone for a time, he would hurry back to be her shadow again.

Emily was certain there was no chance of sneaking food out to Anson before dark. She knew she should try to think of a way, but how would she explain a second walk to Jake? It would be impossible to slip past him.

Wrapped in a shawl, she took refuge on her balcony. It looked down on the valley that dropped below the front of the house, the side away from the barnyard. Here, she had thought herself safe from any reminders of Willa's perfect Jake.

Why did the little girl have to call all his attributes to her attention? She had been content to think of him as her childhood friend, the boy who had teased her, argued with her, gotten into trouble for her.

Yesterday morning she had yelled at him. She was leaving tonight and would probably never speak to him again. She could hardly imagine it.

Somehow, years from now, she would come back

and see her family. It hurt to think that her niece and nephew would grow up without her, but she *would* see them again.

But Jake? Where would he be by the time she was able to return? Would he be married?

She shook away the foolish thought. *She* would be married. And a mother. Her ties to Jake were from her childhood, nothing more. Still she regretted that her last words to him had been in anger.

She felt a sudden chill and wrapped the shawl more tightly around her shoulders. She would find him this afternoon, talk and tease, end things on a more comfortable note. She could even apologize to him now, since she would be gone by tomorrow.

The sound of a horse's hooves caught her attention. She leaned over the balcony to look below her and watched Jake canter past. Had his vacation been brought to a sudden end for some reason? Would he be back before Christmas? Or was he leaving because he was tired of her moody responses to his offers of friendship?

With a sigh, she turned back into her room. It was foolish to think she had that much effect on Jake. It didn't matter anyway. Any chance of settling things with him was gone now. She needed to put him out of her mind and think about her future.

Anson was the one she should be thinking of. With Jake gone there was a much better chance of getting food to Anson. He was probably starving.

The kitchen was empty when she arrived. She hurried to throw together some bread and meat left from the noon meal, knowing Martha could arrive at any moment to begin supper preparations.

She breathed a sigh of relief when she left the
kitchen with the cloth-wrapped lunch tucked under
her arm. She donned her cloak and concealed the bundle beneath it. She said a silent prayer that Christian
wouldn't be watching before she opened the back
door and stepped outside.

No one hailed her as she walked past the barn,
trying her best to look as if she were going for another
of her frequent walks. Still her heart was pounding
by the time the barn was safely behind her.

Anson wasn't where she had met him that morning.
Unwilling to call out for fear her voice would carry,
she looked carefully around her. The thought that he
had left without her didn't fill her with as much panic
as she knew it should.

But he hadn't left. She saw his horse near the
stream in the valley below and carefully made her
way toward it. Anson slept in the sun a short distance
away and woke with a start as she approached.

"I brought some food," she gasped before catching
her breath.

"Good girl."

He made no move to rise but reached out a hand
toward her. She removed the bundle from where she
had tied it at her waist and took it to him.

"You didn't bring a bottle?" he asked.

She hadn't even thought of it. "I was lucky to
sneak this away," she said.

"That's all right." He smiled up at her and patted
the ground.

She sat beside his outstretched legs and watched
him unwrap the lunch. His neatly trimmed hair and
fine, clean-shaven face didn't seem to fit with the

backdrop of winter-bare trees and brown grass. He belonged in his rich home and the fancy clubs of the city. He was giving up a lot for her.

"What will we do in Denver?" she asked.

He shrugged, chewed and swallowed before he answered. "There are a lot of opportunities. Saloons are legal there. I could deal cards, tend bar, work my way up to owning the place. You'd bring in the customers," he added with a wink.

Bring in the customers? Perhaps this was a good time to mention she might be pregnant.

He laughed, bringing heat to her cheeks. "You should see your face. I'm not asking you to slip upstairs with them. Is that what you thought?"

She shook her head but wasn't sure he believed her. This was a side of him she had forgotten, his pleasure at embarrassing her. "Anson, I need to talk to you."

He laughed, leaning forward to pat her knee. "Don't worry, sweetheart. I'll take good care of you. Trust me?"

His half smile was so charming, his eyes so sincere, she had no choice but to nod. He scooted forward, sliding his hands under her cloak to take her in his arms. It was comforting, though not as secure as she would have liked to feel.

"Thanks for coming," he whispered. "I'll see you after dark. Don't forget, only one bag and bring some money. Now, you should get back before you're missed." He kissed her lips hungrily then added, "Though I'd really like you to stay."

His hands caressed her breasts as they withdrew, making her feel uneasy. His touch had never excited her the way Lynnette's books described it, but it hadn't repelled her like this. Perhaps she was experiencing some unmentioned effect of being with child.

She murmured goodbye and started the climb back toward the path. She found herself thinking about Lynnette's books as she made her way home. The heroine always longed for her lover's touch and, though she never got to the details, the reader was led to believe that intimacy was enjoyable to both parties. Emily wondered how her sister-in-law could continue to write that way even after she knew better.

She was so preoccupied that she nearly forgot to use caution when she got back to the ranch yard. Fortunately, if anyone saw her, they didn't question her, and she was able to return to her room to pack.

Sheriff Tom Chaffee was leaving the courthouse when Jake rode up. "I was just going to send someone out your way," he said, when Jake had dismounted. "Come on inside."

Jake didn't like the sound of that. He followed his boss into the building and down the steps to the office, trying to hide his impatience.

"What's up?" he asked, closing the door.

Tom eased into his chair behind the desk before he spoke. "Your friend Berkeley's got himself in trouble again. Seems he demanded money from his pappy, but the old man refused. Said his son stormed out carrying a carpetbag." Tom waved one hand in the air. "Boy says he's never coming back. Old man says good riddance. Whole big fight. Anyway, later that night in comes a report to the police. Some guy, says he runs a dance school, was robbed."

"Dance school?" Jake interrupted. "How much money would there be at a dance school?"

Tom raised his brows. "Well, this particular dance school had a lot of late-night business, if you know what I mean."

"A saloon."

"In our own dry state of Kansas. Hard to believe, ain't it?" Tom gave Jake a wink before he went on. "The guy took a chance coming in. Said he recognized Berkeley as a...uh...student who caused him some trouble in the past. He managed to keep Berkeley from getting much more than a few bucks, but he wants the boy charged for roughing him up."

Jake felt a prickle of fear at the base of his neck. Tom didn't get this much information from a telegram. "When did all this happen?"

"Night before last. Got a complete report this afternoon."

"He could have taken the train here yesterday. He could already be at the ranch!"

"Take it easy, son. We both know that's not likely. More'n likely our boy found some place to hole up. I reckon he'll try again for some money and get caught this time. Or shot."

Jake wasn't reassured. Though he was glad he had come to town to get the information, he regretted deeply leaving Emily at the ranch. He wouldn't be able to make it back before dark, and it got cold when the sun went down. It wouldn't be a good idea to try it, though it was all he could think of at the moment.

Tom spoke again, interrupting his thoughts. "They sent me the report because of the girlfriend, of course.

There is the off chance that he'll try to get help from her.''

"Off chance," Jake repeated, making it sound like a curse.

Tom laughed. "I wired back. Said we already had the girl under surveillance.''

Jake eyed his boss for a moment. Tom found the oddest things to make jokes about. "Not tonight, she isn't,'' he reminded him.

Tom stood up and started around his desk. "Relax, son. The boy isn't coming all this way for a girl. There are plenty closer at hand. Besides, she's got her brother and his family out there. It's not like he could knock on her door and not have somebody else know it.''

Jake stood to leave, trying to believe what his boss said was true. "All the same, sir. I think I'll head back.''

Tom slapped him on the back as he went around him. "You'll freeze your nuts off, boy. Some good you'd be then.'' He laughed and headed out the door.

Jake followed more slowly. Tom might laugh, but Jake knew he was right. Anson was on the run. Who better to offer help than an innocent girl? An innocent rich girl. She had made herself an easy mark. And he had mailed the letter.

He led his horse to the water trough and waited impatiently while he drank. He considered stopping by a restaurant for something to eat but dismissed it quickly. He could wait to eat until he knew Emily was safe.

In a few minutes he was on the road headed toward the ranch. He fought the desire to make the horse run.

Wearing out his mount wouldn't get him there any sooner. Still, he couldn't help imagining that Anson was already there.

It was nearly dark when he crested a hill and spotted a buggy below. It was old and weather-beaten and sat a little cockeyed at the side of the road. As he approached, a man jumped down and hailed him.

"Trouble, mister?" Jake asked, pulling to a stop. The man was about his age, rudely dressed and thin.

"A mite. The horse went lame on us. How much farther to town?"

"About ten, twelve miles or so. Quite a walk in the dark." Jake swung from the saddle, holding the reins with his left hand to keep his right hand free.

"Out of the question, I'm afraid," the man said. He leaned closer. "The missus been ailin'."

"I am not ailing," said a petulant voice from the buggy.

The man rubbed his nose, grinning. "She's in the family way," he whispered loudly.

"Merle! Do you want me to die of embarrassment?"

Merle chuckled. "Is there a farmhouse nearby where we might get help?"

Jake shook his head. "Not close." *And there aren't likely to be many more fools out in the dark.* With a sigh, he realized there was only one thing to do. He turned toward his horse and began removing the saddle.

"Much obliged, mister," the man said. He hurried toward the buggy. "It'll be a'right, Mildred. This fella's gonna help us."

Jake tugged the saddle off the horse's back, cursing

his luck. There was probably only room enough in
the buggy for two. He would have to walk the lame
horse back to town. By then, both he and his horse
would need a rest. He would have to wait until morning after all.

Through the window in the balcony door, Emily
watched the sky darken. It was almost time to go. She
had heard everyone come up to the bedrooms some
time ago. She knew Martha and Perry would have
gone home. And Jake was gone.

Still she waited a few more minutes. She wanted
to light a lamp and look around her room for perhaps
the last time, but she knew she was better off letting
her eyes adjust to the dark. She wandered quietly
around the room, running her fingers over the furniture, touching the old doll on the shelf.

As she caressed the bedspread, she found the little
notes she had left for Willa and Trevor. She had told
them she loved them and would miss them but would
come to see them again someday. The notes would
be a message to their parents, as well, and hers: she
had left intentionally. How long before they gave her
up and let Willa have her room?

She smiled. It would be comforting to think of
lively little Willa moving in. The letter she had dic-
tated to Jake was hidden in the back of the copy of
Pride and Prejudice. In a few years, Willa would decide to read the book and find the letter. And remember her night with Aunt Emily.

It was completely dark outside. Should she wait
until moonrise, or would it be better to be out of the

yard by then? Someone might chance to look out a window and see her.

She decided not to wait. She lifted her carpetbag and went quietly out the door, leaving it ajar for fear the sound of the latch would alert someone. The house remained quiet as she made her way through the dark living room and into her brother's study. She knew where he kept some cash, but she couldn't find it in the dark. She had put matches in her pocket for this purpose and struck one, finding the lamp with the tiny blaze.

Her hands shook as she removed the metal box from the drawer. She never thought she would be stealing from her own brother. Inside was more money than she had expected. Christian must have sold several horses since his last trip to the bank in town.

She couldn't allow herself to think about what she was doing. She grabbed up the money and started to close the box. On impulse, she dropped a few bills back inside, then slipped the box back into the drawer. She folded the bills and stuffed them deep into her bag, blew out the light and left the study.

At the back door, she found her cloak and scarf and finally her gloves. She had two pairs of stockings and a pair of bloomers on under her heavy riding skirt. She even wore two blouses under the matching jacket. She had done it for warmth, but had also been aware that it would leave her with more clothes than the meager choices she could fit in one carpetbag. She felt the chill air only against her face as she went outside.

She found the barn more from memory than from

sight, though there was the slightest gray cast to the
sky. She felt across the rough wood for the handle
and slid the door open enough to slip through. She
closed it behind her and stood still, listening to the
snuffle of the horses in an otherwise silent, black
world.

There was no way she could saddle a horse in
pitch-darkness. She lit another of her matches and
found a lantern hanging on the wall. She prayed no
restless sleeper would look out and see light streaming from the barn's few small windows.

She suddenly felt a need to hurry. She got her saddle from the tack room, and picked the gelding she
had ridden before. Had it really been only a few days?
No. It was another lifetime. A life she had shared with
Jake before Anson had come back for her.

She shed the cloak before she saddled the horse.
The layers of clothes might keep her warm, but they
also made movement more difficult. After several
long minutes, she was ready to tie her bag to the
saddle strings. She led the horse to the door but blew
out the light just before she slid it open. At the last
moment she decided to take the lantern with her and
looped the handle carefully over the saddle horn.

The cloak made mounting difficult, and she led the
horse to the edge of the ramp that led to the upper
level and used it to help her swing into the saddle.
She took one last look at the house, barely visible as
a darker shape against a dark sky, and turned toward
the path where she would meet Anson and her future.

On the far side of the barn, a loud whisper made
her start. "Emily, is that you?"

For a moment she thought she had been caught,

then she recognized Anson's voice. "Yes," she whispered back.

She heard him move closer. He was on foot, leading his horse. "I came up to the barn just before dark. I thought you might wait until moonrise."

"I was afraid of being seen," she answered.

"We'll have to wait here anyway. We'll kill ourselves on that trail in the dark."

Emily dismounted, thinking of the lantern, and found herself in Anson's arms. "I was afraid you wouldn't come," he whispered near her ear. "Did you get the money?"

"Some," she said. "I brought a lantern, too."

"Good girl," he murmured, releasing her. "Light it. We'll walk the horses until the moon comes up."

They made slow progress, leading their horses while Anson held the lantern high to light the trail. Emily let out a shaky breath when the path turned. There was no longer any danger that someone would see the light bobbing on the hillside.

"You all right?" Anson asked. The hand with the reins went around her shoulder, forcing his horse into hers.

Emily turned to quiet the mounts. "Yes, I'm fine. I didn't realize I had been holding my breath until we got away."

"We have gotten away, haven't we?" His smile was more playful than reassuring. "We'll have such a grand time in Denver, child."

"Will you marry me in Denver, Anson?"

"Marry you!" She heard the surprise in his voice. She was surprised, too. She kept her eyes on the rough path.

"Baby, I guess I could marry you, if that's what you want. I just haven't thought much about it."

They were quiet for the space of several minutes before he asked, "Is that what you want?"

"I think that's what I need, Anson."

"Well, I mean for you to have everything you need, little girl. I'd be proud to marry you in Denver."

There was an exaggerated cheerfulness to his tone. He was willing, but not eager, to marry her. But maybe that didn't matter. Once they were married and her baby had a name, they would build a life together.

"Thank you, Anson," she murmured.

They walked on to where the trail began to disappear in the prairie. Emily led the way toward the main road, hoping she was not mistaking distant landmarks in the dark. They had started down a steep slope when the light flickered and went out.

Anson cursed and shook the lantern.

"Do you need another match?" Emily asked, reaching into her pocket.

"What good would that do? The damned thing's empty."

Emily cringed when she heard the crash and tinkle of glass a few feet away.

"Why didn't you fill it before we left?"

The anger in his voice made her want to step away. They seemed to be suspended in total darkness on the slope, however, and she was afraid to move. "I'm sorry," she said, ashamed of the catch in her voice. "I didn't think of it."

"No, of course you wouldn't." His voice dripped sarcasm. "You were too busy planning to get married. Everything else is my problem. You never *think*."

Emily felt tears come to her eyes and was glad for the darkness that hid them. "That's not fair, Anson," she managed.

He muttered a few choice curses. "Well, we're stuck here until the moon comes up. We might as well try to rest."

She heard a pebble slip under his foot as he sat on the ground. She crouched down gingerly, feeling the ground for rocks and sharp, dead grass. After a moment, his hands found her and he pulled her down beside him, wrapping her in his arms.

"I didn't mean to yell at you, little girl," he murmured in her ear. "The moon'll be up soon, and we'll be on our way. Besides, it's time we took a little rest." His lips toyed with her earlobe, making her laugh. "Forgive me, baby?"

"Of course."

She nestled against him, closing her eyes. Sleep was probably out of the question with both horses breathing down their necks, but he was right, she was ready for a rest.

However, rest wasn't exactly what Anson had in mind. His lips moved from her ear to her neck, and he unfastened her cloak.

She grabbed his hand. "Anson, we'll freeze!"

He chuckled. "I'll leave the cloak alone." He pulled the heavy fabric closed but left it to her to rebutton it. While her fingers were busy, he reached for the hem of her skirt, sliding his hand under it.

"Anson, I'm serious," she squealed, drawing her

knees up to her chin and wrapping her arms around her legs. "It's too cold."

"We won't get undressed," he coaxed.

"*You* won't get undressed. I'll still freeze."

"I'll keep you warm." His voice was low and seductive. She wanted to slap him.

"Anson, please. I don't want our first time back together to be on the hard ground with horses about to step on us."

She heard the crackle of dry grass and he gave a startled yelp. "Anson?"

"I see what you mean," he said, his voice some distance away. "Your damned horse just knocked me over. Did you train him to do that?"

Emily couldn't quite swallow a giggle.

"Maybe it was you who pushed me over. Hard to tell in the dark." He crawled back toward her and took her into his arms. "More I think about it, I suspect it was you. I could have rolled all the way down this hill."

"I wouldn't have done that," she said, knowing her urge to giggle was nervousness. Had he given up on his idea of taking her here and now? She was afraid to relax against him no matter how tired she felt.

"You didn't think of it, is what you mean. You never think, little girl."

He pulled her close, snuggling her against him. She tried to pretend that his words didn't sting.

Chapter Five

It was well past midnight when Jake got back to town. His horse hadn't liked being hitched to the buggy and had baulked and misbehaved the entire way. He had finally been forced to tie the lame horse to the back of the buggy and lead his own.

They had made slow progress, especially before moonrise. The buggy was equipped with lanterns, but only one held any kerosene. The light was barely enough to keep them on the road.

Once in town, he stopped the buggy at a little boardinghouse that wouldn't overtax the couple's obviously short funds. "Mrs. Barstow's a light sleeper," he told them. "The bell on the door will bring her out, and she'll find you a place to sleep if she has to give up her own bed."

"You've been most kind, Sheriff," Mildred said as her husband helped her from the buggy.

"Deputy," he corrected for at least the fourth time.

"What do we owe you?" Merle asked hesitantly.

Jake shook his head. "Just part of the job."

"We're much obliged," Mildred said.

"Go on inside," Jake said. "I'll leave the wagon and your horse at the livery."

"I'll be along in a minute to tend to his leg," Merle said as Jake coaxed his horse forward again.

Jake had Merle's horse fed, watered and rubbed down before Merle arrived. The horse had thrown a shoe but was otherwise uninjured. He suggested that Merle look the hoof over carefully in daylight and bade the man good-night.

With his saddle hoisted onto his shoulder, he led his fidgeting horse home. Once the gelding was bedded down, he walked into his little cabin. He was cold, tired, hungry and frustrated. He was no closer to checking on Emily than he had been at dusk. Farther, in fact, because neither he nor his horse would be in any shape to leave as early as he had planned.

He lit a fire in the little stove and sat near it, eating from a can of beans. His feet hurt from walking, but he felt too tired to pull off the boots. The only good part, he thought, as he struggled out of the chair and headed for his bed, was that he was too tired for any worries to keep him awake.

The sun was streaming through his window when he awoke. He threw himself out of bed, then stopped with a groan to flex stiff muscles. Hurrying to the kitchen, he took a look out his east window and was relieved to see the sun had barely pushed its way over the horizon. He had been afraid he had slept until noon. Not wanting to take time to fix himself breakfast, he threw what little food there was into his saddlebags and hurried out to saddle the horse. He could eat as he rode.

Minutes later he was riding into Strong. His practiced eyes scanned the small groups of people waiting at the train depot. A dark head with unruly curls escaping from its pins made him pull the reins so quickly the gelding wheeled in protest.

Her back was to him, the hood of a familiar cloak pushed off her head. A tall blond stranger was beside her. Jake watched her nod, watched her move into his waiting arms. She rested her head against his shoulder as if she were exhausted, or in love.

Jake's blood pounded in his ears until he would have doubted his ability to hear another sound, but a shrill whistle drew his attention. The train was pulling into the station. In moments it would leave again...with Emily aboard!

He dismounted, eager to arrest Berkeley, fearful of what Emily's reaction would be. It would be better to follow, to wait and watch.

He caught a passing boy by the sleeve. The boy turned toward him, startled. "Anthony, I'm glad it's you." He was a good boy, one Jake could trust.

"Mr. Rawlins." Anthony looked confused. "Is something wrong?"

"I need you to do me a favor." He straightened, moving to untie his saddlebags as he spoke. "Take my horse to Sheriff Chaffee. Tell him...tell him I'm following a suspect on the train. He'll know what to do."

Anthony already had the reins. "Anything else, sir?"

Jake searched his pockets for a coin, keeping one eye on the train, and the couple just now boarding.

"No. Here." He handed him a nickel. "Thanks." The last was said as he ran for the train.

He tipped his hat to shield his face as he passed the car that held Emily and Berkeley. He was swinging onto the steps of the car behind them, his saddlebags clutched in one hand, when the train lurched forward. He stumbled, but his grip on the railing held and he easily righted himself and entered the car.

He took a seat, deciding to wait until the train was up to its normal speed before crossing to the next car. As he waited for the conductor to come sell him a ticket, he realized the train was traveling east, toward Topeka. Had Berkeley decided to go back? Had Emily talked him into giving himself up?

His own disappointment at the thought disturbed him. He didn't want Berkeley to do anything noble, anything that might make him acceptable for Emily. He wanted the man to give him an excuse to knock his teeth out.

He was glaring at the closed door at the end of the car when a tap on his shoulder made him jump. One hand snaked toward the pistol at his hip as he turned toward his attacker.

"Ticket?" The conductor's face was bland, evidently used to jumpy passengers.

"I need to buy a ticket," he said, opening his coat and reaching for the small amount of cash he carried.

"Where to?"

Good question. How far were the pair going? Jake allowed the conductor a glimpse of the badge pinned to his shirtfront. "I'm following someone in the next car," he said softly.

"Don't matter. Still got to pay."

Jake bit back an irritated response. "I know that. I just don't know how far he's going."

The conductor nodded his understanding. "The next hub is Emporia. He might change trains there."

"Fine," Jake muttered, feeling a sudden need to be closer to the pair. They could get off sooner, though why, he didn't know. "Give me a ticket to Emporia."

After the transaction was made, Jake, saddlebags slung over his shoulder, jumped from one platform to the other and cautiously entered the next car. He kept his hat low over his eyes, hoping to see Emily before she saw him.

He slid quickly into the empty seat next to the door where he could study the other passengers without his six-foot-two-inch frame being quite so conspicuous. He spotted them immediately. They were sitting halfway down the car, their backs to him.

If he had harbored any doubts that he might have mistaken the dark curls, they dissolved quickly. She was sitting sideways in the chair, her face in profile, as she talked to her companion. Jake could imagine one foot tucked up under her. He had nearly injured himself trying to copy that position as a boy.

She smiled, and Jake's love for her hit him like a blow. How was he going to sit and watch her with Berkeley? How would he resist the temptation to flatten the boy's nose? And when he made his move, however professional he might make it, how was he going to live with the hatred he knew he would see in Emily's beautiful face?

Perhaps all he could do at the moment was follow

them, pray that Berkeley would make a mistake, give him a chance to be Emily's rescuer.

Emily laughed. The sound didn't carry above the noise of the train and its passengers, but he saw it. She leaned forward for a second, resting her forehead against Berkeley's shoulder. His hand came up and caressed the curls at the nape of her neck.

Jake groaned aloud. Hell couldn't have devised a more excruciating torture.

"You're exhausted, baby," Anson whispered in her ear.

"I know," she mumbled, rubbing her face against his coat. "That's why everything's funny."

"Here, get comfortable. You can sleep against my shoulder."

"I think I could sleep against the vibrating window over there." She pulled her leg out from under her and shifted to a better position, never lifting her head from his shoulder.

"I think you could sleep on horseback."

She giggled. "I almost did, didn't I?"

"I was afraid the man at the livery would think I was selling you along with the horses."

Emily sat up abruptly. "You didn't sell Christian's horse, too, did you? You were only—"

"No, no. Just my own." He pulled her back toward him. "Your brother's horse will be waiting for him when he comes into town like you said. How much did you get before you left?"

"What?"

"Money. From your brother. You said you got some."

''Yes, a little.'' She felt an unease she was too tired to analyze.

''Better let me carry it,'' he whispered.

''What?'' She sat up, rubbing her eyes.

''You better let me carry the money. It'll be safer.''

Emily studied the handsome face, too tired to think. He reached toward her carpetbag that sat at her feet, but she grabbed it first. ''All right,'' she said.

She felt inside, finding the wad of bills with her fingers. She carefully separated a few of the bills and refolded them as she pulled them out. ''This is all there was,'' she said, praying he wouldn't know she lied. She didn't even know *why* she lied.

''Is that all?'' he hissed. ''Damn.''

Emily watched him scowl as he counted the money, watched him stuff the bills inside his shirt, watched his face change from angry to cheerful again when he looked at her. ''You did your best, baby,'' he said. ''I shouldn't have bothered with it yet. You need to rest.''

She settled back against the warm shoulder. Sleep. She needed to sleep, or she would be sick. Or maybe that was fear she felt in the pit of her stomach. Anson had sold Christian's horse, she would bet on it, and he had made a bigger fuss about Christian's money than she had expected.

Of course, the train tickets weren't free. They would need food and shelter in Denver until he got a job. He was only being practical.

What would he say when he discovered she had held out on him? If she waited until they were desperate for money, would he be grateful enough to forget that she had lied? Could she claim the bills had become separated accidentally, and she hadn't meant to keep them from him? Only if she pretended to find them the next time she opened her bag. For some reason, she didn't want to give up all the money.

She hated lying! And she used to be so good at it. In her fatigue, she felt herself smile and wondered if she was about to become hysterical. Lying to Anson was nothing like lying to Christian, or even Jake. The worst that ever happened with them was some carefully crafted, often humorous revenge.

God, how they had indulged her. She felt a tear trickle down her cheek and brushed it away. Gone less than twelve hours, and she was already homesick. She wouldn't think about them. She would think about Anson, how much he loved her, and the life they were going to build together.

Her tired brain recalled a different picture of Anson. An Anson furious with one of his friends. She and Anson had gone out drinking with two other couples. She couldn't remember what had started it, but Anson had exploded. The other man, Anson's friend, lost two teeth and gained a broken nose before the others could calm Anson down.

He had become his old self so quickly that Emily had almost convinced herself it hadn't happened, not the way she remembered, anyway. She realized now that she had been a little more hesitant around Anson after that.

She tried to brush the thought out of her tired brain. Everything would be all right. Her baby's father was with her. They would be a family. And she would keep him from drinking. There was no extra money for it, anyway.

Her thoughts turned incomprehensible, and she slept.

Shaking awakened her. The last vestiges of a vaguely unsettling dream slipped away before she had a chance to examine it. A confusing roar surrounded her, and she rubbed her eyes. As soon as she sat upright she felt a sickening lurch in her stomach. For a moment she thought she would retch, but her stomach was empty.

She lay back against the seat, groaning.

"Emily! Wake up. We have to get out soon."

She peeked at Anson with one eye. The train. The escape. The money. All were clear again. But so was the roiling in her stomach. "I think I need to eat something," she said.

The train had come to a near stop, and he stood, taking her arm. "Get your bag. We have to get to another station. I don't know how far it is or how much time we have. We'll worry about food when we get there."

On her feet, she braced her knees against the seat until her head cleared. Anson tugged her arm, and she grabbed the carpetbag, letting him drag her off the train.

Jake had watched the couple closely at each stop. Berkeley let Emily sleep through them all. Until this one. As they neared the Emporia station, he shook her awake. Jake came instantly alert. They would be getting off here, no doubt to change to another line. He would have to be careful not to lose them in the crowds. Or show himself, which would probably prove the more difficult task.

He watched Emily's profile as she came awake. She looked pale and sick. He heard his teeth grind together and consciously loosened his jaw. He couldn't let his anger at Berkeley, or his fear for Emily, cloud his judgment.

As the train came to a lurching stop, the couple stood. He waited until they were moving to the exit ahead of them before he stood, as well, slipping out the door at the rear of the car. He fell back, waiting to see which direction they took then followed, well behind.

Berkeley didn't seem to know where he was going. He dragged Emily off the platform and looked around him. Jake quickly stepped behind a group of travelers, watching cautiously over a young lady's shoulder. The woman gave an indignant sniff, and he looked down into reproving eyes. He opened his coat to reveal his badge, fixing her with a threatening glare. She gasped and sidestepped into one of her companions. He didn't wait to reassure her. Berkeley was on the move again.

Jake was forced to remain beside the Santa Fe depot as the couple crossed the open space between stations. One glance backward would have revealed him to them. Even when they were inside the depot, he didn't dare make his move. He would have been easily spotted through the windows.

Looking around for some way to cross the line of tracks, he spotted a slow-moving luggage cart. It was some distance away but was heading in the right direction. He sprinted the short distance to the cart and kept it between himself and the station until he saw a chance to run from it to the side of the building. A sign between the rafters read "Missouri, Kansas and Texas."

Jake leaned against the wall, wondering how long he would have to wait, praying that they hadn't left this station for another one. He looked back up at the sign. The M. K. T. angled slightly west of north or east of south. Was Berkeley taking his Emily to Mexico? Or Canada? Or was he heading for another hub in Junction City? Lord, if he lost them, it would be difficult to pick up their trail again.

The waiting was wearing on his admittedly short patience. He needed to know he hadn't lost them. He hazarded a peek around the side of the building. There was little activity on the platform. And no sign of Emily.

He stepped cautiously onto the platform, keeping close to the wall. No one took notice of him while he lounged against the wall, thinking. He needed to remain out of sight of the window yet get close enough to glance through it, all the while doing nothing to draw the other travelers' attention. He slid the saddlebags off his shoulder and rested them on the floor beside him, hoping that made him look more relaxed.

As he was about to ease toward the window, Anson Berkeley stepped through the door. Jake's muscles tensed, preparing to dive off the platform and out of sight. But, as Emily did not follow, he remained still. Berkeley, after all, didn't know him.

From under the brim of his hat, Jake watched Berkeley motion to one of the boys loitering near the station.

"Here, boy," Berkeley said. "I'll give you a nickel

if you'll trot over to the nearest restaurant and bring back two dinners.''

"Boxed for the train, sir?" inquired the boy.

"Yes, yes. And be quick about it. We don't have all day."

"Right away, sir."

The boy turned, but before he could go, Berkeley caught up a handful of loose cotton shirt and hauled the boy back around. "Mind you come back, hear? I'll turn you over to the law if you run off with my money."

The startled boy shook his head. "Don't worry, mister."

Berkeley let him go, brushing off his hands and clothes as he watched him dart away. Berkeley turned to reenter the depot. His eyes fell on Jake.

Jake pulled his hat down a little lower and crossed his arms against his chest, pretending to rest. After no more than a couple of seconds, Berkeley turned away. Once he was back inside, Jake let out a sigh of relief. They were here. The train wasn't expected immediately or he wouldn't be ordering dinner.

After a few minutes, Jake lifted his saddlebags and jumped off the platform, sitting on the ground beside the building. Remaining on the platform was too risky. At any moment Emily could decide to step outside.

Berkeley's request of the boy reminded him that he hadn't eaten since the wee hours of the morning. He retrieved a can of peaches from his saddlebags and opened it with his knife. He used the same knife as a fork and ate them slowly, his ear tuned toward the platform.

He would wait. He would jump on the train at the last minute as he had done before, a car behind the couple, if possible. He would buy a ticket to whatever stop the conductor deemed necessary, then watch Emily from the back of the car. When they got off, he would get off.

He wasn't exactly sure what he would do after that. Arresting Berkeley now and taking him back to Topeka sounded very appealing but would, no doubt, make Emily the fugitive's strongest champion. The idea of waiting until he hurt or frightened her made his stomach turn. He thought of the boy's fright when Berkeley threatened him and imagined the same expression on Emily's beautiful face.

The sides of the tin can compressed under his fingers, and he loosened his grip. He wouldn't let Berkeley hurt her. He would stay too close for that to happen. He would find some way to arrest Berkeley without losing Emily in the process.

He almost laughed at himself. When had he started thinking of her as his to lose? Hadn't he decided that he wasn't worthy of her, either? Evidently somewhere deep inside he hadn't been convinced.

Emily looked up from her book and watched Anson pace across the room. It had seemed a little silly to tuck the novel she had started into the carpetbag to take up precious space, but now she was glad she had done it. If only Anson would settle down and let her read.

Every third time he passed in front of her he demanded to know where the boy was with their dinners. It did nothing to help her forget her hunger.

Once she had even offered to let him read her book, but he had only grunted and resumed his pacing. When he was in one of his moods, it was best to ignore him.

She tried to return her attention to the novel. It was one of Lynnette's, a copy signed by "Silver Nightingale" herself. Her heroes were all fairly rugged men; this one was a frontier sheriff. She found herself picturing Jake as the lead, no matter how many times his hair was described as blond.

Anson paused in front of her again. She waited a second before she lifted her eyes from the book. She tried to put a questioning smile on her lips.

"Where in the hell is that boy?"

Emily sighed. "Anson, the restaurants are probably busy this time of day. You said yourself we had plenty of time." Time enough for Anson to have gone for the dinners himself.

"I'm only thinking of you," he snapped. "You were about to faint from hunger when we got off the train."

"I think it was the motion as much as hunger that bothered me," she said, affecting a patience she didn't feel. "I'm right enough now, though I will enjoy the dinner when it comes. And it will come, Anson."

Her smile didn't placate him. He began his pacing again. Once across the room. Twice across the room. Emily reread the last three paragraphs, getting no more out of them this time than she had the last. She was practically holding her breath when Anson stopped in front of her again. She barely stifled a groan.

"He's stolen my money, the little—"

"Anson!" The sharpness in her voice surprised him into silence. She took a calming breath. "Go pace outside, and let me read."

Without a moment's hesitation he snatched the book out of her hands and flung it across the room. Emily leaped to her feet to retrieve it only to be pushed back into the chair. "You could show a little more sympathy," he hissed, "instead of wasting your time on drivel. It's reading tripe like that that's got you so hot to be married."

He turned his back on her and resumed his pacing. Emily came slowly to her feet, her eyes on Anson. When he didn't give her another glance, she walked purposefully toward the crumpled book. She lifted it carefully and smoothed the pages and cover with loving hands. It was a stronger link to her past than she had realized.

Without another look toward Anson, she moved to the door, stepping out onto the narrow platform. She had flung off her cloak when she had entered the depot. Without it, she could feel the cool air penetrate her many layers of clothing. It wasn't so cold that she needed it for the few minutes she planned to remain outside. The chill air helped to cool her temper, as well.

Anson was right. She should be more sympathetic. They had no money to spare, and he had ordered the dinners mainly for her. She, in turn, had buried her nose in a book and left it all for him to worry about. She was even hiding some money from him. Yet...

She had the strongest impression that someone was watching her. She took a quick glance around at the others on the platform. Everyone seemed occupied with their own concerns. Yet the feeling persisted.

Perhaps Anson was watching from the window or door, waiting for her to return and make up. She wanted to let him wait. Maybe this time *he* should come to her and apologize. After all, he had thrown the book and made himself the most annoying pest possible. With a sigh she admitted he would never see it that way. She had provoked him.

She caught a glimpse of movement far to her right. She turned, but no one was there. Perhaps someone had moved along the side of the building. Or someone was hiding there. She felt her skin prickle. She had no desire to investigate.

She was getting cold after all, she decided. As she turned to reenter the building, a young boy, carrying two white boxes, stepped up onto the platform. The boy Anson had hired, she hoped, giving him a smile as she preceded him inside.

Anson stopped pacing to scowl at her. His face didn't brighten when he noticed the boy behind her. "You, there. It's about time."

"Came as fast as I could, sir. A little more money mighta made the cooks work faster, I reckon."

"Oh you do, do you? The promise of a coin didn't make *you* move faster." He took the boxes from the boy, handing one to Emily. Ignoring the boy, he took his own to a chair and sat, preparing to eat.

"I worked hard for you, mister," the boy said, loud enough to attract the attention of everyone in the room. "You promised a nickel."

Anson took a bite of fried chicken. "You took too long," he mumbled around the food.

"Oh, for heaven's sake." Emily put the box aside. From the little reticule that dangled from her waist she pulled a handkerchief, then rummaged for the coin. Afraid Anson would try to stop her, she hurried to the boy. "Thank you very much," she said softly. "I'm most grateful for your help."

"Thanks, pretty lady," he said, giving Anson one last scowl before he turned and ran from the room.

"You're too softhearted," Anson said, grinning at her.

"Thank you," she said, giving him her warmest smile. "And you're a tightfisted grouch."

"Thank you, my dear. I'm so glad we understand each other."

He winked at her, and she giggled. He was being charming again. "It's a wonder what a little food does for your disposition," she said.

"Ah, yes. And what a little charity does for yours."

She decided to ignore him and concentrate on the food. She was so hungry she was afraid of eating it too quickly. She wasn't sure how much time they had left before the train came. Anson was never specific with information like that. He would take care of her; she didn't need to know.

The food was greasy, though still slightly warm, and there seemed to be plenty of it. She ate it slowly, pausing often to give her stomach time to settle. She didn't want to disgrace herself by retching in a public place. Her stomach had been very sensitive lately.

She had finished the meal and was dreaming about lemonade when she heard the train whistle. "Is that one ours?" she asked, coming to her feet.

"Yes. Get your things. I'll be glad to get out of here."

They waited on the platform while the incoming passengers disembarked. That sense of being watched came over Emily again. She looked around, trying to determine the cause. No one was paying either her or Anson any mind, and she decided it was her imagination playing on her sense of guilt for running away. In some deep part of her heart, she must wish someone had followed.

She shrugged it off and followed Anson onto the train. He chose a seat near the front of the car, stepping back to let her sit beside the window. She didn't want Anson to catch her nervousness and refrained from speaking as they waited for the train to move. But the uneasiness didn't leave her even after the train lurched into motion.

It was her conscience watching her, she decided. She had stolen from her brother, lied to those she loved. But, she reminded herself, she had had little choice. Perhaps if her body was more comfortable so too would be her conscience. She stood and shrugged out of the warm cloak. As she folded it into a cushion for her head she glimpsed a familiar figure in the back of the car.

Jake!

Chapter Six

Emily turned and sat so quickly she was sure she bruised her hip. What was Jake doing on the train? His hat had been low over his face, and she was sure he hadn't seen her. But of course he had seen her! Why else would he be here except to follow her? He had been watching her at Emporia.

It occurred to her that he might be another example of her overactive imagination. She wanted to look again to be sure. She couldn't make herself move. Perhaps it was best if he didn't know that she knew he was following her. Oh Lord! She couldn't think. Part of her traitorous heart was singing, "He followed me! He followed me!"

"What's wrong, baby?" Anson asked.

"Nothing." She said it too quickly. He would know she was lying. She leaned against the seat, pretending to try to sleep.

Was that really Jake behind her? And what if it was? Why should she be glad he followed? She should be terrified. Wasn't Anson her only hope for a future—for herself and her baby?

She had to know if she had really seen him. She squirmed in the seat, hoping she looked as if she were trying to get comfortable. After a moment she stood, adjusting her cloak over the seat back. She made the briefest of glances toward the back of the car.

She was turning and regaining her seat even as her brain sorted out the image. Jake was there, trying his best not to be seen. He was slouched low in his seat, his hat pulled down over his eyes. But she didn't need to see his eyes to recognize him. She recognized the dark brown hat and coat, the very shape of his shoulders. She *felt* him, had felt him even at the station in Emporia.

Anson was eyeing her speculatively. She tried again to pretend to sleep, but he wouldn't allow it. Leaning close he asked quietly, "You saw someone, didn't you?"

She shook her head.

His hand closed around her upper arm. "Don't lie to me. Who is it?"

She hated Anson when he was angry. He terrified her. "It's Jake," she whispered quickly. "Jake Prescott. He's just a friend."

"Perhaps it's a coincidence, him being on the train." His eyes were boring into hers, and she couldn't turn away. "You don't believe that, do you?"

Emily shrugged. She had betrayed Jake. She tried to brush away the guilt. Shouldn't her loyalty be with Anson?

"Tell me about him," Anson demanded.

She tried to pull her arm out of his grip but his

fingers tightened. "He grew up on the ranch," she blurted.

"The ranch?" Anson's eyes narrowed. "Does he work for your brother? Could he have sent him after us?"

She shook her head. "He was in town when we left. He's a deputy now."

Anson released her arm and lifted her hand. The change was frightening in itself. "Listen very carefully. He isn't following you. He's following me." Emily started to protest, but a quick shake of his head silenced her. "The police in Topeka are out to get me. They no sooner let me out of jail than they dream up something new to try to pin on me. Your friend's waiting for a chance to arrest me."

"If that's true, why hasn't he already done it?"

Anson shrugged. "Maybe he's afraid I'll hurt you. Who knows what lies he's heard. Maybe he wants to kill me and is waiting to catch me alone."

Emily wanted to pull her hand from his but knew better than to try. "I can't believe that of Jake."

He smiled at her. The violence had left his eyes and she began to relax. "You are such a trusting little girl." He bent forward and kissed her cheek. "That's what I love about you."

"Let me go talk to him," she suggested. "I'll make him tell me what he's up to."

"No. We don't want to force his hand. Just be quiet for a minute and let me think."

She sat in silence while Anson considered their options. She wanted to suggest again that she talk to Jake. Their shared history included countless times when she had talked him into things. It might work one more time. Besides, she felt a growing need to tell him goodbye.

"I'm getting off," Anson finally whispered.

"What?"

Anson waved her to silence. "At the next stop, just before the train leaves the station, I'll get off. You keep your friend on the train."

"He'll just get off one stop later." Why was he running? Why was he leaving her?

"Of course. But that'll give me time to get away."

"What about me, Anson?" *What about our plans? What about our baby?*

"Tell him something to throw him off track. I'll head for Denver. When you know you won't be followed, meet me there."

Why did his plan fill her with panic? "Anson, couldn't we just go back to Topeka and fight these new charges? Can't we clear your name before we start our new life?"

"Don't be such a child, Emily. They won't listen to me. I've been through this already. Just trust me and do as I say."

Emily grabbed his hand. If he left her now they would never be together. Why did that thought come so insistently to mind? She had to tell him about the baby. "Anson, before you go..."

"Americus!" yelled the conductor.

"Open your window," he said.

"What? Why?" Why wouldn't he listen?

"I'll make my move at the last possible moment. You'll have to toss my bag out after the train starts to move."

She blinked at him, unable to comprehend what he

was saying. With a screech of brakes and a resounding whistle, the train pulled into the station.

"Listen," he said, taking her by the shoulders. "You have to do this. I'll wait until the other passengers have gotten off. I'll slip out. You—" He gave her a little shake. "Make sure he doesn't follow, even if you have to trip him. Once the train starts, toss out my bags. I'll need my clothes. Can you understand that?"

"Anson..."

"I'm out of time. Now do as I say."

Anson let her go, and Emily watched a few passengers gather their things and leave the train. A man entered their car and found a seat.

The conductor shouted, "All aboard!" and Anson waited another full minute. Emily thought she could feel a tension in the floor under her feet as the train built up steam. She found she was holding her breath.

The window! She had almost forgotten. She turned and slid it open, just as Anson moved. He was on his feet, running for the door as the train lurched forward. The jump must have staggered him, but he was on his feet when she looked out. She grabbed his bag and shoved it through the window, then turned to make sure Jake was still on the train.

He was standing now. And fixing her with a deadly glare.

Jake couldn't believe it. Emily had helped Berkeley escape. Well, it shouldn't have surprised him. He had known all along that she was going with Berkeley of her own free will. She had given him no reason to hope she would choose the law, let alone him, over her precious Anson.

He lifted his saddlebags without taking his eyes off her, and made his way forward. Her expression held a mixture of fear and hurt, but he tried to ignore it. "Mind if I sit here?" he asked as he slipped into the seat Berkeley had vacated.

"Why did you follow me?" she asked.

Was there a hint of longing in her voice? No, he was imagining again. More likely she was hurt that he had scared off her boyfriend. "Berkeley's wanted for assault and robbery," he said. "Where's he going from Americus?"

She shrugged. "He hasn't done anything. The Topeka police are just out to get him."

Her voice trailed off at the end. So, that's what Berkeley had told her. And she wasn't sure now if she believed him. "Do you have any money?" he asked more gently.

"What is it with you men? Is that all I am, money?"

Now where did that outburst come from? Something Berkeley had said, probably. He put a comforting hand on her clinched fists. "All I want to know is if you have fare back home?"

She looked appropriately contrite. "I can get home." Then her head came up. "What are you going to do?"

"Just go home," he said. He took one more look at her beloved face and fought back an urge to kiss her. Abruptly he stood and hurried toward the front of the car.

* * *

Emily watched in astonishment as the door closed behind Jake. Where was he going? Somehow she had thought she would have his company at least to the next stop and perhaps until a returning train came through. Why wasn't he going to sit with her? Couldn't he even stand to be in the same car with her?

She considered marching into the forward car and demanding to know why he was being so cruel. Of course she knew why. He was almost in love with her. She had realized it, though she hadn't wanted to admit it. Her leaving with Anson had hurt him until he couldn't stand the sight of her.

Well, fine! she fumed. Let him be that way. She didn't want his love, anyway. Then why did it make her feel so sad?

She was lost in thought and didn't notice when the train began to slow. The buzzing questions around her brought her out of her reverie.

"I reckon a bridge's washed out," someone suggested.

"Maybe it's a robbery." This was followed by a few shrieks.

In one instant, Emily knew with a clear certainty what was happening. Jake's badge had been enough to convince the engineer to stop the train. She grabbed her bag and cloak and hurried into the aisle. She excused herself as her bag bumped a woman's shoulder. A child leaned out of his seat, and she waited impatiently for his mother to pull him back in.

What if they didn't stop the train, only slowed it? She hurried to the door and stepped out onto the platform. The train was moving slowly now, or seemed to be until she looked at the ground slipping by beneath her. A little slower, she prayed.

"It's just like jumping from the hay loft," she told herself. Only she had been jumping onto a mound of hay, then. And the loft wasn't moving.

And Jake had always been waiting for her at the bottom.

Jake.

The train had slowed to a crawl, and she tossed the bag and cloak. Whispering a prayer that sounded more like a curse, she stepped off the platform.

The ground came up to meet her faster than she expected. She rolled, as she had been taught to do if a horse threw her. The baby! she thought, coming to her knees. She hadn't even thought of it before she jumped. She pressed her hands to her stomach, but she didn't feel hurt inside. Other than feeling a little bruised, she was sure she was fine.

The train, already picking up speed, clattered past. Jake stood on the opposite side of the track, dusting off his hat. She was relieved to see him. Until this moment, she hadn't considered the possibility that she could have been wrong. She might have found herself stranded here alone.

She came to her feet and watched him pull the hat down on his head. He took two long strides, lifted a pair of saddlebags and slung them over his shoulder, then took two more strides toward Americus before he noticed her bag. He froze for an instant, and she thought a strangled cry escaped his throat.

"Jake," she called.

He whirled to find her.

"I didn't mean to frighten you," she said.

He came toward her. "What exactly did you mean to do?"

She had been feeling guilty about giving his presence away to Anson. She had been relieved and pleased to see him across the track. She had even felt a warm flood of pleasure to discover his concern for her safety. She was forgetting her purpose. She gave her heavy skirt a cursory dusting. "You're going after Anson," she said. "I'm going with you."

He shook his head. "Why didn't you just get off with him?"

She straightened to her full height, which seemed inadequate next to Jake. "I was supposed to keep you on the train."

He put one fist on his hip as he studied her. She didn't like the scrutiny and brushed past him, heading for her cloak. The cold air, or his cold stare, was making her shiver.

"And having failed," he suggested, following, "you decided to tag along and slow my pursuit."

She hadn't actually thought of that, although she should have. After giving the cloak a shake to rid it of dead grass, she wrapped it around her shoulders. "I can't trust you to arrest Anson. You're liable to hurt him in a fit of jealousy."

That was quite an accusation to make to even-tempered Jake, and she expected him to deny it. Instead she heard him mutter "Smart girl" as he brushed past her.

He reached her bag and lifted it, turning toward her with an outstretched hand. "Shall we go?"

They were in a wide river valley where bare trees lined little creeks and all but hid the hills beyond. To their right the thickest growth of trees identified the river. Emily looked for a farmhouse but saw none, though there were some cultivated fields.

"Are we going to walk all the way back? It must be close to five miles!"

"Then your daily walks have been good practice, haven't they?"

He was still waiting for her to join him. She did so reluctantly. With his hand on the small of her back, they started across the prairie along the railroad track.

She had done it again, leaped, this time literally, before she stopped to think. But what else could she have done? She couldn't have simply gone home as Jake had told her. With Jake off the train, she could have gone on to Denver, but she had a nagging fear that Anson might not ever join her there.

She marched along beside Jake and found herself smiling. "I really surprised you, didn't I? Jumping off the train."

"Nothing you do should surprise me."

"Probably not, but it did."

"A momentary lapse."

They trudged along in silence, Emily watching the uneven ground and little else. Each step brought pain to leg muscles that were sore from walking much of the night. A stinging pain in her left heel meant a blister had broken.

When Jake's hand caught her arm, she looked up, ready to voice her misery. His fingers were on his lips.

"I think I hear something. There must be a road nearby."

Emily heard it, too, behind them. It sounded like chickens fighting.

Jake grabbed her shoulders and brought her to the ground just as a wagon burst from a gap in the trees that hadn't been apparent before. "They're singing," she whispered, covering her mouth to muffle her giggle.

"They're drunk," Jake corrected.

"We could get a ride with them!" Emily started to rise, but Jake pushed her down again.

"*I* could get a ride with them. *You're* not riding with a wagon load of drunks."

"You wouldn't leave me here?"

"Of course not!" Clearly she had insulted him.

Emily risked a peek at the wagon. The road was some distance away and, from her low position behind the tracks, she could only make out the top third of the wagon and its occupants over the tall grass. There was little chance of them seeing her and Jake unless they tried to get their attention. They were making enough noise to mask an Indian attack.

With a shove against Jake's arm, Emily turned and sat on the ground. "We might as well get comfortable until they pass," she said. Jake turned and sat beside her.

"He told you he was wanted for robbery and assault?" Jake asked. There was little question who *he* was.

She bent her knee and began untying her left shoe before she answered. "He said the law was after him again. Isn't it a little out of your jurisdiction?"

"A wanted man came into my county. I followed to arrest him."

"Yes, and why didn't you arrest him?" She eased her shoe off, trying to protect her sore heel. A circle of crusted blood decorated her stocking. She pulled the fabric away from her skin, then wondered if that had been wise. Her toes were cold in contrast to her burning heel, and she slid the shoe back on, determining to ignore it. She tightened the laces. "Jake?"

When she turned toward him, he turned away, crouching low to watch the wagon. Their tuneless cries were growing fainter. "They'll cross another creek soon and be out of sight," he said.

"Can't we rest here a little longer?"

He looked at her sharply, suspiciously. "We just got started."

She gave him a sweet smile. "But I want to give Anson a head start."

With a growl he came to his feet and reached down to help her rise. She stood in time to see the wagon disappear in a gap in the trees. With Jake carrying both her bag and his saddlebags, they followed the tracks toward the same row of trees. Emily imagined Americus on the other side.

Jake tossed the saddlebags to his shoulder and took her elbow. She wasn't sure if he was trying to hurry her along or if he had noticed her tendency to limp. It seemed to her they were moving slower now, not faster. But his hand on her arm felt reassuring, and she didn't want to spoil it with any comment.

Jake slowed his pace, wishing he could do something for her blister. He could catch her into his arms and carry her, but probably not all the way back to Americus.

He shouldn't feel sorry for her. She was the one who chose to run away. He hadn't asked her to jump off the train. He would never forget the horror he had felt when he saw her bag and the crumpled cloak lying beside the track. He had thought her broken body lay beneath the cloak. He tightened his grip on her elbow, needing to feel her body move against his fingers.

He had hid his relief behind anger. Of course, it wasn't too hard to be angry with Emily. She never made anything easy for him. He would be nearly in Americus by now if she had done as he had told her. Of course, her company was better than a wagon load of drunks.

When they came to the creek, he helped her up the slight grade to the tracks so they could cross. He let her loose and started across, careful not to catch a boot heel on the ties. Emily, with her smaller feet, could hop nimbly from tie to tie.

"Do you remember the circus we went to as children?" she asked.

He turned to find her walking on the rail itself, her arms outstretched for balance. "Emily!" He reached toward her but didn't touch her. She was beautiful. Her cloak, still buttoned at the throat, had been shoved over her shoulders like a cape to allow her arms their freedom.

"I wanted to walk on the tightwire," she said. He moved along beside her, ready to steady her if she stumbled. "I wanted to fly on the trapeze. I wanted to do everything."

"I remember you tried to stand on the back of a horse."

"I was afraid to straighten up and let go."

"Thank God."

She laughed, as she had always laughed at his worry. He knew then he could never have her. She craved excitement, excitement Anson was more than willing to provide.

He watched her face as she concentrated on the rail. He didn't want to add excitement to her life; he wanted to protect her, shield her. Smother her. No wonder she lost her temper with him so often.

Finally they were across the creek, and she stepped off the rail and made her way back to level ground. He followed a few steps behind. She stopped and looked around, turning to him with a groan. "I was imagining Americus right here," she said, pointing at her feet. "This looks just like the other side of the creek. Only more so."

He laughed. "Poor Emily. You're not enjoying your grand adventure?"

Out of the trees the wind had a biting chill, and he helped her wrap the cloak back around her and raised the hood, skimming his knuckles over the dark hair in the process. He took her arm again and started her forward.

"It is an adventure, isn't it? Two men tried to send me in opposite directions by train, and here I am walking across the prairie instead."

"And, if it wasn't for me," he continued for her, "you would be on your way to…?"

"Forget it, Jake."

"I had to try."

They were quiet for several minutes before Emily

asked, "Would you care at all about catching Anson if I hadn't tried to leave with him?"

Jake chose a careful answer. "I probably wouldn't know anything about Anson if your family wasn't involved."

"There aren't wanted posters on him plastered all over the state?"

"No." Why couldn't she save her breath for walking?

"Then why did you have to follow us? Why couldn't you have just let us go?" The question was a plea but there was curiosity, also, as if she really wanted to know what he had been thinking when he jumped on that train.

"Emily," he said softly. "I couldn't let you go, not like that. This man will hurt you, I feel it. Stopping you was more important to me than stopping him."

She swung toward him. "I knew it! This stupid charge in Topeka was just an excuse. Maybe it was dreamed up entirely by my family. And you're just as bad as they are. Why can't anyone let me live my own life?"

She whirled away. He hung back, watching her stomp across the rough ground. The pace she was setting wasn't going to do her heel any good. He knew, because his own boots weren't designed for walking any more than hers were. When he noticed her starting to favor her left foot, he caught up with her.

"Let's take a little rest," he suggested.

"I wish I had gotten a drink at that stream we

crossed,'' she said, letting him help her to the ground.
''How far do you think we've come?''

''A mile or so.''

She groaned and threw herself backward on the
ground. ''Maybe we should walk closer to the road
and not be so picky about our traveling companions.''

The road had been vacant since the one wagon had
passed and it wasn't so distant that they couldn't
make themselves known to other travelers if something safe presented itself. But if they walked near the
road there would be no hiding from unsavory characters that might be too interested in Emily. No, Jake
wanted to keep them walking just where they were.

However, he had seen signs of a farmstead off to
the north. It was well off the beeline he wanted to
make to Americus, but if Emily was hurting, it would
be better to head for help. ''The farmer will have
water,'' he said.

''Farmer?'' Emily sat up, looking around, then
stood to follow his finger toward a curl of smoke.
''That's as far as the next creek,'' she protested.

''True, but he might be willing to give us a ride
into town.''

Jake judged the farm to be about a mile away, but
travel across the prairie and cultivated fields was
slower going than the packed earth next to the track.
They said little during the half-hour journey.

As they neared the farm, Jake began to have some
misgivings. The place was in terrible shape. The roof
sagged and the door set cockeyed on its hinges. Tools,
broken and otherwise, littered the weed-choked yard.

Emily held back, probably feeling the same uncertainty. "Kinda lacks a woman's touch, don't you think?"

Jake grinned. "At least we can get some water," he said, urging her forward. "Hello!"

A man in tattered coat and pants came around the side of the building with a load of firewood. "Whatcha want?" he asked, carrying the load through the open door.

Jake cast Emily a quizzical look. "I'm not following him in," she whispered.

"Could we have a drink?" he called, stepping closer to the house, equally unwilling to cross the threshold.

"Only got enough to see me through the winter," came the reply.

Jake frowned at Emily, who shrugged in response. Then it hit him. "Water," he corrected.

"Well, that I got." He came back out of the house and pointed to a bucket by the door. "Help yourselves."

Jake watched Emily approach the bucket cautiously. "Do you have a well?" she asked.

"Nope. Bring it up from the creek fresh daily," the man said proudly.

Emily cupped her hand into the water and tossed a few floating specks off the top then drank a handful of the water.

"Good, ain't it?" inquired the farmer.

"Delightful." She turned her back on the farmer and rolled her eyes at Jake.

Jake suppressed a smile. "We're much obliged," he said, stepping forward for his turn at the water.

"We were wondering if we could get a ride into Americus."

As he drank, the man answered, "Ain't no stage or nothin' through here. Too close to the railroad."

"No. I mean, would you be able to give us a ride?"

"Got nothin' to ride," he said. "Just my mule."

Jake looked at Emily. She had fished her gloves out of her bag and was slipping into them. His own hand felt frozen from the water.

"Can't give you the mule," the man said before Jake could respond. "Gotta farm with it."

"Could we borrow it? The lady is worn out from walking." He saw Emily droop a little on cue.

"Ya got yourselves kicked off the train, didn't ya?"

"Not exactly," Jake said. "I'm following a suspect who jumped the train." He unbuttoned his coat to show his badge, hoping it would help get the mule for Emily.

The man laughed. "She a lawman, too? Naw, I reckon ya was kicked off the train. Gettin' a little too friendly, was ya?"

Jake shook his head. "No, it was nothing like that. I'm following the suspect and she's...well...she's following me."

"Ya can leave her here if'n ya want."

The man was trying to get his goat. He chose to ignore him but stole a glance at Emily to see her reaction. She looked more irritated than indignant. Good. A show of temper wouldn't help them get the mule. "Sir, could I rent the mule? I'd leave it in Americus for you."

"Now how would I get into Americus to get my

mule? I'd have to walk. Wouldn't be no easier for me than for you.''

''But the lady—''

''Naw. Walkin'll teach ya to use better manners on the train. Welcome to the water, though.'' With that he turned his back and entered the house, dragging the door closed behind him.

Emily stomped one foot on the ground and winced. ''I say we steal his mule.''

Jake took her arm and led her toward the road. ''Oh, you and Berkeley make a fine pair.''

She jerked her arm out of his hand. ''That's not fair, Jake. I was joking.''

Jake had thought he was joking, too, but on reflection he decided maybe he wasn't. She didn't want to admit Berkeley was a criminal, and he wanted to impress on her that he was.

But perhaps he should give it up. She wasn't going to admit she was wrong, at least not to him. And remaining her friend might be more important in the long run. That way, if she wouldn't listen to reason, at least, she would let him pick up the pieces.

Chapter Seven

Emily was so bone weary when they finally crossed a short bridge and saw Americus, she was practically leaning on Jake. Placing one foot in front of the other seemed to take all her concentration. The sight of the pretty little homes didn't even perk her up. Of course, any house would seem pretty after the shack where they had stopped for water.

She and Jake had barely spoken since that stop. It was almost as if they were both afraid that whatever they said would make the other angry. She wasn't sure what had given her that impression; she was too tired to think.

The sight of their destination seemed to renew Jake's energy, and, as he turned them onto the wide main street, he increased his pace. Emily, hoping to feel the same renewal, made an effort to look around her. Though the town had quite a collection of stores, from drugs to groceries, she felt no lifting of her spirit or her feet.

She wished Jake would slow down. ''M. W. Gibson," she read aloud, hoping to distract him. "Burial Cases and Sewing Machines."

The sign struck her as funny. She bit back a giggle. "Why don't they call it Coffins and Clothiers?"

She had to stop and give in to the laughter. She knew it sounded hysterical, but that just added to the absurdity. "No. I got it," she gasped. "Death and Dressmaking."

She heard Jake chuckle. She wanted him to laugh. "Stiffs and Stitches?" she suggested.

He bent and brought one arm behind her knees. The laughter vanished in a gasp as she found herself thrust against his hard chest. He walked on down the street with her in his arms.

"Oh," she murmured against his neck. "This is a wonderful idea. I wish we had thought of it miles ago."

He didn't respond, and she bent to rest her head on his shoulder, when something caught her eye. "Stop!"

"What's wrong?" he asked, turning his head toward her. His lips were an inch from hers. For an instant she forgot what had caught her attention. She had an overwhelming desire to taste those lips. She licked her own as she stared at his.

"Emily?" A whisper of breath touched her face and she shivered. "Emily?"

It was a plea this time and brought her back to her senses. "That," she said, pointing over his shoulder. "Is that a cow?"

Jake turned. "Yes, that's a cow."

A cow stood placidly grazing in the vacant lot beside them. Jake stood for a moment watching it then started on down the street. "Good," Emily said, resting her head on his shoulder. "For a moment I thought I had gone crazy."

"For a moment, I thought so, too," he murmured.

She decided not to think about what he meant and closed her eyes. She didn't open them until she felt Jake walk up a pair of steps. He set her on her feet in front of a whitewashed door. "Dutton House," he said.

"Nice to meet you, Dutton House," she quipped.

He opened the door, and she preceded him inside, collapsing into the first chair she saw. She listened to the deep resonance of Jake's voice as he arranged for their rooms and a warm bath. In a moment he turned toward her. "Upstairs," he said gently.

She spent a second wishing he would carry her then came to her feet. He took her arm and helped her up the narrow, dimly lit stairs. He opened a door halfway down the hall and set her bag inside. "They'll bring up a bath in a few minutes and a tray a little later."

Emily grabbed his arm. "You're not going after Anson tonight, are you? You won't leave me here?"

He seemed to take forever to answer. She was determined to go with him, but she knew at this moment, if he wanted to leave, she was too exhausted to follow.

"No," he said finally. "I'm going to see if anyone remembers seeing him get off the train this afternoon. Until I find out which direction he went, I have no trail to follow."

"But if you find out, you won't leave tonight?"

"Emily."

"Please."

Perhaps if she knew what he was thinking it would be easier to convince him to wait, to take her with him. She searched his face. His green eyes seemed almost black in the dim light of the hall, but there was a softness about them when he looked at her. She felt her pulse quicken and a quiver spiral though her belly. Then she was lost in his gaze, forgetting everything but his strong, warm body so close to hers and his eyes that seemed to probe her soul.

And his lips. She started to raise her hand, wanting to touch them, when he spoke. "I'll see what I can learn and come back. I won't leave until I've talked to you."

He turned then, opening a door across the hall and placing his saddlebags just inside. He gave her a slight nod as he passed her again on his way to the stairs.

Emily stared after him. What had just happened? Why had her body responded to his? Fatigue must have clouded her brain, she decided, turning into her room.

The room was small and dull with whitewashed walls and a bare floor. There was very little furniture and no wardrobe, merely a few hooks on the wall. But the bed looked inviting.

She had just removed her shoes and stockings when she heard a knock at the door. At her response, a woman carrying a huge steaming kettle and a stack of towels came in followed by a boy with a brass tub and two girls with more kettles. While the girls filled the tub, the boy built a fire in the fireplace.

"I'm Mrs. Dutton. When would you like dinner sent up?"

Emily's stomach growled as if in answer. "As soon as it's convenient," she said, too tired to be embarrassed.

"Very good, miss." Mrs. Dutton herded her helpers out of the room and closed the door behind her.

The tub was steaming. Emily moaned in anticipation. She quickly shed her clothes, frustrated by the extra layers, and eased into the water. She let out a loud sigh of relief as the heat soaked into sore muscles.

She washed quickly, lathering her hair twice, then sank into the water. The tub was cramped, but with some trial and error, she found a comfortable position and laid her head back against the rim. She had just begun to relax when a knock on the door brought a groan of protest to her lips. "Who is it?" she called.

"I have your dinner tray, ma'am," came the muffled reply.

Emily frowned, unwilling to end her bath so soon. "Just leave it in the hall," she called. "I'll get it in a minute."

"Yes, ma'am."

"Ah, dinner," she murmured, relaxing again. "I am starving. I'll get it in a minute."

Jake headed back toward the hotel. First he had sent a telegram to his boss, asking him to let Christian know his sister was safe. Then he had visited a doctor and gotten an ointment for Emily's heel. After that, he had spent nearly half an hour chasing down the man who had been on duty at the train depot that afternoon, but the information had been worth the work.

The man remembered Berkeley well. The fugitive had asked about the next train north and had become furious when he learned he would have to wait two days since the trains didn't run on Sunday. Berkeley, when he had calmed down asked about buying a horse. The station attendant had recommended a nearby livery, and Jake looked up the owner.

Yes, Berkeley had bought a horse and had ridden west out of town. But Berkeley had bought the man's last horse. He suggested Jake try the livery that was connected with Dutton House.

As Jake neared the hotel, he found his thoughts more on Emily than on the horse he needed to buy and the fugitive he needed to follow. He shouldn't have lifted her into his arms, but he had ached for her with every step until he could no longer resist. When he had turned his head and watched that pink tongue trace across her soft lips it had almost been his undoing.

The urge to kiss her had stayed with him. He had nearly given in again in the hotel. That was another in a long list of reasons why he had to send her home. He was likely to give in to the urge eventually, and she wouldn't welcome it.

Maybe he could use that in his favor. If she refused to go home, he could try kissing her. It might make her furious enough to want to get away from him. He found himself grinning when he entered the livery at Dutton House. He made arrangements for a horse and saddle and hurried toward Emily's room.

A tray sat outside her door, and he felt a prickle of alarm when he realized it hadn't been touched. He tapped lightly on the door, needing to know if she was all right but not wanting to wake her if she had gone to bed. The room was quiet.

"Emily?" he asked softly, opening the door to peek inside.

He froze halfway through the door. She had fallen asleep all right, but not in her bed. Her head, resting on the rim of the tub, was turned away from him. Her hair, glistening in the firelight, hung to the floor. One arm was thrown across her chest as if to shield her breasts. It failed miserably. The rosy tips, puckered from the chill in the room, taunted him.

He swallowed, fighting the desire that burned through his body. He couldn't leave her like this: she would catch a chill. He couldn't go wake her: she would die of embarrassment. He took one last look at the tempting mounds he would never taste and slipped back out of the room.

He took a deep breath, struggling to bring his lust under control. He brought one foot down heavily on the floor. "Emily!" he called as he pounded on the door.

He heard a gasp and a splash. "Just a minute."

"Are you all right?" he called, picturing her stepping out of the tub, streams of glistening water cascading down the curves of her body.

"Yes. I just finished my bath. Wait out there."

He imagined her rubbing the towel over her pale skin, turning it rosy in the firelight. Rosy like the tips of her smooth, soft breasts.

He cursed his foolish imagination. His body was all too willing to respond. He bent and lifted the tray, making sure his coat hid all evidence of his lascivious thoughts.

In a moment she opened the door. She had slipped on a modest nightgown and thrown her cloak around her shoulders. "Cold?" he asked.

"I don't have a robe," she answered.

He cursed himself for asking. He didn't need her to say anything that further called her state of dress to his attention. He set the tray on a little table beside the bed.

"I think there's enough here for two," Emily said, taking a seat on the bed. "Pull up a chair and help me eat it. You can tell me what you learned." She threw the cloak off behind her to better free her arms and began building a sandwich out of cold beef and bread.

The only thing Jake could remember learning was the exact color of her nipples. He shook himself and brought a chair to the bedside. He eyed the glass of water, wanting to splash it in his face.

"Did anyone remember seeing Anson?" she asked, before bringing her sandwich to her mouth.

Jake tore his eyes away from her lips. Berkeley. The bastard *would* be on her mind. "Yes," he said, keeping the bitterness out of his voice. "He bought a horse and headed west."

"So that's what we do," she mumbled as she chewed.

"That's what I do." He helped himself to a chunk of meat and kept his eyes off her face.

"I want to go with you, Jake."

"I know you do," he said gently. "It could be hard traveling. I don't know where he's headed or how long it'll take me to catch up with him. You should go back."

She took another bite and shook her head. She acted as if she knew he would give in. It made him more determined.

"The train won't run tomorrow," he said, leaning toward her. "You can stay here, sleep, read, walk around and count the dairy cows—"

"Dairy cows?" She laughed. "You mean there are more?"

"They're all over town," he answered. "There's a cheese factory, so everybody owns a cow or two and sells them the extra milk."

She laughed, handing him a sandwich she had built for him. "That sounds like wonderful fun, but I'd rather go with you."

He shouldn't be sitting here with her like this. Her nightgown was completely modest, covering her from throat to wrists to ankles. But it was a nightgown and made him picture her lying in bed, her dark hair spread across a white pillow, her arms reaching for him.

"Jake?"

The hand stretched out toward him held a sandwich. The fantasy vanished, leaving him aching and surprised at his own foolishness.

"You left me there for a minute," she said, smiling as he took the food from her fingers.

If she knew what he had been thinking... He cleared his throat. "Monday you can take the train back to Emporia. From there, you can head to the ranch or go home to Topeka, take your pick. If you don't want to be with your family, you can go to Berkeley's. When I catch him, I'll get him to Topeka and you can see him there."

"You're giving me choices? I can't believe it." She seemed to think over her options. "I choose...going with you."

He wasn't surprised. "You know I won't hurt him unless I'm forced to defend myself."

"I know." He knew better than to take her sweet smile as acquiescence. "I still want to be with you when you find him."

"That's not one of your choices."

She glared at him a moment before concentrating on her supper. They split the piece of apple pie, and when the tray was empty, Emily took it to the door. Jake couldn't help admiring her backside as she bent to set the tray on the floor.

He had to get away from Emily and cool off. "Could we get that tub into my room?" he wondered aloud.

"It'd be easier to trade rooms."

He eyed the clothes scattered around and gave her a dubious look. She laughed and began tossing articles of clothing over her arm. She didn't seem to notice that several of the items were of a very personal nature. "Done. See?"

He grinned at her, lifting the cloak from the bed. "I'm amazed," he said.

He grabbed her bag on the way out and escorted her across the hall. He opened the door and traded her bag and cloak for his saddlebags.

"Oh, I almost forgot." He took the tiny bottle from his pocket. "The doctor said you should put this on your heel at least four times a day."

"Thank you," she said, taking the bottle from him. Her smile was soft and sweet. She seemed touched by the gesture. He felt himself growing hard again and turned to go.

She caught his arm. "Will you see me before you go tomorrow?"

He shook his head. "I want to leave at first light. You need your sleep."

"So this is goodbye."

She seemed to be leaning slightly toward him. Surely that was his imagination. He was probably the one trying to close the space between them. "Good bye, Emily," he said, turning once again.

"Jake."

He took the last step across the hall before he responded. He should be careful not to be so close to her. "Yes?"

"You might want to go ask for more hot water. I imagine the bath is pretty cold by now."

He nodded, closing the door behind him before he muttered, "I hope so."

Emily woke in the middle of the night, her body tingling from dreams of Jake. As she came fully awake the warm feeling was replaced with one of dismay at the vividness of the dream. "It must have been something I ate," she muttered, rolling onto her side and trying to go back to sleep.

Jake.

Last night she had been ready to let him go. She hadn't known if she would go to the ranch or to Topeka, but she would have all day Sunday to decide. But now, the thought was too depressing. Was she supposed to sit and wait? Quietly listen to her family's condemnation? Drive herself to distraction with worry over her future?

If Anson escaped he would head for Denver, expecting her to meet him there. If Jake caught up with him, he would be returned to Topeka. Somehow her bets were on the latter.

If she was with Jake when he caught up with Anson, would she be able to convince Jake to let them go? Perhaps, if she told him she was carrying Anson's child. That piece of news would come as a surprise to Anson. His reaction might lead Jake to assume she was lying.

She tossed onto her back. Whether it worked or not, it was better than going home to wait. A tiny voice in her brain reminded her that if Anson escaped he might not go to Denver, and if captured, he might not succeed in clearing his name. Her best hope of marrying the father of her child lay in using Jake to help her find Anson and then convincing Jake to let them go.

And that, she thought as she threw off the covers, could only happen if she left with Jake.

She rose and felt along the top the dresser for her reticule. She found the watch she carried inside and read it by the pale moonlight from the window. Ten minutes past five. Jake would probably be leaving within the hour.

With renewed determination, she dressed in the two blouses she had worn the day before, trading the traveling suit for a riding skirt she had packed. She shoved everything else but her cloak into her bag.

In the hall she paused for a moment at Jake's door. She thought about waiting for him there, but he would simply renew the argument from the day before. No, she needed to be ready to leave with him, which meant she needed a horse.

She crept down the stairs and looked around the empty lobby. A lamp burned low on the desk and beside it stood a bell for late arrivals to ring. She had approached the bell when a clatter in the back of the house caught her attention.

Walking through the dim dining room she found the noise was coming from a room beyond. Light shone under the door and the sound of humming and faint smells of cooking drifted out to her. She opened the door cautiously.

The smell of frying bacon hit her like a blow. Her stomach constricted and she raised her hand to her mouth, stepping back into the dining room and letting the door close behind her. Taking slow breaths, she fought the nausea.

The door swung open and the smell hit her again. This time there was no fighting back. She ran across the dining room, through the lobby and out the front door and vomited into the bushes beside the steps. With a groan she leaned against the building, waiting to see if her stomach would settle or repeat the outrage.

"You poor dear," said a voice behind her.

She turned to find Mrs. Dutton in the doorway. "I'm sorry," she managed to say. She brushed her hand across her clammy forehead and shivered in the cold.

"Come back inside." The woman wrapped an arm around her shoulder, helped her into a chair in the lobby and closed the door. "I thought I saw someone at the kitchen door. Then there was your bag on the floor. Why, I didn't know what to think. Are you better now?''

Emily nodded, uncertain if it was the truth.

"When's the baby due, honey?''

Emily looked at her sharply.

"I'm sorry. I just assumed. The smell of food first thing in the morning did it to me every time. Is that nice young man the father?''

Emily considered telling her she was sick from bad food, but thought better of it. The woman would probably know she was lying. Forgetting the woman's last question, she nodded mutely.

"But he took two rooms." Mrs. Dutton seemed to be working out a problem in her head. "Probably to protect your reputation. But Mr. Dutton said he bought one horse." She gently patted Emily's shoulder. "My dear, your man plans to abandon you."

Emily looked at the indignant woman and wanted to laugh. She should probably dab at her eyes instead. "That's why I'm up so early," she said. "I need to buy a horse and be ready to go with him."

"That's the spirit," Mrs. Dutton said. "I'll get my husband to pick out a good one and have it ready. Can I get you anything else, a glass of water, perhaps?''

"That would be nice."

The woman bustled back toward the kitchen, and Emily put her head in her hands. She hadn't meant to deceive anyone, but it did make things easier. The horse would be arranged for while she sat and listened to her stomach protest. The nausea would pass and then she would be starving. She would tell Jake she had been too worried about missing him to bother with breakfast.

Mrs. Dutton returned with a glass of water. "Mr. Dutton is getting the horse now. He'll come and tell you when it's ready."

Emily started to rise. "My money's in my bag."

Mrs. Dutton pushed her back into the chair. "I'll bring it. You just sit right here."

When Mrs. Dutton didn't come back immediately, Emily decided she must have had to return to the kitchen. Closing her eyes, she leaned her head back. She hadn't gotten enough sleep last night to make up for the ordeal of the day before.

She smiled to herself when she remembered Jake swinging her up into his arms. A tingling started in her nearly settled stomach and spread through her body clear to her toes and fingers. For a moment she could remember the warmth of his strong body, the smell of his skin.

Caught up in the memory, she inhaled deeply. All she smelled was the oil lamp and a faint scent of bacon. Her stomach clinched again. She waited a moment to see if it would settle, then threw herself out of the chair and through the door. The remaining contents of her stomach joined the rest on the ground.

She groaned, leaning against the building. What a rotten trick God played on women.

With unsteady steps she went back to her chair. Mrs. Dutton had left the water and she finished it, hoping to clear the taste from her mouth.

In a few minutes, Mrs. Dutton returned with her bag and cloak. "There's a little something for later tucked inside," she said. "Are you sure you'll be all right?"

"Yes," Emily croaked. She cleared her throat to steady her voice. "Yes, it'll pass soon."

Mrs. Dutton knelt beside her. "Honey, I could ask my husband to talk to your man—"

"No!" She saw the shock on Mrs. Dutton's face. "I mean no, thank you. We'll be fine." She could just imagine Jake's reaction to Mr. Dutton's little talk.

Mrs. Dutton came to her feet. "All right. Whatever you think is best." She patted Emily's shoulder again. "Just rest here till my husband comes for you."

When she was gone, Emily closed her eyes. She imagined Jake going to the livery to get his horse and finding Mr. Dutton with a shotgun accusing him of abandoning a ruined woman in his hotel. Jake would call her a liar then, and he wouldn't be far wrong.

She wondered what time it was but didn't want to bother finding the watch in her reticule. She was sure nearly an hour had passed since she had left her room. Jake could come down and find her any moment. She would rather he find her in the stable ready to follow. It would give him less chance to argue and she needed every advantage.

With that in mind, she donned her cloak and grabbed her bag. Outside, she cringed at the mess she had made beside the door. What a miserable thing being pregnant was; it was a wonder any woman was willing to go through it more than once.

At the livery next to the hotel, she found a man saddling a pretty bay gelding. "Are you Mr. Dutton?"

"You must be the little lady what needs a horse."

He came forward to shake her hand. "Do you like this one?"

"He looks like a fine horse, Mr. Dutton." Emily moved to stroke the horse's head.

"Yes, he's a fine animal. Your man wanted him last night but my price was too high. Course, I'll knock a few dollars off for a lady."

Emily grinned at him. Poor Jake. He must be running a little low on cash. He had paid for both rooms and the meal, and the medicine for her blister. Now she was getting the better horse. Well, they could trade once they got under way.

Mr. Dutton quoted a price that seemed more than reasonable to Emily. She fished the roll of bills from her bag and counted out the amount, thankful she hadn't given all the money to Anson.

"Wouldn't you be more comfortable waiting inside?" Mr. Dutton asked.

"I think I'd rather get acquainted with my new horse, if you don't mind."

"Here. Hop up, and I'll adjust the stirrups."

Mr. Dutton helped her into the saddle and went to work on the strap. "Where you folks headed?" he asked.

Emily said the first thing that popped into her head. "Denver."

"That's a long way for a young lady on horseback. Be best to wait and take the train." He finished one stirrup and slid it over her foot to check its length. He walked around the horse. "Not my place to say."

"Jake wanted me to take the train," she said, not wanting Mr. Dutton to decide to lecture Jake. "We have someone we're hoping to…look up on the way."

"That'll be good," he said. "A place to take a few days rest. My Wilma, when she was carrying the young'uns, she didn't have the energy to make a trip to the grocers, let alone across the country like you. I remember one time…"

As he talked, Emily's attention was drawn to the tall figure just inside the lamp-lit barn. She didn't hear the rest of Mr. Dutton's story. All she heard was "carrying the young'uns," repeated again and again as Jake walked slowly toward her.

Chapter Eight

It shouldn't have surprised Jake to find Emily in the barn. Even the fact that she was aboard the expensive gelding with Mr. Dutton fussing over her shouldn't have surprised him. But telling himself not to be surprised didn't change how he felt.

Mr. Dutton, aware finally that he had lost Emily's attention, drew his story to a quick conclusion. "I'll have your horse saddled in a jiffy, Mr. Rawlins."

With the older man gone, Jake approached Emily. He considered demanding she tell him what she thought she was doing, but he already knew: she was being spoiled and stubborn. He could forbid her to follow him, but she would anyway. He had nothing to use as a bribe or a threat, no power over her whatsoever.

Finally he asked, "Did you sleep well?" He took comfort in the fact that she hadn't expected a quiet question.

"Not especially," she said.

"Too bad. Maybe you have a guilty conscience." He found her bag on the floor nearby and tied it behind the saddle. He checked the length of her stirrups, making a minor adjustment on one. How many times had he done this for her at her brother's ranch?

Jake moved to the horse's head and stroked the long neck. The gelding stood patiently, a good sign. At least his Emily would be riding a well-behaved horse.

He looked up to find her watching him. She was pale and drawn in the lantern light. Surely his crack about her conscience hadn't had that much effect on her. "Are you all right?" he asked.

She nodded mutely.

Mr. Dutton joined them, leading the nearly white mare he had purchased. "Here you go, Mr. Rawlins. Saddle's a bit used, like I told you, but I think it'll do well enough."

"Thanks," Jake said, taking the reins. He tossed the saddlebags into place and tied them.

"I filled the canteen like you wanted. Threw one in for the lady, too."

Jake watched him smile up at Emily as he handed her a dripping canteen. He took his own and murmured another thanks.

"Like I was telling the lady," Mr. Dutton went on. "There's nothing quite like a family. No, sir. It's a wonderful thing to watch those young'uns grow, have a wife you call your own."

Jake spared him a glance as he adjusted the stirrups and checked the cinch. Odd conversation to be having with Emily. Unless...what had Emily been telling him?

"Tell your wife thanks for me," Emily said hastily. She seemed to be trying to silence the man.

Jake swung into the saddle and eased his mount near Emily's. "Ready?" he asked. At her nod he rode through the tall doorway and into the quiet street. Dawn was just starting to add a touch of color to the shadowed buildings and bare branches. It was cold, but not the biting cold of a winter storm. The weather had been kind so far. He waited until Emily joined him then started down the street, turning on a worn track that led west of town.

"If you had any sense you'd be back there sleeping," he said.

"No one's ever suggested I had any sense, so here I am."

Her voice wasn't quite as carefree as her words. Jake would have liked to see her face, but she had raised her hood, hiding it from view. He wondered if privacy might have been her motive as much as warmth.

She made no effort at further conversation so he left her to her thoughts. His own could use some sorting. He was chasing a fugitive across open country when he had had ample opportunity to arrest him yesterday. His reason for not making his move rode at his side. Maybe he didn't have any more sense than Emily.

A few miles out of Americus, they forded the river, dismounting at the western shore to rest and let the horses drink. The water was cold and Emily used her scarf to dry the horses' legs. Jake watched her efforts with some surprise.

As she tied the ruined scarf to the saddle horn, she asked, "How do we know we're following Anson? He could go off in any direction."

"Good question," Jake said, coming to stand beside her. "I guess we just head toward any house we see, ask if they've seen anyone that fits our boy's description. If they haven't, we keep asking till we find someone who has, then hope they saw which way he went."

She turned her head upward to look at him. Her hood slipped, letting the sunlight glint off her dark hair. "Meanwhile, he gets farther ahead."

"Until he stops somewhere. The whole process could take weeks, even months."

He watched her eyes grow large at the prospect. He should tell her he would give up long before that; Berkeley wasn't worth it. In fact, he would like nothing better than for the man to disappear forever. But he wanted Emily to go home. It didn't hurt to let her picture a monumental task before them.

"Then we better be on our way," she said, lifting her foot to the stirrup. With a sigh, Jake helped her aboard, then caught up his reins and mounted. He should have known Emily wouldn't be easy to discourage.

For the next half hour Emily thought about what Jake had said. Somehow she had pictured them following Anson's tracks until they caught up with him on the trail. She realized how foolish she had been. Still she had to find Anson, and Jake was her only hope. But the longer it took to find Anson, the harder it might be to convince Jake to let them go.

A little cluster of houses became visible from a hilltop and Emily rode on with renewed hope. If nothing else, stopping at a town broke the monotony. The road bisected the tiny village and Emily gazed curiously at the buildings. All of the shops were closed, some of them permanently. It was Sunday, she reminded herself. But that didn't explain it entirely. "Where is everyone?" she found herself asking aloud.

"My guess is most moved to Americus when the railroad came through," Jake said. "There's someone."

He reined his horse off the main street toward a man who had just emerged from his barn. "Good morning," Jake called.

The man waved and sauntered over to meet them. "What can I do for you?" he asked.

"We were wondering if you've seen a man," Jake began, dismounting. Emily slid to the ground, also, feeling she should take advantage of every opportunity to stretch her legs.

"He would have passed by yesterday afternoon," Jake continued. "A young man, early twenties, medium height, thin, with straight blond hair. He had a dark gray overcoat and a light gray hat. He was riding a black gelding with a white blaze and one white stocking. Might have been in a hurry."

Emily was a little surprised at the details in Jake's description, but he was a lawman after all. She tucked her gloves in her waistband and untied her carpetbag, withdrawing the food Mrs. Dutton had packed for her. The morning sickness had passed some time ago, but she hadn't wanted to slow up their travel by admitting she was hungry.

"Rode through, like you said," the man answered. "Then kept on going. The road ends up there at the cemetery, but I figured he was heading for one of the ranches out that way.''

''Much obliged,'' Jake said. He turned to remount when he noticed Emily. ''A little early for dinner, isn't it?''

Emily paused with the biscuit and bacon at her lips. ''About right for breakfast, though.'' She took a bite and mumbled, ''Want some?''

''No, thanks.'' He came around the mare and retied her bag in place. ''Can you eat while you ride?''

''Sure, hold this.'' She rewrapped the sandwich and handed it to him, jumping to the stirrup and into the saddle. She had wanted to show him she was completely capable of mounting alone, but he held the food with his left hand, using the other to give her a boost as she swung aboard. He handed back her breakfast. She caught his hand before he could withdraw it. ''I'm not trying to slow you down, Jake,'' she said.

He nodded but his eyes told her he was a little skeptical. She tried not to feel hurt. What reason had she given him to trust her? She watched him mount and reined her horse around to ride beside him again. When they were back on the main street, she looped the reins loosely over the saddle horn and went back to her food.

''Did Mrs. Dutton fix you breakfast?'' she asked between bites.

''You could call it that.''

''Wasn't it good? This is delicious.''

''The food was fine. The lady was not particularly friendly. What did you tell her this morning?''

Emily looked at him sharply. She forced herself to

chew, trying to look at ease. "I don't know what you're talking about," she said.

"I'll bet." He spurred his horse forward as it went up the slope of a hill, and Emily nearly dropped the last of the biscuit as her horse trotted to catch up.

"I'm not responsible for any conclusions the Duttons came to," she said. Seeing his raised eyebrows, she added, "Whatever those conclusions were."

He laughed. It sounded a little more cynical than she would have expected from Jake. It reminded her that they had been apart for some time prior to the past week. She had grown up. Of course he had changed, too. She was suddenly curious about his life now, but before she could ask, he spoke again.

"You may not have lied to the Duttons, but I bet you know what they were thinking and did nothing to correct them."

His green eyes on her were too knowing for Emily to try to hedge. She imitated an indignant Mrs. Dutton. "What kind of man abandons a lady among strangers?" She shook her head and clucked her tongue as she supposed Mrs. Dutton might have done. She didn't want him thinking about Mr. Dutton's references to families.

With the last bite in her mouth, she brushed the crumbs from her fingers and slipped her gloves back on. With the reins in hand again, she looked around her. They were up in the hills now, well above the river valley, in country rougher than that around her brother's ranch. There were trees in the watercourses and winter-dead prairie everywhere. They were heading straight west without a trace of a road to follow.

She couldn't imagine Anson riding through here.

He must have felt desperately alone. She looked for any signs of life and finally made out a trail of smoke above a hilltop slightly to the right. "I bet Anson headed for that," she said, pointing.

"My guess, as well," Jake said. "He'd be looking for a place to spend the night."

"You were already watching for smoke?" she asked.

"For some sign of a farm or ranch, yes."

She watched his profile as they rode toward the smoke. "Have you followed suspects before?" she asked.

"Once or twice. But never with such charming company."

She knew he was teasing, but she smiled anyway. "Tell me what it's like being a lawman."

Jake considered the question for a moment. "I think it's something I always wanted to do, even when I was a boy." He didn't add that it wasn't something he wanted to do for the rest of his life. Emily wanted to be entertained; she didn't want to hear about disappointments.

"You never told me. I always thought you would raise horses like Christian."

"Well, I miss that a little, I admit. And I guess I never talked about it because I didn't suppose I'd ever go ahead and leave the ranch." *Until I saw you grow into a beauty I could never have. Then I had to get away.*

"So what's it like? Have you shot anyone?"

He ignored the last half of the question, not wanting to talk about the one life he had taken. "Part of it's boring," he said. "And you get called out to listen to ridiculous disputes between neighbors. But once in a while, I feel like I've helped someone.''

They reached the top of the hill and discovered the smoke was behind yet another rise. ''Right now is one of those boring times,'' she said. ''Tell me an example of helping someone.''

Jake smiled at her. ''You're not going to make it through weeks of tracking Berkeley if you're bored already.''

She shrugged.

''All right. A story.'' His first thought was the couple he had helped to town the night before he saw Emily at the train station. But he hadn't been acting as a deputy then. Something about that story tugged at his subconscious, but it didn't materialize. He brushed it aside when he thought of an earlier incident.

''Just last week I rescued a kitten from a tree.'' He tried to keep a straight face as she laughed. ''It might not seem like much to you, but one little girl was impressed.''

''I'll bet she was. Did they do an article in the paper? Hero Saves Life in Treetop Rescue.''

Jake shook his head. ''I don't seek glory, Emily dear,'' he said dramatically. ''I wish only to serve.''

That brought on more laughter. They rode down the last slope toward the ranch house with Jake trying to think of more stories that would keep her laughing. All the while he wished he could be telling her his dreams.

Emily watched the details of the ranch yard come into view. The house was built of stone, not as large as Christian's but nice enough to give the place an air of prosperity. The other buildings looked neat and well cared for.

The moment of closeness with Jake seemed to dissolve as the silence grew between them. Soon they would find out if Anson had passed this way.

As they pulled up in the yard a young man about Emily's age came out of the house to greet them. He was followed quickly by an older couple.

"Passin' through?" the young man asked, grabbing the reins and helping Emily dismount. When the man didn't draw away from Emily, she backed up a step.

Jake had dismounted and approached the older couple. "We're following someone," he said. He described Anson much as he had to the man in the little town.

The couple nodded. "Eldon Starky," the woman said. "He spent the night with us. Real nice fellow."

Emily glanced toward Jake to see his reaction. She would have loved to gloat over the man's description of Anson as nice, but the fact that he used an assumed name took something away from the compliment.

Jake didn't glance in her direction, but the young man watched her with open admiration. She left the gelding in his hands and walked quickly to Jake's side.

"Did you hear that, honey," Jake said, putting his arm around her. "We're less than half a day behind Eldon."

For all appearances he seemed nothing more than pleased by the announcement, but the tension in his arm made her wonder if he had seen the young man's advances. His possessiveness was certainly just for show. "My name's Jake Rawlins and this is Emily."

The man took his hand. "Garvey. I'm Will and my wife's Opal."

"You folks'll stay for dinner," the woman announced. "Billy'll feed your horses. Come on inside."

As the Garveys ushered them into the house, Emily raised an eyebrow at Jake. He had let them believe she was his wife. His smile gave nothing away.

Near a huge fireplace, Emily slipped the cloak off and chose a straight-backed chair, afraid of leaving dust on the velvet cushions of the settee. Jake, after removing his coat and gloves, stood near the fireplace. "We can't stay long," he told the rancher.

"Don't think of leaving soon, when dinner's about ready." Will sat down in a large leather-covered chair. A nearby table with a pipe and pouch marked the chair as his. "Nice weather for travel," he continued. "Can't be sure it'll hold, though."

"I've thought of that," Jake said. "How far north to the railroad?"

"Twelve, fifteen miles or so. Council Grove is straight north of here. Nearest railroad is south, though. Less than ten miles to Strong."

Emily saw Jake cast her a speculative glance and felt her heart sink. If Jake decided to take her home, she might never find Anson. She had a strange urge to rest her hand on her still flat stomach as if to comfort her child, or herself. She gripped her hands together on her lap instead.

"Your friend was asking the same questions," the rancher went on. "We told him it would be better to head for the railroad, but he rode out of here going straight west. Said he was enjoying the scenery.'' The memory made the rancher chuckle.

"What's west of here?'' Jake asked.

"Not much. A few ranches. Diamond Springs if you jog north a little. We told Eldon about a friend of ours six, eight miles farther west. Recommended he stop there for food and water. Do the same for you.''

As Jake listened to the directions, Emily excused herself and sought out the kitchen. Thinking of going back without Anson made her too restless to sit still. "Can I help?'' she asked when she found Opal working at an iron stove.

"Sure, honey. You come stir the gravy while I check the potatoes. I tossed in a few extra when we saw you coming. Don't have too many visitors out here. Told your friend the same thing when he rode in yesterday.''

"How did An—Eldon seem to you?'' After she asked she wasn't sure exactly what she wanted to know. Was he well? Was he scared? Did he mention a woman he had left behind?

"He seemed fit to me,'' she said. "A little saddle sore, but he tried not to let on, you know what I mean.''

Emily stirred the gravy, wishing she understood her own reaction to news of Anson. She should be hanging on every word. She should be filled with longing to be with him again. She shouldn't be counting herself lucky to be with Jake instead.

"If Eldon knew you were coming along behind him,'' Opal said, removing a tray of chicken from the oven where she had kept it warm, "I'm sure he would have waited. Ain't much fun traveling all alone."

So she had been right when she had thought Anson would be lonely. She tried to build up more sympathy for Anson. She certainly wouldn't want to be crossing the prairie alone.

Her thoughts were interrupted when the woman took the spoon from her and poured the gravy into a large bowl. She had set the chicken and several other dishes on a table at the other end of the room. "Have a seat," she said. "I'll go call the men."

Billy had evidently finished with the horses and joined the men at the fireside. He led them into the kitchen. Emily had waited to take a seat, wanting to sit as close to Jake as possible—and far away from Billy.

It worked and yet it didn't. Billy ended up across from them where he leered and winked. She gave him one cold stare then tried her best to ignore him.

Jake seemed oblivious to Billy's behavior. He talked about ranching and horses, occasionally fishing for any information they might have gotten from Anson or Eldon as he called him.

Emily listened, impressed with the way he put the old couple at ease.

Billy's ankle bumped hers. She slid away, trying to take up less space under the table. The leg found hers again. She looked up to discover his stomach pressed against the table. He must have been sitting on the very edge of his chair.

A moment later the leg brushed her again. Emily resettled herself in her chair, scooting a little closer to Jake. He cast her a quizzical look. She tried to tell him with her eyes that she was being bothered by the fool across from her, but he went on with his conversation with the rancher.

Billy grinned while he shoveled more potatoes into his mouth. He raised a piece of chicken, opened wide, and let out a cry of surprise. The next moment he disappeared.

Everyone around the table stood to see Billy sprawled on the floor, his overturned chair lying beyond him.

"Land sakes," murmured his mother. "Get up and sit still."

"Sorry, Ma," he muttered, brushing crumbs off his shirt as he stood. "The chair just jumped out from under me." He retrieved his chicken leg and his chair and sat, giving Jake a speculative glare.

The others sat back down, and Will and Jake resumed their conversation. Emily mentally measured the distance from Billy's chair to Jake's against the length of Jake's legs. He must have done it. She ate cautiously, afraid a giggle would escape and choke her. She couldn't wait to get away from the house and let out the laugh she was holding in.

Evidently Jake didn't want to linger, either, and a few minutes later he was thanking the Garveys and helping Emily back into the saddle. She tried to give the three a pleasant smile but found herself nearly laughing when she turned to Billy. He returned her regard with a sullen frown.

They headed out onto the prairie, following a faint trail. When the ranch house was a safe distance behind them, Emily gave in to gales of laughter.

"Jake," she managed to say after a full minute, "the poor boy might have choked to death."

Jake was smiling but he evidently didn't see the humor in it Emily did. "He needed to learn some manners."

Emily wiped tears from her eyes. "I thought you hadn't even noticed what he was up to. Then all of a sudden—" She was overcome by another fit of laughter.

Jake laughed with her this time, or perhaps at her. She didn't care. It felt good to share a secret with Jake.

"I was waiting for you to do it," he said. "Then I realized your legs might not be long enough. He was so close to the edge all it took was a tap."

"You were great," she said. "I don't think you even flinched. His parents never suspected you did it."

"Billy knows. Or I hope he does. Think about it. He was making eyes at a man's wife with the man sitting right there. He could get shot for that."

"Except I'm not your wife."

She thought she saw something flicker in his eyes before he responded, "He didn't know that."

"Well," she said, not liking his serious tone. "I thought your response was completely fitting. It was as heroic as saving the kitten."

He grinned at her then. "Why thanks, ma'am. I'm glad to be of service."

The smile stayed on Emily's face as they rode on in silence. The thought occurred to her that she was having a wonderful time. Jake was by far a better traveling companion than Anson had been with his complaining and flights of temper.

Of course that would probably change in a few hours when she became tired. It happened every day. Her energy gave out, forcing her to bed for a nap. Only today there was no chance for that. How would Jake react if she asked to stop and rest? Would he suspect her of deliberately slowing them down?

For the first time she wondered if perhaps she should have gone back as Jake had asked. Alone, Jake had a better chance of catching Anson and bringing him back to Topeka to clear his name.

No, she decided. Without her along, Anson wasn't going to cooperate. He would resist and end up getting hurt. Or hurting Jake. She needed to be along to see that both men remained reasonable.

She didn't want to acknowledge it, but in the back of her mind remained the thought that Anson wouldn't clear his name if he went back to Topeka. That she and Anson needed to get away and start over.

Anson had to marry her before she gave birth to a fatherless child. And somehow she would have to keep Anson out of trouble in the future. The desperate nature of her situation weighed on her, making her feel tired already. There were hours of travel ahead of her before she could even ask to rest.

Jake kept a careful eye on Emily as they traveled. By early afternoon, he had called a rest at a little creek. She had fallen asleep on the ground in a matter of seconds. He let her rest much longer than he admitted and insisted she treat the sore on her heel before they started off again. But now, after barely two more hours of travel, she looked drawn and exhausted.

He remembered her pale cheeks this morning when they were leaving Americus and worried that she might be ill. But she had seemed fine all morning and had eaten quite heartily at the Garveys, even after the midmorning snack she had called her breakfast.

Suddenly the folks he had helped with the broken wagon came to mind. "The missus been ailin'," the man had said. "She's in the family way." That was what had been nagging at him. That, and Mr. Dutton's conversation in the stable. Not to mention Mrs. Dutton's cold shoulder!

His Emily was expecting!

For a second he had trouble catching his breath. Fortunately Emily was so preoccupied with her efforts to stay awake she didn't notice his unusual behavior.

Fury swept through him as the realization sank in. The urge to strangle Berkeley that he had had on the train came back to him tenfold. The bastard had seduced her, or worse, forced her!

He gave himself a few minutes to enjoy his anger then tried to look at the situation more logically. Emily claimed to be in love with Berkeley, though that didn't rule out seduction. Berkeley had come for her, so he must have some regard for her. Or her family's money.

He didn't want to give Berkeley credit for any tender feelings toward Emily. He wanted to believe that an honest man would have married her before he took her virtue, or at the very least immediately after.

Logic told him that might have been Berkeley's

plan, and his own arrest and Emily's subsequent departure from Topeka had interfered. Still, the man should have stayed out of trouble!

Now Emily was the one in trouble. The child explained her determination to find Anson. He chose to ignore the possibility that she was motivated by love. And what did she expect when they found him? That her old friend would simply let them go?

He turned his full gaze on the woman at his side. She was barely able to keep her eyes open. He moved in close enough to touch her arm. "Do you want to rest again?"

"No, no, I'm just bored, I guess. Tell me some more exciting deputy stories."

He couldn't force a smile. "Tell me where Berkeley's going," he said.

She shrugged, but he didn't believe her. If she had stayed behind in Americus, would she have headed west to join her lover? Perhaps even that would be better than letting her follow along. He could catch up with Berkeley and bring him to wherever Emily waited. Perhaps he could convince Berkeley to do what was right.

But the thought nearly made him ill. He couldn't believe that Emily, even in her condition, would be better off married to Berkeley. It would only be a matter of time before he did something else that landed him in jail.

Whatever might be best in the long run, the immediate problem was clear. He could not allow a soon-to-be mother to continue this journey.

Chapter Nine

They made two more stops before Jake started to worry about getting to the ranch Garvey had described. After each stop Emily seemed to revive, but an hour later she was nearly dosing again.

Finally Jake pulled up alongside the gelding. "Come over and ride with me."

"What?" she mumbled, visibly trying to shake off the drowsiness.

"Come over and ride with me. If we stop again, we won't make it to shelter before dark."

Emily let him lift her from the saddle into his lap. The gelding, after a moment's hesitation, followed along behind.

With his arms around her, knowing she was no longer in danger of falling, he felt confident they would make better time. What he didn't count on, was how quickly his body would respond to having her in his arms. Her body, even through the bulky clothes, felt soft and yielding, molding quickly to his as she laid her head on his shoulder.

"I'm sorry I'm slowing us down," she said. "I guess I'm not used to riding all day, anymore."

"It doesn't matter." Surprisingly he meant it.

"I used to, you know, ride all day I mean. Mostly with Christian, but sometimes with you."

"I remember," he murmured, resisting the urge to caress her cheek.

She sighed so deeply it was almost a yawn. "Tell me what Garvey said about the rancher."

Jake smiled. She wanted him to keep her awake. "The name's Kinney. That's about all I know. Mostly Garvey talked about how to find the ranch."

"I wonder if Kinney has a son," she said.

"If he does, we may ride right on by."

He could feel her body shake as she laughed, then the sweet torture as she snuggled closer against him. "Wake me when we're close," she said.

Jake agreed. They rode in silence across the prairie with Jake turning occasionally to make sure the gelding followed. He found himself reflecting on how right it felt to hold Emily, to touch her and protect her. He was almost grateful to Berkeley for giving him this opportunity. Almost.

Just as the sun was setting, he crested a hill and could see the ranch yard below. "We're almost there, sweetheart." The endearment was out before he realized it. He hoped she was too sleepy to hear. "Wake up, Emily," he said, somewhat louder.

She stirred in his arms, a sweet snuggling movement that made him want to hold her forever. She rubbed her eyes and looked around her. "How long did I sleep?"

"Maybe an hour, I'm not sure."

She cringed. "I bet I put your legs to sleep."

She squirmed a little as if trying to redistribute her weight. He caught her waist to hold her still. He had spent the past hour in a mild state of arousal. It wouldn't take much for it to turn very uncomfortable. Not to mention how embarrassed, or even disgusted, she would be if she felt the evidence.

She had turned to look at him, uncertainty written on her face. He loosened his grip on her waist. "You'll bruise yourself on the saddle horn," he said.

Damn, he thought. What if she had already noticed his state and thought he was making suggestive comparisons? He took the opportunity to check on the gelding and was glad to find her watching the house when he turned back.

A burly man, presumably Mr. Kinney, stepped out of the house, throwing on a coat as he came. He was followed by, not one, but three big strapping boys. "Damn. Don't these ranchers raise anything else?"

Emily stifled her laughter against his shoulder. "Poor Jake. I've always been more trouble than I'm worth."

"I didn't say that," he mumbled.

The young men stepped into the yard to meet them. Two caught the horses while the tallest hurried to their side. "Hand her down to me," he directed.

Jake reluctantly complied. Instead of lifting her to the ground, the young man kept her in his arms.

"I can walk," she protested, mischief plain in her voice.

"Yes, ma'am," the boy said, striding toward the house.

Jake dismounted and hurried after him.

"Best put the lady down, Matthew," remarked the father, casting a wary look at Jake. Jake hoped the man hadn't seen murder in his eyes.

He stopped to introduce himself and mention that Garvey had directed him there.

"You'll stay the night, of course," Mrs. Kinney said.

"I'd appreciate it," Jake answered, while visions of Emily being carried off to Matthew's bedroom filled his head.

Kinney directed his remaining two sons to take care of the horses and led Jake inside. The spacious room was furnished with heavy furniture that looked home-made. Emily was ensconced by the fire that Matthew was turning into a roaring blaze.

Jake took a nearby seat and caught Emily's smirk before he turned to Kinney. "We're following a young man. He should have come through here about midday."

Kinney listened to Jake's description. "Haven't seen him. We can ask the boys though. You seen anyone, Matthew?"

The young man shook his head. "I'll go help with the horses and ask my brothers." With a respectful nod at Emily and Jake, he left the house.

"What's he wanted for?" Kinney asked.

Jake cast a quick glance at Emily and saw her eyes narrow. Garvey had assumed they were friends of Berkeley's trying to catch up with him. Kinney noticed the badge and came to a different conclusion. Emily evidently thought he had said something outside.

"I'll see if Mrs. Kinney needs any help," she said

to their host. Without another glance at Jake she followed Kinney's directions toward the kitchen.

Jake watched her go, feeling an odd sort of loss. He needed to send her home, and the only way to do that was probably to abandon her in the middle of the night. But he wasn't about to do that here with Matthew and his brothers.

"Garvey recommended your place," he said, turning back to his host. "Both to me and to Eldon."

"And Eldon guessed you or somebody was following," Kinney provided.

"Where else would he have stopped for food? He's not a man used to roughing it."

Kinney nodded his understanding. "I can draw you a map of the area, locate all the ranches and farms, and the little towns. If you don't mind me asking, why is the young lady along on a manhunt, Deputy?"

"It gets complicated."

"It usually does."

Emily had found Mrs. Kinney mixing up batter for corn bread. She wouldn't hear of Emily helping. "I'll have this in the oven in no time. I thought I'd scramble some eggs. Not a proper supper, but it's food and it's fast."

"Anything will be fine," Emily said, taking a chair at a nearby table.

"We ate about an hour ago," the woman said, spreading the batter efficiently into a pan. "With a crew like mine, there's never much left over."

"I'm sorry to put you out," Emily offered. "And I meant it when I said I'd like to help."

"Well, first off," she said, greasing a huge skillet,

"I'm so used to scurrying around in here I'd probably bump into you if you tried to help. Besides, you're not putting me out at all. I'd go to most any lengths to get a female to talk to. The boys say that's why they let me milk the cow." She laughed heartily.

Emily laughed, too, remembering her summers on the ranch with her father and brothers. The house-keeper, Jake's mother, had been there of course, and Emily had usually had a week-long visit from her friend, Rose, on the neighboring ranch.

"How many?" Mrs. Kinney asked, breaking eggs into the skillet.

"Four or five will probably be enough," Emily said.

"Oh, honey, won't your man eat more than that?" She turned back to the stove. "I'll fix ten. Somebody'll finish up what you folks leave. So tell me where you're from and where you're going."

Emily thought a moment, wondering what Jake was telling Mr. Kinney. He had let on that she was his wife before. Maybe she could avoid the subject. "I grew up in Topeka mostly," she began. "My brother has a ranch not far from Strong. I visit there a lot."

"And the man you're with, that your husband?"

So much for avoiding the subject. What was the best way to go here? Whichever way she guessed, Jake could be telling her husband the opposite. Her silence had earned her a questioning look from Mrs. Kinney. With a sigh, she decided on the truth. "No. We're just traveling together. We've been friends since we were children, though. Sometimes Jake lets people think we're married as a way of protecting me."

"Ah." Mrs. Kinney broke the yokes with a large spoon, using a little more force than necessary. "But if we think you're married, we'll put you in the same room. That's his idea of protecting you?"

Emily tried not to laugh at the woman's indignation. "I'm perfectly safe with Jake. If you gave us separate rooms he'd probably spend the night outside my door with a shotgun across his knees."

Mrs. Kinney raised an eyebrow. "That doesn't sound like a childhood friend to me."

"No," Emily said. "It sounds like a brother."

"Hmm," was the reply. "We'll wait and see what he told my husband. But—" she pointed the spoon at Emily "—if he said you two are married it's because that's what he's wishing was true."

Emily shook her head, but Mrs. Kinney nodded in response before turning back to the stove. "I saw his face when Matthew carried you into the house."

"He had just been teasing me about the Garvey boy," Emily insisted.

"And why was that? Because Billy Garvey made eyes at you, if I'm not mistaken."

Emily smiled, remembering the look on Billy's face as his chair flew out from under him. "Something like that," she said.

"Then he saw my handsome boys and felt threatened." She nodded again. "He told my husband you're married."

Emily laughed, wondering if further argument wouldn't just reinforce the notion in the woman's mind. Jake was fond of her, she knew that. A few times she had thought there was something more in his eyes. No matter, it would disappear quickly when he knew about the baby.

She felt suddenly worn-out, not so much physically, as she had slept off and on all afternoon, but emotionally. The baby and Anson weighed on her mind almost constantly. What would happen to her and the child without Anson? And life with Anson had also lost its appeal.

And Jake. Was he truly falling in love with her? If he was, there didn't seem to be any way to avoid breaking his heart. Dear, trusting Jake thought way too highly of her. Perhaps she should tell him about the baby and be done with it.

No, she dared not. He would abandon her for sure. And she needed his help to find Anson. Even though a part of her hoped he would never be found.

She was pulled out of her reverie by the arrival of one of the boys. "Ma'am," he said, nodding in her direction. "Is there coffee, Ma?"

"There's always coffee, Mark. Go tell your pa to bring our guest in. Their food's almost ready."

"Yes, ma'am."

He left the room, and Emily grinned after him. "That's a very polite young man," she said.

"I had to teach them manners," she said. "Otherwise there'd be no living with them, there're so many. I kept hoping I'd get a girl, but the Lord was punishing me for something."

Emily smiled. She wouldn't mind having a boy; in fact, she usually pictured her baby as a boy. She thought of holding little Trevor and felt her eyes mist as they did when he nestled against her. She shook off the feeling quickly. This woman seemed to guess everything. She would probably see the tears and know she was pregnant—and unmarried.

Jake and the others came in, taking her mind off her troubles. Jake took a seat next to her, casting her a questioning look. She smiled, wondering what he had seen in her face.

Mrs. Kinney brought plates of eggs and the pan of corn bread. She sent Mark after some molasses and her husband for the coffee cups. One by one the boys came in, filling coffee cups for themselves and taking seats at the table.

Emily stifled a laugh when a fourth son came in. Jake kicked her lightly under the table.

Kinney introduced the boys as they came in. Matthew, Mark, Luke and John. Each time, he introduced Jake and Emily as Mr. and Mrs. Rawlins. Mrs. Kinney cast Emily the same knowing look every single time.

When all the boys were around the table, Jake described Anson to them. They all shook their heads. They hadn't seen any strangers all day.

"It's like I guessed," Kinney said. "He avoided us because he knows someone's on his tail."

"Let's get back to that map," Jake said, having finished eating.

"The Rawlinses will need a place to sleep," Mrs. Kinney said, looking pointedly at her oldest son.

"My room's the biggest," Matthew said, coming to his feet. "I'll go change the sheets."

"Matthew can bunk with me," Mark said, sliding his chair away from the table. "I'll go straighten up a mite."

"May I have the rest of the eggs?" asked John.

"If Mrs. Rawlins has had enough." At Emily's nod she added, "Share with Luke."

"I'd rather have some of the corn bread," Luke said. "That is, if Mrs. Rawlins has had enough."

"Go right ahead," Emily said, grinning at the earnest face. Mrs. Kinney may long for female company, but she certainly didn't have much to complain about in her sons.

"I imagine you're tired," Mrs. Kinney said. "Let me show you where you can wash up. Did you boys bring in the bag I saw tied behind the saddle?"

"Yes, ma'am," they said almost in unison. "And the saddlebags, too," added Luke. "They're just inside the back door."

Emily stood to follow Mrs. Kinney and both boys jumped to their feet. "Good night," she said.

"Good night," they echoed, waiting until she left the room to resume their seats.

"If you let those boys out where women are, they're going to get snatched up real fast," Emily said as she followed Mrs. Kinney.

"You should see the way the girls at church fall all over themselves around them. The girls are scared of me, though."

"You're kidding."

Mrs. Kinney drew herself up and scowled down at Emily. Emily laughed. "Why?"

"I think my boys deserve brave women, don't you?"

Jake studied the map Kinney had drawn. The railroad from Emporia to Junction City ran at an angle across the upper right hand corner of the page. From the ends of this, two railroads ran west and southwest.

Berkeley wouldn't head south for the Santa Fe; he had already left it behind at Emporia. The nearest station was still Council Grove on the diagonal line, roughly north of Garvey's ranch.

"My guess is he found one of the other ranches," Kinney offered. "Got directions from him. Hard to guess, though, when you don't know where he headed."

"Yeah. Or he might have gone back to the railroad. That was his original plan, and it'd be faster. I imagine he's plenty tired of riding." Jake straightened, shifting his weight to the other foot. He was tired of riding himself.

"He's turned cautious, though. He may be afraid the stationmasters have been alerted."

"That's pretty vain," Jake said. "Nobody's particularly interested in finding him, but me. What about Diamond Springs?"

"Little place. He could have gotten food in the store there. It's close by."

But in the wrong direction. Jake had to get Emily to a town with a train station. He couldn't continue to drag her around looking for Berkeley. It was half a day's travel to Council Grove; he would leave Emily there. She could sell her horse and take the train home or back to Strong or off to wherever Berkeley had told her to meet him. He could spend the afternoon, and perhaps the next day, checking the ranches and farms Kinney had indicated. If nothing turned up, he would admit defeat.

Kinney folded the map and handed it to Jake, who

stuffed it into his shirt pocket. "It don't seem right letting you share a room with the young lady."

"I told you, I'm not letting her out of my sight."

Kinney raised a hand. "I understand and I went along with the lie to the missus and the boys, but if you aren't worried about her running off to meet this Eldon, I don't quite see the point."

He had said their story was complicated, but it had gotten more so when he had tried to explain it to Kinney. The man had gotten the impression that she was virtually his prisoner. He was willing to say anything to keep him from knowing he was in love with the fugitive's woman—pregnant woman at that.

"I'm hoping she'll talk in her sleep," he said. "I think I'll turn in."

"I'll show you the way," Kinney said, rising.

Upstairs, Kinney stopped in front of a closed door. "I want to trust you, son. That's why I'll allow this. But keep in mind, my room's right below."

"Yes, sir," Jake said, waiting for Kinney to turn away before he opened the door. A lamp on the dresser burned low, casting a soft light over the tidy room. He could see Emily asleep on a narrow bed. He slipped inside the room and closed the door as quietly as possible.

He walked slowly toward her. Her dark hair was in a thick braid that lay on the covers as if it had been flung aside. Little tendrils curled around her face. He found himself kneeling beside the bed brushing the soft hair off her cheek.

Why did she have to get mixed up with Anson Berkeley? Why couldn't she have fallen in love with him? The thought made him want to laugh. He had avoided her for three years because he knew that wouldn't happen.

He was a little surprised to realize that the baby didn't change the fact that he loved her. He had been so angry when the realization had first come to him that he hadn't been aware of anything else. But his anger had been directed at Berkeley, not Emily. All afternoon as he had watched over her, he had thought of the baby only as it related to Emily's strength and health.

Now he thought about it as another human being, a tiny child who knew nothing of his parents' misjudgments. He pictured a toddler Trevor's size with Emily's fine features. He would look like Emily's brother Arlen, he realized.

Or he might look like Berkeley.

He decided to hold on to that thought. He had begun to think of the miniature Arlen or Emily as his own, an impossible thought. He gave the soft cheek one more caress and turned away.

He found an extra quilt at the foot of the bed, blew out the lamp and lay down on the rug. It made a hard bed, but he was tired enough it didn't matter.

Emily sat up cautiously. With her elbows on her knees she put her head in her hands and waited for the wave of dizziness to pass. Now, if she could somehow avoid the kitchen.

She was alone, but a quilt tossed over the back of a chair indicated that Jake had spent the night in the room. She pictured him sleeping in the chair, its back pressed up against the door, the quilt wrapped around his shoulders, a shotgun across his knees. The picture made her laugh out loud.

Laughing made her feel good. She decided that would be her cure from now on. She would laugh to dispel the illness she felt almost every morning.

She dressed quickly, straightened the room and took her bag with her downstairs. The big living room was far enough away from the kitchen to be blessedly free of cooking smells. Her cloak hung near the front door, and she left her bag on the floor beneath it. She was relieved to find Jake's coat hanging there. Was she still worried that he would leave her?

She thought on that as she moved back into the room and sat down in a chair. She was most certainly slowing him down, and now their trail seemed to have disappeared. She knew Jake and Mr. Kinney had talked into the evening about where they should look next. Perhaps Jake had decided to give up.

The thought filled her with a familiar dread. What if she never saw Anson again? She decided she wouldn't miss him exactly, but without his name she and her baby would be outcasts. She had to find him.

She heard someone clear his throat and jumped. One of the boys, Luke she thought, stood just inside the room. "I didn't mean to startle you, ma'am."

"That's all right," she said, regaining her composure. "I was just lost in thought."

"Ma said to tell you to come eat whenever you want."

"Thanks," she said, uncertain what to tell him. She couldn't eat now, but she would be starving later. Though it would make her seem completely spoiled, she saw no other choice but to ask. "I don't like to eat this early,'' she said finally. ''Could you ask her to pack something I can take with me?''

''Yes, ma'am,'' he answered politely. He gave her an odd look before he turned and left the room.

So what if Luke thought she was spoiled? So what if the whole family did? She was leaving in a few minutes, and Jake's opinion was the only one that mattered. He already thought she was spoiled. Besides, anything was better than throwing up and having Mrs. Kinney guess her state.

And give it away to Jake!

She didn't have to wait long before Jake and the elder Kinneys joined her in the living room. Jake headed straight for the door. ''Ready?'' he asked.

''Yes,'' she said, rising. She turned first to the Kinneys. ''I appreciate your hospitality.''

''Our pleasure, dear,'' Mrs. Kinney answered. She brought a cloth sack to her. ''This is for later.''

''Thanks,'' Emily said, feeling embarrassed. She hurried to tuck the sack into her carpetbag. Jake waited with her cloak. She let him help her into it and followed him out the door.

Two of the boys stood in front with the horses saddled. Jake tied her carpetbag in place and checked the gelding's cinch before he helped Emily aboard. There were more goodbyes once he was in the saddle. In a few minutes they rode out of the yard.

''Wait a minute,'' Emily said. ''Isn't this the way we came?''

''Not exactly.''

''It seems to be,'' she said, irritated that more information wasn't forthcoming.

Jake turned and grinned at her. "How would you know? You were asleep most of the afternoon."

She bristled at his gibe. "Maybe. But I can see the sunrise and know we're headed east."

"Northeast," he corrected.

"Toward the railroad?" she asked suspiciously.

"Berkeley didn't go to Kinney's ranch. We don't know where he went when he left Garvey's yesterday morning. His talk of enjoying the scenery and his intention to head straight west could have been intended to throw us off his trail. The most logical thing for him to have done was head for the railroad, and the nearest station is still Council Grove."

"So that's where we're going? And you'll ask everybody in town if they've seen him?"

"Something like that," he said. "It'll take us half a day to get there, and you can spend the afternoon sleeping in a hotel room while I ask around."

She turned in the saddle to glare at him. "I don't have to sleep the entire afternoon."

"Really? You could've fooled me."

It sounded like his typical teasing, but there was no sparkle in his green eyes. Either he was truly irritated at her or something else bothered him. She wondered if it might be her morning eating habits. Perhaps he had been embarrassed by her request. Well, he could think what he wanted as long as her secret was safe.

Chapter Ten

The day had begun as warm as the past week, but by midmorning the temperature dropped. Emily drew the heavy cloak more snugly around her. "Do you think it'll snow?" she asked.

"Probably," Jake answered. "Though this time of year it usually doesn't amount to much."

"That's reassuring," she said, shivering. Of all the times to decide not to wear double layers! But it had been so nice yesterday.

"You'll be warm soon. It's not much farther to Council Grove."

"Will we spend the night there?"

"That depends on what I find."

She turned to scowl at him, but he was looking straight ahead. He had been stingy with information all day. She had a feeling he was planning farther ahead than he let on. Was he considering giving up? What would she do then?

Perhaps, she decided, if he said the trail was lost and it was time to go back, she would tell him about Denver. Odd that she had treasured that little bit of information, almost as a last hope of escaping with Anson. Confidence in Anson had faded considerably since they had parted on the train, and now she wasn't sure the information had any value even to Jake. Was Anson really planning to meet her there?

She wanted to laugh at herself. If she told Jake now, her sole purpose would be to keep him from giving up. And she wasn't even sure he would believe her.

All the way to Council Grove, Jake reconsidered his decision. He had to get Emily off a horse and onto the relative safety of a train and ultimately home. She wasn't going to go willingly. Abandoning her in Council Grove seemed the only solution.

He had trouble feeling good about it, though. If there was no sign of Berkeley in Council Grove, maybe he should give up and escort the lady home. That way he would know she was safe.

But was she really? What about the baby? He would be taking her home to face disgrace, without the child's father available to make it right.

No, it was better to send her home and continue his search. A glance in her direction helped to reinforce the decision. Her shoulders were hunched against the cold, and she was shivering. Yes, he needed to send her home. He should have done it sooner.

The sky had turned a heavy gray by the time they rode into Council Grove. Jake pulled up at the Hays House in the center of town. "Hurry inside," he said. "I'll see to the horses."

"Shall I order your dinner?" she asked.

He hesitated just a moment. Would it be easier to leave her now? But the temptation to spend a little more time with her was too great. "Whatever you're having," he said. "I'll only be a few minutes."

He put the horses up in the livery across the street. He described Berkeley and his horse to the proprietor, but the man hadn't seen either. The first few flakes were falling when he hurried back to the restaurant. He shed his overcoat, hat and gloves at the door and joined Emily at the table she had taken near the fire.

"Thawing out a little?" he asked as he took the seat across from her.

"Mmm, it feels wonderful. I ordered us steaks, thick and rare. I've been longing for one for days."

He grinned at her. "Are you paying for them?"

She grinned back. "I can."

"I thought so, considering you could afford a better horse than I could."

"Yes, I noticed that, too. I thought about offering to trade, but the gelding has such a smooth gait I decided against it."

He laughed. She was so beautiful in the glow of the fire. Her cheeks were rosy, and little wisps of hair danced around her face as she moved. This was Emily the way he dreamed about her. He wanted her so sharply he found himself needing to break the spell. "Was your horse bought with Berkeley's ill-gotten gains?"

Her smile faltered for a moment then it was back. "I'm afraid it was my own ill-gotten gains," she said, feigning remorse. "I stole it from Christian."

He knew his jaw had dropped. Was he surprised she had taken money before she left, or that she would admit it now? "Emily, you've been swiping things from your poor brother all your life. How much did you take?"

She shrugged. "I gave part of it to Anson. He wanted to carry it. But I held some back."

He gazed into her serious eyes. "Why did you do that, Emily? Hold out on Berkeley?"

She shrugged again.

Their conversation was interrupted by the waiter with their steaks. They were both quiet for a few minutes as they started their meals.

"Could it be," Jake asked, watching her closely, "that you don't trust Berkeley?"

She looked up at him, pain evident in her eyes. "I don't know," she whispered. "I think I wanted to save some back in case..."

"He deserted you?"

"No," she responded quickly. "In case we didn't need it, and I could return it to Christian."

She was sullen now, hurt and angry. He had pushed too hard. But it would be easier to walk away from her like this than the teasing beauty of a few minutes ago. He finished his steak in silence.

The waiter refilled his coffee cup and offered them dessert. They both declined and the waiter took Jake's empty plate and left.

"I need to start asking around," he said gently, longing for her smile in spite of himself.

"Who will you ask?"

"The stationmaster, the local law, at the livery stables. Any place else I can think of."

"How long will it take?"

He hesitated, feeling guilty already about leaving her. "That depends on what I learn," he said.

"Of course. Shall I just wait here?"

"You can, or you can get a room upstairs and rest."

"You think it'll take a while then?" She shoved her plate aside.

"It could take all afternoon, especially if he hasn't been here."

"I see your point. Ready?" She reached into her purse and deposited a few bills on the table before she stood.

He felt a pang of guilt for letting her pay, for letting Christian pay, but his own funds were running low. He would make it up to Christian somehow. He couldn't help the thought that bringing Emily home safely was all Christian would ask. And leaving her here might *not* be the best way of doing that.

They grabbed their coats and went through the connecting doors to the hotel. A tiny room provided space for a desk at the base of a flight of stairs. Jake rented a room in Emily's name and brought her the key. "Room three," he told her. "Shall I order a bath or anything else?"

"No, I'll be fine." She took the key and headed for the stairs.

"Emily." She stopped and turned. What did he want to say to her? Goodbye? "I can have your bag sent over from the livery," he offered.

"Don't bother. I won't need anything out of it unless we spend the night." With a wave she turned and went up the stairs.

Jake watched her until she disappeared. He should

put her out of his mind. He needed to get to work. He turned to the man behind the desk and recited his description of Anson Berkeley.

An hour later he sat in the sheriff's office and repeated it for perhaps the twentieth time. No one had seen any stranger who came close to the description.

"Don't recall hearin' nothin' from Topeka about this fugitive," the sheriff said. The joints of his chair screamed in protest as his massive body tipped it back on two legs.

"It's not that important a case, I suppose."

"Not important, huh?" The chair banged back to the floor. Jake wondered how it could still hold the man's weight. "The minute I get back from dinner, I hear there's outside law askin' after some city fella. You've bothered nearly everybody in town. Sounds like you think it's important."

"It's become personal, sir."

The sheriff laughed. "Best kind, ain't they?"

The sheriff stood, probably a practiced tactic at intimidation, and gazed down at Jake. Jake tried not to squirm.

"Do you suppose, Deputy, if I know that you rode in here right about noon with a pretty dark-haired girl, ate at the Hays House, bought one room—" he waved one finger in the air "—one room then went around describing this city fella to everybody who would listen, do you suppose I would also know if this city fella ever set foot in Council Grove?"

"Stands to reason, yes."

"Now think of all the trouble you would have saved if you had come to me first." A smug smile curled his lips.

"You weren't in, sir."

The man laughed and dropped back into his chair. "I like you, boy. I wish I could help you, but your Berkeley fella ain't been here."

Jake withdrew the map from his pocket. "A rancher named Kinney drew this up for me last night," he said. "Berkeley was last seen here at the Garvey place. These are the homesteads Kinney thought he might have gone to for food and shelter. Can you add any more?"

The sheriff drew the map toward him and tapped it here and there with a thick finger. "It's pretty thorough. There's a little farmstead here." He felt around on his desk for a pencil and added another dot before handing it back. "You gonna check all these places?"

"I thought I'd give it a try." Jake folded the map and returned it to his pocket. "If he turns up later, hold him for me. If I don't find anything I'll be headed back this way."

He stood to go, but the sheriff's voice stopped him. "One question, Deputy. How does the girl figure into this?"

Jake considered a moment. He couldn't bring himself to say she was in love with the fugitive; he would choke on the words. If the sheriff's grapevine was as efficient as he claimed, he was going to know in short order that she was no longer traveling with him. "It's personal, sir," he finally said.

This sent the sheriff into gales of laughter that followed Jake out the door.

The snow had come down steadily since he left the restaurant. The wind was up now, blowing snow off the roofs and making it hard to tell if any new snow was still falling. The sun was weak, filtered as it was through the heavy clouds.

Jake's heart was heavy, too, as he trudged toward the livery. At the door, he glanced across the street to the upstairs windows of the Hays House. He resisted the pull and entered the barn. He didn't know which window was hers anyway, he told himself.

As he saddled the white mare, he noticed Emily's carpetbag waiting beside her saddle. He was tempted to have it sent across the street. He hated to think of her venturing out in the cold to get her bag. But if somebody brought it to her now, wouldn't that alert her to his absence that much sooner?

His horse was ready to go and still he hesitated. It had turned so cold. He would compromise. He left the mare standing and grabbed the bag. Across the street he deposited it near the desk. "Give this to Miss Prescott when she comes down," he said, then hurried back across the street.

He headed out of town turning almost due south toward a small farmstead roughly halfway between Garvey's and town. It was the nearest spot on the map and as good a place to start as any. He tried to frame what he would ask the farmer, plan where he would go from there, but his mind lingered instead on Emily.

How long would she wait before she went looking for him and discovered he had abandoned her? Would she be frightened? Angry was more likely.

Yet she was young and alone in a strange place. She was bound to feel betrayed. He pictured her big brown eyes looking lost and vulnerable and cursed himself.

She was resourceful. She had managed to buy a

good horse in order to go along in the first place. She wouldn't have any trouble getting home—or away to meet Berkeley.

He tried to put that last thought out of his mind. In its own way it was more upsetting than the lost little girl he had pictured earlier.

No, he told himself. She could take care of herself. Didn't she always do as she pleased anyway? She had run away with her lover, jumped off the train and forced him to take her with him. She wouldn't have any trouble.

Suddenly Jake realized he shared the trail with a northbound traveler. He should have seen him some distance away but had been too lost in thought. As they neared each other he tipped his hat to the man who responded in kind.

He rode on, trying to put Emily out of his mind. He was a lawman on the trail of a fugitive. Why was that so easy to forget? Perhaps he should go back to training horses. Maybe then he could keep his mind on what he was doing. He laughed out loud. He seemed to recall Christian's mind wandering a great deal the first summer Lynnette was on the ranch. It seemed it wasn't the job at all, but the woman that was to blame. Or the man's feelings for her.

The little farmhouse came into view, nestled near a stand of trees along a creek. The smoke rising from the rock chimney spoke of a warm, inviting fire. But he had a lot of ground to cover. He would ask and be on his way.

Emily awoke feeling more rested than she had in days. She wasn't sure how long she had slept, more than an hour, she was sure, perhaps two. She stretched and padded to the window in her stocking feet. The snow that had looked so lovely drifting down had turned to a dirty mess in the street. She touched the glass and remembered watching Jake walk away, the light snow dusting his dark coat and hat.

"Hurry back," she whispered, repeating the wish she had murmured before.

Maybe he *was* back. Maybe he had taken another room and was even now waiting for her to wake up. There could be a note on her door or a message waiting downstairs at the desk.

Without bothering to treat the sore on her heel, she sat on the bed and slipped into her shoes. In a moment she was running downstairs. She was a little surprised to find herself so elated but didn't stop to wonder about it.

"Is there a message for Miss Prescott from Jake Rawlins?" she asked the clerk, giving him a sunny smile.

"Oh, yes, ma'am." He reached beneath the desk and came up with her carpetbag. "He said to give you this when you came down."

"Ah, my bag. Did Mr. Rawlins take another room?"

"No, ma'am. I saw him ride out of town."

Emily froze. She hadn't heard him right. "He didn't leave town."

"Oh, yes, ma'am. That white mare he rides is pretty distinctive. I saw him walk her right down the street. Will you be staying the night?"

"No." She grabbed up the bag. "I'll be leaving, too."

She stomped up the stairs and back into the room. "How could he do this!" she raved, searching through her bag for more clothes to put on. She was going after him.

She didn't know where he was headed. She didn't know how to find out except to ask people which way he had gone. That hadn't worked too well for Jake after Anson left the Garveys. It probably wouldn't work for her. She could end up lost. Besides it would take too much time.

She buttoned the blouse hastily, tucking it into the waist of her riding skirt. She knew she should put on a second pair of stockings but she hated to take the time. God knows how much of a head start Jake had.

"Darn him," she muttered, flinging the cloak over her shoulders and snatching up the bag. "Just when I was starting to…"

She froze, bringing her fingers to her lips. She had been about to say—no, she wouldn't even complete the thought. She wasn't in love with Jake.

She groaned, forcing herself to leave the room and move down the stairs. If she was in love with Jake, this latest trick ought to end it! "Just when I was starting to *trust him*," she said deliberately.

On her way to the door a plan took shape. Maybe more of an impulse than a plan, but she acted on it. She turned back to the clerk. "Where can I find a lawman?"

The clerk blinked at her. "Sheriff's office…" he pointed.

"Thank you very much." She smiled sweetly, left the hotel and slammed the door behind her.

"He's supposed to be my *friend*," she raved under

her breath as she marched down the boardwalk. "He acts so *sweet*. So *considerate*." She heard the words on her own lips and thought of them as curses.

She nearly walked past the sheriff's office. She saw the sign out of the corner of her eye and backtracked a step. She took a deep breath, hastily considering just what she was going to tell the sheriff. It came to her in an instant. Turning her anger to sorrow, she walked into the room.

"You have to help me," she wailed. "My husband—" She gulped a mouthful of air and swallowed it. "My husband's abandoned me!" Her voice croaked quite convincingly.

A huge man stood and came toward her. His scowl made her wonder for an instant about the wisdom of this particular course of action. But she was already committed. She sniffed noisily.

"Mr. Rawlins is your husband? He checked you into the hotel as Miss Prescott."

She had no ready explanation. "Ohh!" she wailed, doing her best to dissolve into tears. They had come so easily the past several days, where were they now?

"There, there, miss…er…ma'am." He patted her back awkwardly. "He's looking for his fugitive. He said he'd be coming back this way. I'm sure he wanted you to wait for him."

Wait here for him! Fat chance! "No, he was lying. He's…he's…not after a fugitive." Oh Lord, what kind of a mess was she getting herself into. Yet she needed to find Jake.

"Now, ma'am, he asked everyone in town about this Berkeley fella. He's determined to find him. Said it was personal. You'd best just stay here and let him do his job.''

"Ohh," she wailed again, buying herself time to think. Personal, huh? "Berkeley's not a fugitive," she said between huge sniffs. Nothing seemed to bring those tears! "He's just a friend. Jake is so…jealous." Dropping her bag and burying her head in her hands, she sobbed, trying to irritate her eyes in the process.

"Not a fugitive?" The man's voice sounded furious.

She shook her head without lifting it.

"We'll find him," the sheriff announced, turning to grab his coat.

"No, wait! I have to go with you."

"Now, ma'am, it's cold out there. I'll round up some boys, and we'll bring him back to you."

She lowered her head and sobbed into her hands. "I have to come with you!"

"There, there," he said, patting her shoulder again. He turned and opened the door, and she grabbed up her bag and followed him out.

He began yelling orders to passersby. In a matter of minutes a crowd had gathered. "You all seen the stranger came in about noon. Most of you talked to him. It turns out he's a scoundrel set on deserting this young lady."

Emily took that as a cue to sob daintily.

"We're goin' after him. Anybody seen him ride out, step up here and report."

Emily stood back watching the proceedings. The sheriff, her ally now, incited the indignation of nearly every man in the crowd. She began to worry for

Jake's safety. Well, *he* shouldn't have abandoned her, she decided.

"This man could be dangerous," the sheriff was saying. "Any of you that looked into his cold blue eyes—"

"Green," she interrupted before she could stop herself. She suddenly had everyone's attention. "They're green," she repeated nervously. "And not especially cold."

"There, there," repeated the sheriff, patting her shoulder.

The crowd murmured its compassion.

At the sheriff's word they scattered to ready their horses. She found, as they gathered again, that the man at the livery had saddled her gelding for her. She gave him a tremulous smile before he helped her aboard and tied her bag on behind.

The sheriff wasted no more time. Emily found herself nearly galloping out of town between the sheriff and a rancher who had evidently met Jake along the road. She almost expected to overtake him immediately. Surely Jake wasn't pushing his horse this fast.

After several minutes of breathless riding, they stopped at a farmhouse. The sheriff seemed to have a good idea where Jake would go. He dismounted, had a few words with the farmer, who pointed the way, and swung his considerable bulk into the saddle again. The posse, as Emily was now thinking of the group, took off in a new direction.

After a few more minutes, they spied a lone rider ahead of them. The horse was white. The sheriff gave a triumphant shout and spurred his mount to greater speed. Emily and the rest did likewise.

The rider pulled up at the sound. He looked around, considering perhaps the chances of running or heading for cover. But there was no cover. He dismounted, thrusting his coat behind him to expose the handle of a gun in his belt.

"Jake!" Emily screamed, realizing it was more of a warning than anything else.

"We got him," the sheriff assured her.

They came up to Jake and made a rough circle around him. His eyes flicked to Emily then concentrated on the sheriff. She wished he would look at her again. He was missing her smirk. She raised a hand to her mouth to hide it from the posse.

"Young man," the sheriff began sternly. "We take our marriage vows seriously around here."

That brought his eyes back to Emily. She tried to look the part of the abandoned wife by giving him a beseeching smile. "Why did you leave me, darling?" she choked. She wanted to throw in a couple of sniffs but was afraid she would giggle.

Jake didn't answer. He turned his attention back to the sheriff, evidently uncertain what the big man would decide to do. It occurred to Emily that he might decide to exact some punishment. She jumped off her horse and ran to Jake, throwing herself into his arms. "Darling," she crooned, "you won't leave me again, will you?"

"Don't suppose it'd do much good," he muttered.

"'Pears to me," the sheriff said, "a gal'd be better off a widow than tied to a man what runs off and leaves her."

Jake's body didn't stiffen but Emily's did. Lord, she had never dreamed the sheriff would react so strongly. She turned her face into Jake's chest and sobbed noisily.

"You give up this notion of tracking down your wife's friend," the sheriff said. "You be good to the little woman, and let the past go. I got your promise?"

Jake was silent. Emily poked him in the ribs. How foolish was he?

"Oh, yes, sir, you have my promise. I should never have let the *little woman* out of my sight in the first place."

Emily leaned back to scowl at him, but his eyes were on the sheriff.

"That's good, boy. You see you remember that." He waved his arm and turned, walking his horse back the way he had come. The rest of the posse regrouped behind him, each man giving Jake a cold glare as he turned away.

Jake sighed, drawing Emily gently away from him. He gazed down into her eyes, and she waited to read his reaction. Was he furious with her? She really hadn't stopped to consider how he would feel.

"I had to find you, Jake," she blurted. When she realized how close she had come to telling him why, she added, "I need you to help me find Anson."

She wanted him to pull her back into his arms; it had felt so right. But it had only been part of the act. And she couldn't have him. He would have no feeling for her but contempt once he knew about the baby.

A voice in her head suggested she not tell him, not ever, but she brushed it aside. She was capable of considerable dishonesty, but she wouldn't seduce Jake and try to pass the child off as his. She had to find another solution to her predicament. Anson, her best hope, seemed more like an additional problem than a solution.

Jake must have read the turmoil in her eyes because he stepped forward, cupping her cheek with a gloved hand. "Are you all right?" he asked.

She felt the tears come to her eyes. Sure, *now* she could cry. "I need you to help me find Anson," she repeated, though the truth was she simply needed him.

He gently folded her into his arms, and she wondered if he had read more than she suspected in her face. She melted into the embrace, for a moment feeling warm and safe.

Maybe not so safe. A fire leaped to life in the pit of her stomach and spread heat through her limbs. She tried to ignore it. She knew what it was. Desire. And it was more a trick than anything else.

She started to pull away but only got far enough to find her face scant inches from his. His breath was coming in short shallow puffs. Not a good sign. Never a good sign.

But she couldn't step away from him. It was as if his gentle hands on her shoulder blades held her in an iron grip. His eyes were half closed, his lips slightly parted. She found herself drawing nearer. Or he was. She couldn't tell. At any rate, his lips were closing in on hers.

The heat inside her intensified, making her tremble. Against all reason, she wanted to taste those lips. She no sooner thought it than it happened. Warm firm lips embraced hers, and her body molded against his hard torso. No reasonable thought seemed possible beyond the knowledge that the man she loved held her in his arms.

He raised his head a fraction, and she sighed, parting her lips. "I love you" was on the tip of her tongue.

She jumped away, clamping a hand over her mouth. She hadn't said it, surely! She stared at his startled expression. Would he look more surprised if she had confessed her love? She waited in dread for him to speak.

He took a deep breath and let it out slowly, as if he were fighting for control. "I'm sorry," he said finally.

Sorry? She must not have said the words aloud. What was he sorry about? Was he taking the blame for the kiss? She should let him. She should play the innocent. He had taken advantage of her.

She lowered her hand. "It was my fault," she heard herself say. Well, she had thrown herself into his arms for the sheriff's benefit. But the kiss had just…happened.

He grinned at her, not at all the reaction she expected. "Women have taken the blame for men's lust for centuries. Who am I to argue?"

Lust? She had fallen in love, and all he felt was lust! She shouldn't be surprised. Men were all alike. And she had thought Jake was special. She whirled away and caught up the reins to the patient gelding.

Jake was behind her, his hands on her waist before she got her foot in the stirrup. He was going to apologize for the cruel remark. He was going to kiss her again. She was about to turn toward him when he tossed her into the saddle.

"Up you go, little woman," he said.

Oh, it was going to be easy to get over Jake. She wanted to kick him, but he caught her foot and guided it into the stirrup.

He rested a hand on her knee and looked up at her. "Emily," he said softly, "I left you in town because I wanted you safe. But I didn't want you to be afraid. My conscience has tortured me ever since. I'm glad you found me."

He turned and mounted the mare, eased along beside her and started them down the trail. Emily stole glances at his profile. Had he really forgiven her for the scene with the posse? Was one "little woman" all she was going to hear about it?

He had always been forgiving. Lord knows she had given him plenty of practice over the years. Maybe it was just habit. Maybe he cared so little about her it was easy.

Maybe he was just the sweetest man she had ever met.

Lord, how was she going to fall out of love with Jake Rawlins?

Chapter Eleven

No one was home at the next farmhouse on the map. Jake considered waiting a bit but after watering the horses, he decided to follow the creek to the next one. Emily seemed to be holding up better than she had the day before. The good rest after dinner had evidently made the difference. Or the excitement of rounding up a posse and chasing him down had.

Jake hid his grin from her as they followed a dim road that skirted the narrow fields along the creek. The shock of finding a mob coming up fast behind him had been followed by an even greater shock when he recognized Emily. And that had been followed by a calm acceptance. Of course she would find a way to catch up with him. He should have expected it.

And now here she was, beside him again, where she belonged. His heart felt lighter than it had all day. How he had missed her!

He wanted to see her face, but it was hidden by her hood. He leaned forward to peer up at her. A frown creased her forehead; she was deep in thought and didn't notice his scrutiny.

He straightened, concerned. Could she be in pain? "Emily?" he said, regretting the alarm he heard in his voice.

She straightened abruptly. "What?"

"I didn't mean to startle you," he said. "I just...are you all right?"

"I'm fine."

She hadn't looked fine a moment before. "Emily, don't think your little trick with the sheriff has somehow ended your right to complain. If you need to rest, I want you to tell me."

"Jake," she groaned, frustration clear in her voice.

"What?" he asked gently. "What did I do?"

She sighed and glared at him. He was completely at a loss. It hit him, then. The kiss. She was bothered by the fact that he had kissed her. She was probably afraid to be alone with him, now. And he wanted very much for her to feel safe.

The kiss had been an awful mistake. He had known all along that if he ever gave in to the temptation he would regret it. It had just seemed so right at the time. And he could have sworn she kissed him back.

He remembered every detail. Her body softly pressed against his. Her hands clutching his coat. Her lips, warm and pliant, returning the pressure of his kiss.

So that was what was bothering her. The fact that she *had* returned the kiss. She had been unfaithful to Berkeley.

He tried to stop the grin he felt spreading across his face. He had never been quite so aware of his own ego before this moment. He felt too damn good to even consider apologizing.

He glanced her way and discovered her scowl had deepened. "What?" she demanded. "Why are you grinning?"

"You first," he said, making an effort to be serious. "Why are you frowning?"

"You're impossible," she said. "I should hate you!"

"Why?" He truly was bewildered now. "Because I left you? Or because I kissed you?"

"Yes. Yes. And for other reasons. I should hate you. But I can't!" She slammed her gloved hand down on the saddle horn and it made the softest of thuds.

He laughed. He knew he shouldn't. He should take her unhappiness seriously, no matter how little sense it made. "You're angry because you can't hate me? Of course you can't hate me. We've been friends forever. That's what friends do. They get angry, and then they forgive each other."

"I don't want to forgive you," she muttered.

"I wish you would forgive me, but that's your choice. You know, I could be angry at you for bringing that sheriff down on me like you did."

"I *know*," she said through gritted teeth as if that somehow made it worse. She took a deep breath, trying to pull herself together. "Tell me why you were grinning."

He grinned again. "Because you kissed me."

"I took the blame because I had thrown myself at you for the sheriff's benefit. But I didn't kiss you."

He nodded. "I was there. You kissed me."

She was angry again. "Oh, this is good. This is better. I can be mad at you for this. I didn't kiss you. How could I kiss you? You're taller than I am."

Jake laughed, though half of what she said hadn't made any sense. "I didn't say you were the only one kissing. I'm just saying I wasn't, either."

She glared at him, opened her mouth, but he spoke first. "The next farm." He pointed to the house a few yards in front of them. She had evidently been unaware of it until now.

Emily lagged behind a little as Jake approached the house. She had to get her temper under control. She knew she was being unreasonable but he had been so...so...solicitous. Here she was trying to fall out of love with him, and he was worried that she didn't think she could complain anymore.

Then he laughed! The arrogant bastard thought she was worried because of the kiss! As if she had even given it a second thought. And *he* hadn't been the *only* one kissing, he said. Well, she *liked* kissing. That's all there was to it. She would even kiss him again if he wanted to. It didn't mean anything!

Lord, had she gone crazy? She didn't dare kiss him again!

Emily joined Jake in the yard. He hadn't even dismounted before an old man stepped out of the house holding a shotgun.

"Good afternoon," Jake said pleasantly.

The man seemed able to resist Jake's charm, even if she couldn't. He didn't lower the gun. "Whatcha want?"

"We're following a man. He would have come

through here early yesterday afternoon. A young man, early twenties, medium height, thin, with straight blond—''

The man swore and spat. "Little thief."

"That's the one," Jake said.

Emily gasped indignantly, but Jake ignored it.

"He come ridin' in askin' to buy some feed for his horse. While I was off to the barn, fillin' a nose bag, he come inside and took my wad. Thirteen dollars I had saved. Didn't notice it was gone till this mornin'.''

"Sir, you must be mistaken. Eldon wouldn't—''

"He was headed toward the Fuller place," the man said, ignoring Emily completely. "I'd a gone over to check on 'em but my horse is lame.''

"I'll check on the Fullers," Jake said. He dismounted and walked toward the man. "Can you find their house on this map for me?''

The farmer set his shotgun aside to study the map.

Emily watched them as they conferred. She should dismount and stretch her legs, for who knew how far it was to the Fullers'. But she didn't think her legs would hold her if she tried to stand. Could Anson have really robbed this poor man? She looked around the plain but tidy yard. He couldn't easily spare any thirteen dollars.

She fumbled with her reticule under her cloak. She still had more than twenty dollars left. She counted out thirteen, wondering what the man would say if she offered it to him. She hesitated until Jake turned to remount his horse then kneed hers closer to the farmer.

"Eldon," she began. "The man who was here, I can't believe he stole your money."

"Somebody did, lady, and weren't nobody else around." He started to turn away.

"If Eldon stole it, I can get it back from him," she said quickly, handing him the roll of bills.

The man took the money hesitantly. "He kin?"

"Of sorts," she said, wondering if that would make it easier for him to take it.

"Keep him away from me," he said, entering the house.

Emily turned the gelding around and joined Jake. They left the yard side by side.

"Are you going to live your life paying Anson's debts?" Jake asked.

"Please, Jake," she murmured. "Anson didn't take any money. I just wanted to help that old man."

A glance at Jake's face told her he didn't believe her. She wasn't sure she believed it herself. "How far to the Fullers'?" she asked, wanting the subject changed.

"Just a few miles."

The few miles were ridden in silence. Emily wondered what Jake was thinking but was afraid to ask for fear he was gloating. Anson was living up to all his predictions, or so he thought. She wasn't sure what she thought anymore. She shivered under her cloak, knowing that the cold that crept into her limbs came from the inside.

The clouds that had lifted almost unnoticed seemed to lower again. More snow, Emily thought, but it hardly mattered.

* * *

The Fuller farmstead finally came into view. It was a tiny place, barely more than a shanty. A young man stepped out as they drew up near the door. He looked younger than Emily, at least younger than she felt.

"Can I help you?" he asked.

Jake dismounted and began his now-familiar description of Anson. The boy nodded. "Came through here yesterday afternoon. Watered his horse but didn't stay long."

As he spoke a girl, wrapped in a worn shawl, stepped out behind him. He drew her close to his side. Emily stared at them. They looked so young.

"Did he take anything?" Jake asked, drawing Emily's scowl.

The couple looked at each other and shook their heads. "Don't have much," the boy said. "Leastwise nothin' he could steal." He and the girl exchanged fond smiles.

"Want to come inside and warm up?" the girl asked. "I got coffee on."

A polite refusal was on the tip of Emily's tongue when Jake spoke. "Thank you. It'll be good to stretch our legs."

He turned to Emily and helped her dismount as the boy took up the reins. "I'll water the horses at the creek for you," he said.

"Why are we stopping?" Emily hissed in Jake's ear as they walked toward the open door. "Shouldn't we be hot to the trail of your supposed thief?"

"You're cold," he said, bringing her inside.

"Come on over," the girl invited. She had moved two chairs close to a little iron cookstove, the only heat in the small cluttered cabin. When they were seated, she pressed chipped mugs of coffee into their hands.

"Did yesterday's visitor say much?" Jake asked their hostess.

"Well," she said, and crossed her arms and frowned. She hadn't taken a seat herself; Jake and Emily occupied the only two in the house. "He was interested in how long we'd been here, how we were gettin' on. We thought he might be looking for a place for himself."

"Did he ask if you were puttin' any money aside?"

Emily wanted to kick Jake for asking such a question, but she was too intent on waiting for an answer.

The girl nodded slowly, her little face showing alarm. "I told him how I'd just put three dollars butter-and-egg money in the bank."

"He can't get it there," Jake said, sipping his coffee.

"If I hadn't mentioned the bank, might he have tried to rob us?"

Jake gave her a charming smile. "You're safe now," he said.

The boy came into the house, shucking his heavy coat. "That man through here yesterday was a robber," his wife told him.

Emily rolled her eyes toward the ceiling.

"Just be a mite more careful with strangers," Jake suggested, rising. "Thanks for the coffee."

Emily set her half-finished coffee aside, muttering, "We're strangers." She reached for her cloak the same moment Jake did. Their fingers brushed and she drew away. If he noticed, he showed no sign. He settled the cloak around her shoulders as he thanked the boy for caring for the horses.

In the saddle again, Jake led the way to the road. He unfolded the map and studied it. "There are two more farms here along the creek, then we need to head up into the hills toward a ranch."

"Where are we spending the night?" Emily asked.

Jake turned toward her. "Tired?"

"Disgusted."

He grinned. "Want me to take you back to town?"

"Jake, whatever happened to innocent until proven guilty?"

He didn't answer. She watched him refold the map and stick it inside his coat. "We can try a couple more houses before we stop for the night. It'll get dark early, though."

He seemed to be oblivious to the desperation she found closing in around her. Of course, he didn't know about the baby. All he cared about was catching Anson; he had already decided the worst about him.

But she had to believe it wasn't so. If Anson was really a thief...

No. She wouldn't jump to conclusions. And she wouldn't borrow trouble. She had plenty as it was.

The next farmhouse was barely two miles from the last. It was larger and older than the young couple's. A man walked from the barn as they rode into the yard. He seemed wary at first but relaxed when he noticed one of his visitors was a woman.

"We're looking for someone," Jake said, dismounting and walking toward the farmer. He launched into his description. The man listened carefully, nodding when he finished.

"You a friend of his?" There was open accusation in his tone.

Jake opened his coat, revealing his badge. "He's a fugitive," he said.

The man nodded grimly. "He was here. The missus offered him supper while I took care of his horse. I came inside to find him poking around. I ran him off."

Emily closed her eyes. She wanted to believe he was just curious, looking at some books or something. Somehow she couldn't bring herself to voice the suggestion aloud. Then another thought occurred to her, and she threw herself off the horse. "Mister," she said, rummaging through her reticule as she came toward him. "Did he look like this?"

He took the small framed picture she held out to him. After studying it a moment, he handed it back saying, "That's him."

Emily sighed, replacing the picture. She had a sudden need to lean against Jake, but he didn't seem to notice she was even standing beside him.

"Which way did he go?" Jake asked.

The man pointed north. "Off across country. I told him I was going to warn my neighbors up and down the road."

"Did you?" Jake asked.

The man scuffed one toe on the frozen ground. "Naw. I figured the threat would be enough. I didn't want to leave the missus alone for fear he'd come back."

Jake nodded his understanding and thanked the

man as he turned to help Emily remount. Emily followed him out of the yard. They headed north, across open prairie.

"Do you know how helpful that picture would have been in Council Grove?" he asked.

She looked at him, glad that he didn't seem angry with her. "I didn't want to be helpful," she responded. It was only half the truth. She had forgotten she had the picture with her until this moment. It wasn't as if she looked at it every night.

"But you're willing to be helpful now?"

Emily studied him for a moment. Why hadn't she realized how handsome he was until it was too late? And kind. Even when he was angry he was unfailingly kind.

"I had to know for sure," she whispered finally.

He kneed his horse closer to hers. "It'll be all right," he said, resting one gloved hand on hers. "You'll see."

She nodded, turning away. She didn't believe it for a moment. They rode on in silence. The prairie was slower going than the road, however crude it had been. The horses picked their way carefully between clumps of dead grass and rocks and prairie dog holes.

The sky was taking on an ominous cast by the time they neared the ranch. Emily noted with some satisfaction that the house was stone, but it was small, unlikely to have a spare bedroom for passing strangers. The thought was reinforced when a man stepped out of the house, followed by a round-faced youth, and half-a-dozen little faces peered at them through a large window.

A few minutes later, Emily found herself being

ushered into the house. Six pairs of eyes studied her from across the cramped little room.

"He come through here all right," the man was saying. "Spent the night."

Emily's eyes met Jake's, and she saw him hesitate for a moment. Turning back to the rancher, he asked, "Was anything missing?"

"Missing?" He seemed perplexed for a moment, then realization dawned. He moved across the room, lifting a battered tobacco tin from the clutter on a stone ledge above the fireplace. He opened it, stared inside and seemed to deflate before their eyes.

He turned to the flock of children. "Did any of you see that man take our money?"

Six little heads shook from side to side in unison.

He muttered a curse and replaced the can on the ledge. "I just didn't think about it at all. It was late and cold and the man needed a place to sleep. Hate to think it ain't safe to offer a man Christian hospitality."

Emily hadn't realized her knees had gone weak until she felt Jake's arm slip around her waist, supporting her.

"Ah, the lady's plum wore-out," the man said, helping her into a rocker that sat before the fire. "Maybelle, see how Ma and April are coming with dinner."

The tallest child, who might have been eight, scampered away.

Jake and the rancher took seats. Emily half listened to their conversation as she rocked, feeling the warmth of the fire dissipate the chill, except for the chill around her heart.

Before she could slip too deeply into self-pity, the youngest child, a toddler not much more than a year old, started edging toward her. He was watching the chair more than her, rocking his little body occasionally in time with it.

Emily smiled at him, leaning forward slowly. When she reached her arms toward him, he crossed the rest of the distance and let her lift him to her lap.

"August! Don't you be botherin' the lady," his father said gruffly.

The baby's response was to snuggle deeper into her lap and close his eyes.

"You're going to spoil that young'un."

None of the children were alarmed by their father's harsh tone. His bark, Emily concluded, was worse than his bite. "Am I in your mama's chair?" she whispered to the little boy.

A sticky little hand reached up and touched her mouth for a second then curled under his chin again.

The remaining four children were slowly creeping closer. One little girl put her hand on Emily's knee and was surveying her lap as if looking for room for her. An older child pushed her back.

"August thinks if you don't talk to him you'll forget he's there and rock him longer," explained a boy who might have been six. "Ma falls asleep sometimes when she rocks him."

Emily could imagine. With this many children, the poor woman must be exhausted.

The little girl made another effort to climb the rungs of the chair. "Junebug!" her father exclaimed.

She threw herself onto Emily's lap, and August

made room for her. "Safe," chirped the girl, and both babies laughed.

"Bah." The man looked truly disgusted. "You're gonna scare the lady outa ever wantin' kids." He went back to his discussion with Jake.

Maybelle came back into the room and announced, "Ma says ten minutes." She pushed at her father's legs until he moved them aside, giving her room to sit on the chair with him. "The boys are supposed to wash their hands."

"Girls, too," said the boy standing beside Emily.

Maybelle shook her head, leaning toward her brother with narrowed eyes. "Girls aren't dirty."

"Are too!"

"Well, I'm dirty," Emily said, hoping to forestall a fight. She turned to Maybelle. "Can you show me where to clean up?"

Junebug had slid from her lap when she leaned forward, but August refused to leave his curled position. His eyes were shut tight, and he made little snoring sounds. Emily held him over the floor, but his legs remained curled under him. June knelt in front of him and tried to pull his legs down, only to have them spring upward again. The snoring sounded a little like giggles.

"Put the kid in his crib," the father said, coming to his feet. "If he's asleep, he don't need no supper."

The baby suddenly dropped his legs toward the floor.

"He was faking," one of the children informed her solemnly.

Once all the children had washed, they filed into the big kitchen to take their seats at a long table.

Besides the six children Emily had met in the living room, there was a twelve-year-old girl who had helped with dinner and a fourteen-year-old boy who had put up the horses. The ages and names—minus the bugs and belles their father had added—were given by their mother as they took their seats at a long table.

Conversation was impossible at the table, but Emily noticed that the man, Mr. Kraus she discovered, didn't mention the loss of their money to his wife. She wasn't sure what he and Jake had discussed in the living room before dinner. It didn't matter. Jake would make his decisions without her anyway.

For the first time she wished she had stayed in Council Grove. She didn't want to hear about Anson stealing from anybody else.

The thought brought her eyebrows together. Did she believe it now? Was there any faith in Anson left at all? Very little, she realized. What other explanation was there? A thief was following Anson, stealing from everyone he met? Anson had given them the slip and they were following a stranger who looked like him? A part of her, she realized, would have liked to believe something of the kind.

When the meal ended, the men and most of the children returned to the living room. Emily stayed to help the woman clean up. Anson, she realized, hadn't once been mentioned at the table. Mrs. Kraus hadn't yet been influenced by Jake's remarks.

"Did you have a visitor here last night?" she began.

"Why, yes," the woman answered. "A nice young man, tall and blond. Do you know him?"

Emily smiled. She set a stack of dishes near the sink and wiped her hands on the apron the woman had loaned her. "I think so," she said. Her reticule was hanging around her waist, and she pulled it open, feeling inside until she found the picture. "Did he look like this?"

The woman gazed at the picture without touching it. "Yes, that's him."

She had known it would be. There hadn't really been any question that Anson had been here. Only whether he had stolen from them or not. There was little question of that, either, she supposed.

Emily helped Mrs. Kraus, April and May with the dishes then joined the others in the living room. June climbed onto her lap while Mrs. Kraus rocked August. The other children played in small groups, being carefully quiet most of the time.

Emily didn't listen to the conversation between Jake and Mr. Kraus. She snuggled the little girl close, watched the fire and tried to think of what to do. There seemed no good way out of her situation. Her baby still needed a name, but the name of a thief?

Maybe it was time she went home in disgrace. Her family would eventually forgive her. Christian and her father at least. Mother and Arlen would take longer, but they all truly loved her. And they hated Anson enough they would easily blame him entirely.

She closed her eyes for a moment. Why hadn't she listened to them? Why had she been so taken in by Anson's charm?

For some odd reason Jake's opinion of her mattered more than her family's. She didn't think she could bear to see his reaction to her confession. But she would have to. Tonight.

She took a deep breath, hoping to dispel the pain that constricted her heart and lungs, and forced her body to relax. She tried not to think of anything but the small warm body curled in her arms. She didn't know she had drifted off to sleep until she felt the child being lifted from her lap. The other children had disappeared and in a moment the couple went up a flight of narrow stairs.

"They left blankets," Jake said. All the lamps had been put out, and he stood between her and the fire, looking slightly uncomfortable.

"Are we husband and wife again, Jake?" She had meant it to sound teasing, but instead it came out breathless, leaving the oddest sensation in her chest.

"It seemed the easiest thing to tell them. You trust me, don't you, Emily?"

"Of course," she said, coming to her feet. Trust wasn't exactly the problem.

He knelt to spread the blankets on a rug before the fire. "Aren't they something?" he asked, grinning up at her. "All those children. I thought Christian and Lynnette had their hands full."

Emily knelt to help him make their bed. "Do you want that many children, Jake?" She had no idea why she was asking a question like that. Because babies were on her mind, she supposed.

He shrugged. "I guess I never thought about it. Remember I grew up without any brothers or sisters. Well, you and your brothers seemed like mine."

Emily didn't like him thinking of her as a sister, though she wasn't sure why it mattered. A few times she had thought… But no. Even if she had seen something more in his eyes, it would be gone as soon as he heard her news. Maybe acting as a sister would make what she had to say easier. "I need to talk to you," she whispered.

His head came up and his hands went still. She hadn't realized how desperate she sounded until she saw his response. In a moment he was moving again. "Here. Slip off your shoes and get comfortable."

As she obeyed he found the bottle of ointment in her bag and handed it to her. "Thanks, doc," she teased.

In short order he had her half-reclined against his strong chest, her legs covered with a blanket. She was aware of his strong warm muscles against her back. "Now talk to me," he whispered close to her ear. "You can tell me anything you want."

"I'm ready to go back home now," she said. It had been easier than she expected, perhaps because she didn't have to see his face. "I don't care whether you keep hunting for Anson or not."

He didn't say anything. She wasn't sure what she expected, but surely he had some comment. She turned toward him. "Did you hear me?"

"I'll get you home," he said, taking her shoulders and settling her back against him. "Is that all you wanted to tell me?"

She took a deep breath. "No."

She couldn't find the words. She wanted to put herself in a good light, find some way to tell him that wouldn't mark her as a fallen woman. She almost laughed at herself. As if that were possible.

She felt a pin slip from her hair and reached up to find Jake's hand there. "You can't sleep with your hair pinned up. Let me take it down while you talk."

"Jake, it's not something I can tell you while you fuss with my hair."

"After, then," he said.

She felt the heavy mass slip to her shoulder and his fingers comb through it. She sat quietly, almost holding her breath. He parted the tresses and pleated them into a simple braid. She wanted to ask him if he knew her brother used to braid her hair every night when she was a little girl at the ranch, away from her mother. Did he need one more reminder that she was almost like a sister to him?

She was in love with him, and he wanted to be her brother. Would he be more willing to forgive a sister what she was about to tell him?

"Do you have a ribbon to tie it off?" he asked.

"In my bag."

He handed the braid over her shoulder, and she took the end, sitting up straight in the process. He rolled away for a moment and rolled back with the carpetbag. With one hand, she rummaged inside until she found the ribbon and tied it around the end of the braid. By the time she was finished, he had set the bag aside and was ready to settle her against him again.

It seemed unreal, leaning against Jake, feeling his cheek rest against her hair. She could almost pretend she was a child in her brother's arms. Almost. The heat that curled through her body like wood smoke was something else altogether.

His lips brushed against her temple and the slow fire turned to a blaze. She found her heart pounding and her breath catching in her throat. She had to put a stop to this. And she knew just the way.

"I'm going to have a baby."

Chapter Twelve

Jake pressed his lips against her temple again. It had felt so good the first time, he couldn't resist. "I know," he whispered. "It'll be all right."

She threw herself forward and turned to face him. "Did you hear what I said?"

He raised a finger to her lips. "You'll wake the children."

She sighed heavily, raising her eyes to the ceiling.

He had to fight the urge to grin at her exasperation. "A baby. I know." He coaxed her back into his arms, this time half-turned toward him with her head on his shoulder. He was braced against the front of a heavy chair. His shoulder blades protested but the rest of his body ignored them.

"How long have you known?" she asked.

"Long enough to think of a solution."

Her arm wrapped around his chest, and he closed his eyes, aware of every inch of her body that touched his, even through all the layers of clothes.

"There is no solution," she whispered.

She sounded close to tears. He didn't think he could handle tears. "Marry me," he said.

She sat up again. His body missed her immediately, but it did make it easier to think.

"Emily," he began, wanting to be reasonable. "You can't marry Berkeley. He would make you miserable."

She turned away. She was still in love with the bastard. The knowledge sent a shaft of pain through his heart. Perhaps that was what made him willing to risk hurting her. "Is that the name you want for your child? Berkeley the thief?"

He heard her sob and wished he could call the words back. "Emily." He reached toward her.

"I know," she said, slipping from his touch. "I don't want to marry him. I don't want to ever see him again."

"Then marry me."

She turned to face him again. Her face was in shadows, but he could see the uncertainty there. "Why would you want to marry me?" she whispered finally.

A laugh broke from his lips before he could stop it. She drew farther away, but he moved with her. "Emily, I'm sorry. I wasn't laughing at you. I thought it had been obvious. I've been in love with you as long as I can remember."

They were both kneeling on the spread blankets, lit only by the fire. Her shocked silence suggested he had done a better job hiding his love than he had thought. "I love you," he whispered into the silence.

"Like a sister," she whispered back.

He almost laughed again. Instead he gently lifted

her hand and drew it to his chest. "Feel the way my heart is pounding. A sister wouldn't do that to me."

He released her hand but it lingered. He found himself leaning toward her. "One kiss should prove how I feel."

The hand on his chest suddenly stiffened. "No," she said. "I...I knew you felt...something. But how can you love me now? I carry another man's child."

A lock of hair had missed the braid, and he reached up and brushed it off her cheek. "The baby is a part of you," he whispered. "How can I not love it?"

To his complete surprise she sank to the blankets and buried her face in her hands. "What? What did I say?"

"Stop it," she sobbed. "Stop being so nice."

He tried to draw her into his arms, but she pushed him away.

"Stop being what?" he whispered, his hand hovering just above her shoulder.

After a long, painful moment, she sat up. The firelight glistened on tears before she brushed them with the backs of her hands. "Stop being so nice!" she hissed, giving him an ineffectual punch in the shoulder for emphasis.

He knew he shouldn't grin at her. She was obviously exhausted. The decision to tell him about the baby couldn't have been easy for her. He should let her spend her emotions, not tease her. But still. "Nice?"

She glared at him then muttered, "You're impossible."

Some of the tension seemed to have left her, and he drew her carefully into his arms, coaxing her to lean against him again. He waited until she was re-laxed before he spoke.

"Emily, we've known each other since we were children. I think it's safe to say we're friends." He waited for her nod of agreement. "I'm asking you to consider me as a solution to your problem. I promise to love your child as my own. And God knows I'll be a faithful husband."

She tried to turn to look at him, but his hand on her cheek kept her head pressed against his shoulder. He hadn't meant to sound so vehement that it sparked her curiosity.

He went on quickly, "I've already admitted to lov-ing you and I think you have enough respect and fondness for me that you could learn to love me."

He smiled to himself, quite satisfied with the speech he had rehearsed in the hope that she would choose to tell him about the baby.

"That won't be a problem," she muttered.

"Which?"

"Loving you," she said, resisting his efforts to keep her snuggled against him. She gave him another punch in the shoulder, and nearly lost her balance. She rearranged herself to sit beside his outstretched legs facing him.

"It's impossible not to love you," she admitted grudgingly. "I've tried for days. And stop grinning at me. I'm not nearly as nice as you are. I'll drive you completely crazy!"

"I'm looking forward to it," he said, bringing him-self upright. He brushed the errant lock off her cheek again and cupped her face with his hands. "I prom-ised you a kiss."

"Did I say I wanted one?" But even as she whispered it, she leaned toward him.

"I promised myself a kiss, then." It was more the truth anyway.

He took her lips slowly, savoring the flavor, the feel of them. With the slightest urging of his tongue she parted them for him, letting him taste the soft sweetness of her mouth. Her tongue came to meet his, reluctantly at first, then more boldly.

He felt her tremble and realized she was pressed close against him, her hands clutching his shoulders. The smell of the wood in the fireplace, its gentle crackling, seemed to be part of Emily, part of the fire he felt raging inside him. He wanted her desperately, as he always had. He wanted to lower her to the blankets and plunder more than her lips.

But she hadn't offered him that. She hadn't even offered him the kiss. Still he knew her body responded to his touch, and he took hope from that.

Slowly he raised his head, breaking off the kiss before it consumed him. To his surprise, Emily collapsed against him, breathing hard. He was glad she couldn't see the arrogant smile that was surely on his face.

"Is that a yes?" he asked after a time.

She righted herself then. "Jake, are you sure? I mean the baby could…"

He raised her head with a touch to her chin. "Could what?"

She hesitated another moment. "Could look like Anson."

"Anson's not bad looking," he said.

Emily was not to be teased out of her worry. "But every time you looked at him—"

"I would see a little child. Emily, it wouldn't be impossible for us to have a fair-haired baby. Look at your father and at Christian. We'll tell everyone the baby looks like them, and they'll see what they expect to see."

She gazed at him, as if trying to read the truth. He spent the time watching the firelight glisten in her soft dark hair. Finally she drew his attention back to her lips. "Darn it, Jake, you're going to be nice about this, too, aren't you?"

"It's an annoying habit, I know, but you'll get used to it. Now, you need to get some sleep. Did you want to…uh…take off your…anything." He had thought the tightly fitted blouse and heavy riding skirt looked confining but discovered he couldn't say it aloud. She was scowling at him. "I was thinking of your comfort, Emily."

They were still sitting close together on the blanket. He didn't know what she was thinking. He was thinking of her lying naked in his arms. He should never have mentioned undressing.

In another moment he would be kissing her again. He wasn't sure he would be able to stop this time. He moved away from her abruptly, rising to sit in a chair and remove his boots. She took off the little purse that hung from her waist, but nothing else.

He stretched out on the blanket and drew her into the crook of his arm. She felt perfect nestled against him, but it was hours before he could sleep.

Emily had been half-aware of someone walking through the room earlier, but she had fallen back to sleep. She felt so cozy she didn't want to move. Something was tugging at her mind, something she would only understand once she woke up. Still she fought it.

Her cheek felt an odd tickle. She tried to twitch it away. The tickle grew worse until she had to brush at it with her hand. She let her arm fall back to its former position.

Jake gave a soft grunt, and Emily came fully awake. She was snuggled up so close to Jake she was almost on top of him! They were both fully clothed, thank goodness, but still, she was using his shoulder as a pillow. Her arm was around his chest, no doubt accounting for Jake's audible protest when she dropped it. Her leg was— She drew it quickly away.

The tickle came again, along with the realization that she was being watched. She turned slowly and looked up at three little children, each munching solemnly on a biscuit. They were standing so close, the crumbs were falling in her face.

One little child gave her a masticated-biscuit grin.

Her stomach rolled over. She closed her eyes, fighting down the nausea. She was aware of Jake moving beneath her, making her feel seasick. More crumbs fell in her face, and she knew she was losing the battle.

She flung herself upward, suffering a wave of dizziness. Before she had fully righted herself, Jake was beside her.

"What's wrong?"

Her only answer was a groan. She wrenched away from him and ran for the door. The cold air dispelled the dizziness but stung her face and feet. She hardly noticed. She emptied her stomach on the bare ground just off the stone step.

"Emily." Her name was whispered in her ear. Jake was holding her upright, she realized, or she would have dropped to her knees.

"Better?" he asked.

She waited a moment to answer, wanting to be sure. "I think so," she murmured finally.

"Then come inside before you freeze."

He led her to the fireside and kicked the blanket aside so he could move a chair closer. When she was seated, he knelt in front of her, taking her feet into his hands, rubbing first one and then the other.

"Are you sick, Emily?" he asked gently.

"No," she moaned, grateful that the children had fled. "It happens every morning.

"But you haven't even eaten."

"Don't mention food! Please." She let her head lull back against the chair. "I'll be all right. Your feet are cold, too, Jake."

"Put your shoes on," he said, moving to bring them to her. "In case…"

"Yeah," she said, fully aware of what he was thinking. She kept her eyes closed for another couple of minutes, not sure she wanted to bend over. Jake's warm hands lifting her foot as he dabbed the heel with the ointment made her feel pampered.

"How do you get these on?"

She opened her eyes at the question. He had one stocking spread across his lap and was pushing the open end over her toes.

She giggled, and he looked up to give her a heart-stopping grin. "You have to roll it," she explained, reaching for the garment. With deft movements she scrunched the stocking in her hands until her thumbs were in the toe. She slipped her toe inside and pulled it smoothly over her knee.

Only then did she realize the show she was providing. Jake, still kneeling on the floor was getting a close look at nearly the full length of her leg. She dropped the riding skirt back into place.

A second passed. Jake shook his head, as if to clear it, and raised his eyes to hers. She glared at him. She could just guess what he was thinking. What all men were always thinking.

Before she could say something scathing, he mumbled a short "Sorry."

Why did she feel like forgiving him? It hadn't been his fault, she reasoned. And he hadn't taken any kind of advantage, merely looked. She felt herself softening. It must have shown on her face because Jake's expression relaxed a little. She was close to smiling after all when he handed her the other stocking.

She snatched it out of his hand. Did he think she would do it again? He continued to kneel in front of her, as if that were just what he expected. She cleared her throat loudly, bringing him out of his lust-filled trance.

He rose to his feet, looking appropriately embarrassed. "I'll...uh...go in the kitchen and get some brea—sorry. I'll be back in a few minutes."

Emily watched him hurry out of the room, and found herself wanting to giggle. She reflected on her reaction as she slipped on the other stocking and pulled on her shoes. Why didn't Jake's interest fill

her with dread? Why wasn't her stomach churning?
He had asked her to marry him, and she had agreed.
Sometime soon, he would have the right to take what
she had so foolishly given Anson.

And she was no innocent girl. She already knew
that the warmth in her stomach, the tingling on her
skin—those very things that she felt now as she remembered Jake watching her bare leg—were tricks to
make a woman willing to participate in a most un-
satisfying and even humiliating act.

So why did she want to giggle at Jake?

She leaned back and closed her eyes, swallowing
the sound before it escaped her lips. Because she was
going crazy, she guessed. Maybe hysteria was another
of the joys of increasing. At least her morning sickness had passed in record time.

Less than an hour later, Emily found herself on her
way back to Council Grove. The fourteen-year-old
Rodney was riding with them. Mr. Kraus had been
hesitant to leave all the chores to his wife and children
and had decided instead to send the boy in to report
the theft.

Jake, she had learned, had paid the family for their
hospitality, she kept a few coins and left the last of
Christian's money tucked under the bedding she had
folded and stacked near the hearth.

Rodney, away from the competition of so many
siblings, found an easy audience in Jake and talked
nearly the entire ride to town. She heard about all the
other children and every humorous, and not so humorous, stunt any of them had ever pulled. She also
learned that Rodney still attended school, though he

missed a lot if his father needed him, and he wanted to be a lawman when he grew up.

Emily was glad to be excluded from most of the conversation. She had begun to worry about their greeting once they arrived in Council Grove. She had told the sheriff that Anson wasn't really a fugitive, merely a friend of hers. Jake wasn't doing his duty as a deputy, merely acting the jealous husband. Perhaps they could get in and out of town without the sheriff learning she wasn't really Jake's wife. Yet.

Even that hope shattered a few miles short of Council Grove. Jake, having exhausted Rodney's entire store of tales, dropped back to ride next to her. "I'll take Rodney with me to talk to the sheriff, then I'll find a preacher."

Her mind was blank for a moment. She wasn't positive, but she thought it was Tuesday. Hadn't they left Americus on Sunday? "Preacher?"

"To marry us," he clarified.

Emily felt the blood drain from her face. "Marry us? Here?"

He answered quietly, "If I take you home first, your mother will want to turn the wedding into a big affair. That could take months to arrange." He gave a significant glance toward her middle.

Of course he was right. She didn't want a big wedding, and she certainly couldn't afford to wait months. Still, she wished things were different.

Jake was watching her, looking slightly worried. Was he afraid she would argue with him? Or afraid she wouldn't? Lord, if things were different, as she had wished, he wouldn't be marrying her at all.

He had told her last night that he loved her, but he

was so nice, of course he would say that. She vowed right then to do her best to make him happy. She *was* in love with him, and maybe, if she loved him enough, she could make his love true as well.

She felt a smile tug her lips. "Shall we ask the sheriff to be a witness?"

Jake shook his head, laughing. "He already thinks we're married, remember? On second thought, maybe you should come with me to his office. He might lock me up if he thinks I've abandoned you again."

"I suppose I should do a little explaining."

His smile became a wide grin. "I think I'd like to see that."

She tried to scowl at him, but in the face of his grin, it was impossible. "Couldn't we just tell him that in light of our earlier…er…problems, we want to renew our vows?"

Emily expected a hasty refusal. Instead he agreed, making her instantly guilty. Her story to the sheriff had made Jake look like both a poor husband and an irresponsible lawman. And he was going to let her stick to it.

When they finally reached town and turned down the street toward the sheriff's office, Emily's stomach was in knots. She was usually hungry by this late in the morning, and she supposed that could be part of it. But mostly she dreaded facing the huge sheriff again.

She recognized a few men on the street as members of yesterday's posse. Their curious stares did nothing to relieve the tension. In fact, she noticed more than a few of them moving down the street parallel to them.

"We're drawing a crowd," Jake commented cheerfully.

"Shall we invite them all to the wedding?" Her voice sounded a little more sour than she had intended. His response was still a laugh.

In front of the office, Jake swung down and came to help Emily dismount. Rodney had stepped up to the door only to have the sheriff barge through it, nearly knocking the boy off his feet.

"Well, now," said the sheriff, hitching up his pants. "I didn't expect to see the two of you around here again."

"At least we're together," Jake offered.

"Mr. Sheriff," Rodney began.

"Did you find the old boyfriend?" Emily was glad his glare was directed at Jake and not her.

"No, sir," Jake answered

Emily wanted to crawl into a hole somewhere. But she needed to straighten things out for Jake. "He really is a—"

"Mr. Sheriff," Rodney tried again.

"Whatcha doin' back here, then?"

Emily, Jake and Rodney each tried to answer. It was Rodney's voice that carried above the rest. "My pa was robbed!"

A gasp went up from the gathering crowd.

"Maybe you three should step into my office," the sheriff said, waving the others away.

Inside, the sheriff lined up the chairs and seated his guests then leaned against his desk to tower over them. Jake motioned Rodney to speak first.

"Pa—that's Waller Kraus—he said to tell you that a young blond fella spent the night at our house night before last and stole fourteen dollars and twenty-seven cents from a tin on our fireplace. I was to describe him if ya wanted.''

The sheriff raised an eyebrow toward Jake.

''It was Anson Berkeley. The boy I was following.''

The eyebrow shifted in Emily's direction.

She took a deep breath. ''He really is a fugitive. I lied to get you to help me catch up with Jake.''

Jake cut in quickly, ''I did leave without telling her what I planned.''

''But only because he knew I'd follow.''

The sheriff waved his hand to end the argument. He directed his gaze at Emily. ''Are you at least his wife?''

She and Jake answered at once. ''No.'' ''Yes.''

The sheriff grunted. ''Do you two ever agree on anything? Which is it?'' Before they could both speak again, he pointed at Emily. ''You first.''

''We aren't married. I wanted—''

Jake interrupted. ''But we're going to be.''

''Did I ask you to talk?'' growled the sheriff.

Rodney's young voice filled the room. ''What about the man what stole Pa's money?''

The sheriff sighed. ''All right. You—'' his finger pointed at Jake ''—tell me the whole story, I mean about the robbery, and you two be quiet.''

Emily listened while Jake related what they had learned from each of the farms they had visited the day before. She produced the picture from her reticule at an appropriate time. The sheriff's glare silenced any words she might have added.

Finally, with both the sheriff and Rodney satisfied,

they rose to leave. "You run over to the café and get some grub, boy," the sheriff told Rodney. "Tell 'em I sent ya. I'll round up one of my deputies to ride home with you. He'll visit with your pa and your neighbors, and we'll see what we can turn up.

"Can't make no promises, though. Most likely, someone'll catch him in the act and put a bullet in him." The last was obviously intended to reassure Rodney that justice would eventually be served.

"What about you two?" asked the sheriff, tossing a huge arm over Jake's shoulder and another over Emily's. "I'm not sure I should let you run around loose. You've proved to be a mite disruptive."

"We're going to get married," Jake said without hesitation.

The sheriff laughed. "Is that a fact? I think I'll tag along to make sure."

He withdrew his arms to open the door. Emily flexed her shoulders, hearing a satisfying pop, and followed Jake outside. And stopped in her tracks.

A crowd of people waited for them. They were a quiet bunch, but she detected a murmur of disappointment at seeing them emerge. Were they hoping at least one of them had been arrested?

She felt the heavy arm go around her shoulders again and discovered the sheriff had stepped between her and Jake.

"Folks," the sheriff boomed. "These two young people are gonna get married."

"Ain't they already married?" asked one observer amid the murmurs of the rest.

"Appears not. Somebody get a parson."

"Which one?"

The sheriff turned to Emily. "Do you prefer Catholic or Protestant? We ain't got a real big choice."

"Protestant," she said past the lump in her throat. She truly wished she had held to her earlier lie. She would much rather get married quietly, without the help of this overbearing sheriff. She tried to look past him to see Jake's reaction, but the man was too big.

"Four o'clock," boomed the sheriff. "Give the ladies time to whip up the usual."

"The usual?" Emily's words were lost as she found herself thrust into Jake's arms. She clung there trying to sort out what she had missed. The crowd gave a hearty cheer and dispersed in several directions. Their horses were led away by one stranger, her bag and Jake's saddlebags carried off by another.

"What's going on?" she asked.

"They're making the arrangements," Jake whispered.

"You two go get some dinner. The preacher'll find you to discuss any details. You need a dress or a Bible to carry or anything like that?"

She stared at the sheriff. It was Jake who answered. "I think we can find everything she needs. Let me feed her before she faints."

"Faints?"

"She had to…skip breakfast."

The sheriff's wide face broadened into a lascivious grin. "Did she now?" He slapped Jake on the back so hard they both nearly fell over. "That's a boy." He chortled then grew serious. "You marry her, ya hear? Don't try to duck out on her again. I'll tell the liveryman not to let you have your horse, or any other, if I have to."

"That won't be necessary, sir," Jake said.

To Emily's immense relief, he led her away. By the time they were outside the restaurant, she was feeling more her old self. "Is the whole town invited to our wedding?"

"That's what I understood."

"Will the sheriff bring a shotgun?"

"Count on it."

"Oh, Jake." She turned into his arms. "I'm sorry."

"Don't be," he whispered. "I'm marrying the woman I love. The details don't really matter. Besides, I wouldn't mind sharing the event with the whole world, or even a town full of strangers."

He took her arm and led her into the restaurant, helping her out of her coat and gloves. The waiter hurried to direct them to the table they had occupied the day before. Emily, her back to the huge fireplace, watched Jake's face as the waiter hurried away.

The humor of the situation finally hit her. "It looks like you're really stuck with me, Jake. The sheriff'll never let you escape."

"Do I look like I want to cut and run?" He was smiling, too, his green eyes sparkling. "I've imagined you as my wife since I was eighteen."

Emily laughed, trying to remember what she had been like at thirteen. "And before that, darling?" she asked, trying to sound flirtatious and overdoing it.

"Before that," Jake said, leaning toward her and taking her hand. "I thought you would have made a wonderful little brother."

"You say the sweetest things."

The waiter arrived in time to see the couple holding

hands and smiling at each other across the table. He let out a heavy sigh of contentment as he put plates of steaming pot roast and vegetables in front of them.

"It's on the house," he said in a suspiciously choked voice before hurrying away.

Chapter Thirteen

Emily soaked in a tub of hot water the hotel had provided. When she and Jake had finished their meal, they had learned that Emily's carpetbag had been moved into the room she had occupied for a short time the day before and Jake had been assigned the room across the hall. Jake, however, had been informed that baths were available in the back room of the barbershop, with a strong hint that he also visit the front room.

Emily squeezed out the sponge and watched the water trickle into the tub. In just a few hours she was going to marry Jake Rawlins. Every time she thought about it she wanted to laugh hysterically. A month ago—a week ago!—she wouldn't have believed it.

Her baby would have a name, and a good name at that. And more important, it would have a daddy. Jake was incredibly handsome, kind, far kinder than she deserved, and she knew she loved him. He even acted as if he loved her, too, though she wasn't sure she could believe it.

The water was growing cold, and she reached for

the towel, wrapping it around herself as she stepped from the tub. Someone had built a roaring fire before she had been shown to the room and it still sent out an abundance of heat.

Emily applied a second of the four towels the maid had left to her hair as she took a seat before the fire. A moment later a soft tap sounded on the door.

"Who is it?" she called.

"It's me, Hannah. Don't worry about being decent, honey."

"Hannah?"

"The sheriff's wife." The woman had opened the door a crack and peered inside.

Of course the sheriff's wife would expect to barge right in. Emily tried to give her a smile and found it wasn't at all hard when it was returned in such a pleasant way.

Hannah stepped inside and closed the door, revealing an arm laden with garments. "Abel, that's my husband, said you were about my size."

They eyed each other critically then both realized at the same moment what they were doing and laughed.

"This was my wedding dress," Hannah said, holding it by its wooden hanger. It was white with a sprinkling of pale pink roses and dark pink trim. She shook it out before slipping it onto a peg on the wall. "And a few underthings." These became a huge pile over the back of a chair. "What else do you need?"

Emily, still clad only in a towel, shifted uncomfortably in the chair. "Are you sure you want to loan me those? I mean, you don't have to just because your husband..." Oh Lord, what had she been about to suggest? That the poor woman disobey her huge, domineering husband? "You could tell him I refused."

Hannah looked genuinely disappointed. "You don't like them?"

"No, that's not what I meant." She rose and walked across the room, clutching the towel in place. "I mean, surely you don't want to loan all this to a stranger. And if your husband gets upset—"

"Abel?" Hannah laughed incredulously. "He never gets upset. He's just a big ol' softie."

Emily blinked her amazement.

"You will wear them, won't you?" Hannah asked eagerly.

Emily smiled. "Yes, I'd love to wear them."

"Good. You rest now. I'll come back at three and help you dress and fix your hair."

Emily stopped her just before she opened the door. "Why did your husband decide on four o'clock for the wedding?"

"To give us time to cook, of course. There'll be a big potluck dinner at the opera house and dancing. We need an excuse to celebrate."

"But it's only five days until Christmas."

"Exactly. Five whole days to wait."

In a moment Emily was alone again. She finished drying her hair and slipped into clean drawers and a shift from her bag. She crawled into the bed and tried to rest, but found her mind too cluttered with random thoughts.

Her mother was missing her wedding. She would soon belong to Jake. Anson had escaped and was probably even now stealing from someone who had offered him help.

No matter where her mind wandered, it always came back to the thought of spending the night with Jake. Of course, she had spent the night with him last night. But tonight would likely be different.

She shouldn't dwell on it; it might ruin her high opinion of Jake. She tried to turn her thoughts to arriving home in time for Christmas, but her concern for her welcome there interfered with the joy of the image.

She was too pent up to rest. Oddly enough, her first thought was to go to Jake. He was probably in his room across the hall by now. A few soft words from him would reassure her.

She shook her head at her own foolishness and went to stand by the window. Snow was falling again, coating the roofs and tree branches, mixing with the mud on the street. She felt a wave of homesickness and supposed that accounted for her wandering thoughts most of the afternoon.

She stayed where she was, watching the light snowfall accumulate here and there until she heard Hannah at the door. The older woman's chatter quieted Emily's nerves, and she soon found herself seated in front of the small mirror while Hannah arranged and rearranged her hair.

Finally, after what seemed like an excruciating amount of time, Hannah helped her into her cloak and took her downstairs where the sheriff waited to take them to the church.

"Where's Jake?" she asked when they started off without him.

"My deputies were to see him to the church," the sheriff answered.

"Deputies?" She wanted to ask if they had come equipped with leg irons.

"All but Hank. I sent him out with the Kraus boy. He'll likely be back in time for the party, though."

The sheriff, she learned, was not only planning to give her away, he and his wife were going to stand up with them. "I'll see this done proper," he told her with a laugh.

The moment she stepped through the door a whining organ began to play. Hannah thrust a bouquet of dried flowers into her hands and whispered, "You wait here about five seconds." Giving Emily's dress and hair a last adjustment, she turned and began slowly down the aisle.

"Five seconds," whispered the big man, clearing his throat.

Oh my. The sheriff was actually nervous. Hannah was about halfway to the front before Emily registered two things at once. Jake stood beside the pastor, waiting for her. And the church was completely packed.

She fought the urge to giggle.

"Has it been five seconds? I forgot to count," whispered the sheriff.

Emily shrugged and tugged his arm. Together they started down the aisle, much faster than Hannah. They had nearly caught up with her before they reached the front. Emily was grateful to be handed over to Jake and have the ceremony begun.

The pastor had promised them at dinner to keep the

ceremony short and simple, and he was true to his word. In less time than it had taken Hannah to fix her hair, Emily found herself being introduced to the crowd as Mrs. Jake Rawlins. To her astonishment, several women were weeping and sniffing into their handkerchiefs.

Jake's very public kiss was brief but sweet and filled with promise. Emily wanted nothing more than to escape with him. Instead, the sheriff and his wife whisked them off to the opera house where they stood at the door and greeted the well-wishers.

When everyone was assembled, Jake and Emily were directed to the buffet table and encouraged to take some of everything. Several women seemed to be watching closely, noting, evidently, whose dishes they sampled and whose they passed up. Emily tried to take at least a taste of everything that Jake didn't.

They were then seated at the front of the room surrounded by the sheriff and his wife. Emily, feeling too nervous to eat, did her best to anyway. She remembered Christian and Lynnette's wedding dinner and didn't want to invite any jokes about keeping up her strength.

When Jake finished eating and declined the invitation to get seconds, Emily hoped again for a chance to escape. Instead, the sheriff stood and offered a slightly embarrassing toast to the new couple, which Jake took good-naturedly.

A band struck up a number, and Jake and Emily were thrust onto the dance floor. The dance was far too fast to allow for talking and, though a few couples joined in, most seemed content to stomp and clap and watch the young couple. As soon as the music ended, Emily whispered breathlessly, "Can we go now?"

"Aren't you having fun?" His grin made her want to punch him.

Three toasts and four dances later, they made their escape. The sheriff drove them the short distance to the hotel with half the town running along behind. Once through the doors, Emily breathed a sigh of relief.

The hotel clerk followed them inside. "I've moved your things into Room three with the lady's, Mr. Rawlins," he said breathlessly. He went behind his desk to search for a key.

Jake took a step toward the clerk. He seemed about to protest. "That will be fine," Emily said quickly, gaining a surprised glance from Jake.

The clerk smiled pleasantly and handed over a key. He brushed past them and hurried back to the party.

Emily and Jake started up the stairs. "You were going to ask for separate rooms, weren't you, Jake?"

"Don't take offense, Emily. I didn't want to rush you."

She took his hand and drew him into the room, giving him a smile she hoped was more teasing than shy. "You've made quite a sacrifice for me, Jake. I think this is the least I can do."

He closed the door behind them and turned to light the lamp on the wall before he answered. "Do you feel like you're making a sacrifice, Emily?"

Her already tense nerves wound a little tighter. What sacrifice was she making? Did he think she still cared about Anson? She shook her head, uncertain what he was asking.

He stepped closer, his voice low. "Is making love to me a sacrifice?"

"No," she whispered. "More a...gift."

He touched her cheek lightly, making her tremble clear to her toes. "A gift? Perhaps. But Emily, I had hoped you would want me as much as I want you. It should be something we share."

They hadn't yet removed their coats, and Emily suddenly felt unbearably warm. She stepped away and slid the cloak from her shoulders, tossing it over a nearby chair. He had been standing too close, anyway. In another second she would have wanted him to kiss her. *He* seemed to want to talk.

"Something we share," she murmured thoughtfully. She certainly enjoyed sharing Jake's kisses. But the rest...

Jake turned from her, perhaps reading the skepticism in her eyes. He removed his coat, tossed it over the back of the chair next to the door then put his gun belt over it. He walked to the window and stood looking out on the dark street.

She hadn't wanted to hurt his feelings. "Jake," she said softly. "I will share whatever you want. But let's remember, I've done this before."

He turned toward her, his face unreadable. She shouldn't have mentioned Anson, even indirectly. Before she could decide how to correct the mistake, he spoke. "Emily, I don't care about the past. You're giving me your future, and I'm giving you mine. That's far more important than anything that's gone before."

He took a step toward her, but only one. Emily started forward, too, but stopped. He seemed to have something more he wanted to say and was perhaps as aware as she that it was easier to talk with some distance between them.

"I slept with you in my arms last night," he began after a moment. "It felt right to have you beside me. But I can't do that again without wanting more."

"I know," she said quickly. "I don't expect—"

A raised hand silenced her. He went on quietly, "I want what we share tonight to reflect all the love I feel in my heart, but you see, Emily, I've never done this before."

She stared at him. When she realized her mouth was hanging open she snapped it closed. She had hoped that most married men stayed faithful to their wives, but she had assumed that all single men sampled whatever was available. Unless...

She swallowed a lump in her throat. Perhaps he had no interest. That was, of course, a shock, but after a moment of reflection, she decided she could live with that. "It doesn't matter, Jake," she said.

He smiled at her. She still wasn't sure if she understood.

"You have to accept the blame for my inexperience," he said.

"Me?" Lord, had a childhood prank of hers caused some injury? She felt herself growing light-headed.

"Every time I had the opportunity I would end up comparing the woman to you. None of them ever came close. All these years, you are all I've wanted."

Emily took a deep breath. "I don't know what to say. I feel more guilty than ever about my own past."

He moved toward her quickly, taking her arms. "I don't want you to feel guilty. I told you so you'd be patient with me."

She had to laugh. "Jake, there's nothing much to it. I'm sure you'll figure it out."

To her relief he grinned at her. "I didn't say I was completely ignorant. I got the usual speeches from both my mother and my father. Of course, if I remember right, they pretty much contradicted each other."

Emily giggled. "You got speeches from both your parents?"

"I was an only child."

It felt so good to laugh with him again. She threw her arms around his neck, thinking of him more as her old friend and less as her new husband.

His mind had evidently taken a little different turn. "Let's start with something simple," he whispered, "like a kiss."

Shivers shot through her body. Whether it was from his breath on her ear or the tone of his voice, she wasn't sure. Suddenly she was aware of the closeness of his body, the pounding of her own heart. She drew away enough to make her lips accessible without being aware of doing so. One moment, her face was buried in his shoulder, the next, it was rising to meet his kiss.

Desire uncurled in the pit of her stomach and flooded her senses. All she could taste, all she could smell, was Jake. All she could hear was her own blood humming with his. All she could feel was Jake pressed against her body.

Or almost. She realized she was pushing so close

to him he had to shuffle one foot to keep his balance. Her own knees were less than steady.

He broke the kiss and grinned down at her. "I think we did that pretty well, don't you? What shall we try next?"

It took Emily a moment to find her voice. "Well, I'm a little worried about ruining a borrowed dress so, would you do the honors?"

She turned her back, and he moved her slightly for better light. "Hmm, a million buttons, I see." He loosened the top one and planted a kiss at the nape of her neck. "I feel like I'm opening a Christmas present early."

Emily bit her lip to keep from giggling. Her stomach seemed to be filled with butterflies. She felt a second kiss on her back an inch below the first, followed quickly by a third an inch lower still. With each button, his kisses worked down her back. Even through her undergarments, his lips felt hot and moist. The suppressed giggle turned into a moan. By the time he slipped the gown off her shoulders she was ready to believe there *had* been a million buttons.

The dress pooled at her feet. She knew she should step out of it and put it on the hanger. She wasn't sure her legs would cooperate. If Jake hadn't come around and taken her hand, encouraging her to step toward him, she might have collapsed onto the floor just like the dress.

He led her to the bed, where she gratefully sat down, and he hung up her dress. "You did that very well, too," she murmured.

He grinned at her, looking more wicked than she

had ever seen her Jake. Obviously he knew he was turning her into a pile of jelly.

"Now the shoes," he said. And he untied them, one then the other, slowly slipping them off her feet and setting them aside. His fingers trailed up one leg, starting at the ankle, all the way up to the top of her stocking, then slowly back down, bringing the stocking along. When he started up the second leg, she found the anticipation almost more than she could stand.

When both stockings had been removed, she gave a great quivering sigh, wondering what he planned next. After a moment, she realized her eyes were closed and opened them to find him grinning down at her.

"Here is where it gets difficult. All this feminine mystery." He indicated her petticoats and corset. "I don't know how they come off."

"Good," she said, feeling a little of her reason returning. "Because I think it's time you caught up."

She stood and slipped her hands under the lapels of his suit jacket and ran them slowly up to his shoulders, forcing the jacket up and off. She slipped her hands down his arms, enjoying the flex of hard muscles until the jacket hit the floor. "We should hang that—"

She didn't get any farther. His lips were on hers, teasing them open. His tongue slipped inside, stroking her senseless again.

When he finally raised his head, she gasped for breath. "Where were we?" she murmured.

"Here," he said, lowering his lips to hers again.

Well, he certainly had the kissing figured out. If he

could make her feel like this first, she didn't think she would mind the rest.

This time when he raised his head, it took her more than a moment to collect herself. She sighed. And he grinned.

"Pleased with yourself, aren't you?" Some of the teasing was lost in the breathlessness of her voice.

"Pleased with you," he said. He pulled the end of the string tie and loosened his collar. "Buttons," he said.

She hadn't thought about this when she had been so bold about removing his jacket. He had buttons on his shirt and would expect the same treatment he had given her.

Her cheeks warmed a little at the prospect. She caught a light in his eyes reminiscent of a much younger Jake daring her to try something. She stepped forward, opening his shirt at the throat, and deposited a quick kiss. Her lips encountered smooth warm skin where she had expected cotton.

Perhaps he hadn't had any clean underwear. It seemed too intimate a question to ask. The incongruity of that thought, considering what she was doing, nearly made her laugh.

She flicked the next button open and kissed the exposed skin. There were a few soft hairs she would want to explore later. She continued her journey downward over his hard chest and lean stomach, until she was stopped by the waist of his trousers.

She drew away as he yanked the tails free. She worked the last few buttons loose. Sometime while she was occupied, he had slipped the suspenders off, and they dangled at his thighs. She drew the shirt over his shoulders exposing a broad expanse of chest. She spread her fingers and ran them through the mat of hair, being careful not to touch his nipples. That would have been too forward.

He lifted her chin with a fingertip and captured her lips again. The fire had scarcely subsided from the last time, and she moaned, clinging to his bare arms for support.

"Now," he said, when his lips had freed hers. "It's your turn again. Show me how all these ruffles are removed so I'll know next time."

Something deep in her stomach gave an excited lurch at the notion of a future filled with this sort of activity. He grinned at her, and she remembered what she had been asked to do.

"This has buttons," she said, indicating her corset. She sucked in to make it possible to undo them through the stiff fabric. She sighed with relief when she was free.

Jake took the garment and tossed it aside. "It looks uncomfortable."

"It makes me sit up straight."

"I would imagine. Now the rest."

Emily had to laugh. "You even sound like a little boy at Christmas."

He demonstrated his impatience by grabbing her shoulders and branding her with another searing kiss.

When he let her go, she had to clear her throat twice before she could speak. "These tie here," she croaked. Her hands were shaking. She found the ribbons at her waist and untied all three petticoats, letting them drop to the floor as one.

She stood now in her loose shift, wrinkled from the

tighter garments she wore over it. She thought she should feel chilled, being left with so little, but she found herself heating under his appreciative gaze. The fire, and hence its light, was to her back, she realized.

He was standing in his boots and pants. Of course, she didn't expect him to open the latter until he was ready to...

She found herself biting her lip. She had been having so much fun she shouldn't have ruined it by thinking about later. Still, Jake was smiling at her so she tried not to worry.

"Can you take that off?" he asked.

"Jake." Surely he didn't mean for her to stand in front of him completely naked!

"It won't be the first time I've seen your bare skin."

She gave a nervous laugh. "If you're remembering the time I escaped from the bath, and you were the one who brought me back to the kitchen, it doesn't count. I've changed a little since I was three."

"You can't possibly remember that."

"No," she said, putting one fist on her hip. "I just heard about it often enough."

He laughed, a deep husky laugh that didn't sound at all like Jake. "I was thinking of Americus." He crossed the short distance between them. "You were in the tub. Asleep." His fingers were in her hair, scattering pins along with her thoughts. "But there were bubbles, and it was dark. I want a better view."

Distracted by the feel of her hair tumbling down her back, she didn't realize he had untied the drawstring at the neck of her shift until she felt him ease

it over her shoulders. The shift joined the pile of petticoats at her feet.

His exasperated sigh made her giggle. She still
wore a pair of ruffly drawers.

"I think women's clothes are designed for the sole
purpose of frustrating men," he said. "But I'll try to
be patient."

The length of one finger rubbed the underside of a
breast. It seemed to swell toward him. Her breath
stopped in her throat, and she swayed. Strong arms
caught her waist and steadied her. In a moment she
found her breasts flattened against the hard muscles
of his chest, her nipples tickled by his hair. His lips
were working their magic again.

The next moment, she felt her drawers slip past her
hips. He had found the ribbons easily now that he
knew what he was looking for.

He scooped her up in his arms and carried her to
the bed. He laid her down gently and kissed her lips
thoroughly then pulled her arms from around his
neck. "I'll be right back."

She groaned in protest, but he was already gone.
She opened her eyes and found him across the room,
sitting to remove his boots. She couldn't pull her eyes
away as he stood and reached for the closure of his
trousers.

"More buttons," he offered, coming toward the
bed.

Emily gasped. He wasn't serious! She could feel
her cheeks flaming.

"That's all right," he whispered, bending to kiss
her lips. "I can do it myself. You can do it another
time."

She didn't know whether to be relieved by the reprieve or appalled by the promise. His lips settled over hers, and she forgot entirely what was bothering her.

When she opened her eyes again he had dropped his pants, revealing cotton drawers. Emily mimicked his earlier sigh, drawing his attention. She was rewarded with a wicked grin. The drawers, she realized, left little to the imagination. They fit the contours of his hips and thighs, and displayed evidence of the effects of their undressing games and kisses.

While she watched, he shed the last garment and climbed into bed beside her. She got barely more than a glimpse of his erect member. Now, she thought, bracing herself.

Instead, he took one puckered nipple in his mouth and teased it harder with his tongue. Emily felt as if she had spent an hour spiraling off to the heavens and settling back to earth. As he leisurely toyed with her breast an odd impatience built at the juncture of her legs. Desire was playing with her senses, she decided, promising her pleasure she knew better than to expect.

It felt too wonderful for her to try to fight it, though, even if it meant increased disappointment later. She closed her eyes and let the sensations sweep her away. She felt the mattress sag as he shifted his position, bringing his mouth to the neglected nipple.

Hot liquid need replaced the impatience. She found herself clinging to Jake, calling his name.

Exactly how he had insinuated himself between her legs she wasn't sure, but she felt his manhood nudge against her womanhood. Too enthralled to think clearly, she thrust upward, drawing him inside.

The sensation was impossibly new. His member glided in, filling her senses the way his kisses did. He moved slowly, whispering things she couldn't understand in her ear. She felt herself tremble all over.

In frustration, she wrapped her legs around his thighs and pulled him deeper, bucking up against him. She was spinning off to the heavens again, this time so quickly she had the fleeting thought that she might not come back. She heard Jake's cry mingle with her own.

Then something seemed to burst inside her. All the tension in her body released at once and she was floating, lost and uncaring. And then she settled back, not the disappointing return of her senses, but a most beautiful, peaceful return.

Jake had collapsed on top of her, his body still except for his pounding heart and labored breath. His head was on her shoulder, and she threaded her fingers through his damp hair. He murmured something incomprehensible, and she smiled.

She had thought to give him a gift and ended up with a surprise of her own.

He rolled off her in a moment, his groan making her giggle. "Be good," he scolded, drawing her toward him to nestle against his shoulder.

She wondered if she should tell him that it had been so much better than anything she had experienced with Anson, but he probably didn't want to think of Anson now. Someday, she promised herself.

She snuggled close, preparing to sleep, too tired to want to get up and blow out the lamp. But after dozing for what seemed like only a few minutes, she woke to find his hand caressing the curve of her hip, the swell of her breast. And she found herself wanting him again. To her surprise, the feeling was mutual and they began a slow exploration of each other's bodies, until they were both hot and hungry.

The second time seemed even more explosive than the first and left them both exhausted. They wrapped themselves in each other's arms and slept.

A light tap on the door woke Jake just before dawn.

Chapter Fourteen

Jake tried to ignore the tapping. Maybe it was his imagination. He snuggled closer to Emily's warm body.

The knock came again, just a little louder. Whoever it was, was going to wake Emily, too, if he kept at it. Jake drew his arm from under her head and climbed carefully out of bed. He grabbed up his drawers and stepped into them as he crossed the room.

He slid his pistol free of the holster and opened the door a crack. It was the sheriff.

"Get your clothes on. We found Berkeley."

A moment later Jake was staring into an empty hallway.

Berkeley. Did he care anymore? His first impulse was to crawl back into bed.

But Berkeley had used Emily and betrayed her. Here was his chance to bring the man to justice.

He left the door open a couple of inches to let some light from the hall sconces into the room. As he dressed quickly he whispered, "Emily."

She gave a soft murmur. It sounded so content he had to smile.

"Emily, I'm going with the sheriff to bring in Berkeley. I should be back by...well, I don't know when I'll be back. Just wait here for me."

She mumbled something. The only word he recognized was his own name.

By now he was strapping on his gun belt. "Did you hear me, darling?"

"Mmm-hmm."

It sounded affirmative. He slipped to the bedside and kissed her cheek. She murmured a response, her lips curling in a sleepy smile. He grabbed up his coat and, as an afterthought, his saddlebags, and left the room, closing the door quietly behind him.

Outside he found the sheriff mounted and waiting. His own mare was saddled and tied to a hitching post. The moment the sheriff saw Jake he turned his horse into the street and headed out of town. Jake tied on his saddlebags and caught up with him in a few minutes.

The town they left behind was still asleep, shrouded by a fresh layer of snow. The first hint of the sun, veiled by gray clouds, was on the horizon. The sheriff headed southwest across open country.

"Here's the deal. The Reeves boy came to my house. His pa caught a thief red-handed and winged him. Reeves is holding him at gunpoint. I sent the doctor on ahead. I thought you'd like to be in on the arrest since the thief matches the description of your boy."

"I appreciate it."

The sheriff grinned. "You looked like you appreciated it when you opened the door."

Jake chuckled. "It's damn cold out here, Sheriff. Especially compared to where I was."

The sheriff laughed.

After a time Jake asked, "Where's the Reeveses' place?"

"Not too far. It's one of the dots on your map you never got to."

"Figured as much," Jake mumbled. "Where's the boy, by the way?"

"At my house. The missus is feeding him breakfast."

Jake nodded his approval. The boy, at least, was out of harm's way. "What about the rest of the family? Who all's there?"

The sheriff turned to look at him. "You think this fella might be dangerous? I just figured him for a sneak-thief."

"He's wanted for assault in Topeka. And any desperate man is dangerous."

"You got a point. As far as I know, all that's there is the couple."

It was full light by the time they rode into the farmyard. The doctor's horse was tied out front. The sheriff and Jake dismounted, tying their horses nearby. The sheriff, seeing no need for caution, stepped up to the door, but Jake made a quick scan of the yard, noting several outbuildings and a woodpile.

A middle-aged woman opened the door. "Sheriff! Thank God!" She turned, motioning him inside. Jake followed the sheriff.

"Reeves! What the hell happened?" The sheriff hurried to the doctor's side.

Jake put the pieces together quickly. Berkeley had somehow turned the tables on Reeves, injuring the farmer in the process. It was he who the doctor had found in need of his services.

While the farmer tried to explain the details to the sheriff, Jake started toward the door, intending to take a look around. The sound of running hooves propelled him forward. He stepped out on the porch in time to see his white mare disappear over a hill.

He came to a decision quickly. Without a backward glance, he vaulted into the saddle of the sheriff's horse and took off after the fugitive.

The sheriff was only a little slower than Jake. He stood in the doorway, gaping as his own horse disappeared. He swore eloquently for a full minute.

"Reeves! You got a horse?" he demanded as he turned back into the house.

"I got a mule," responded the injured farmer.

The sheriff let loose another string of oaths before he remember Mrs. Reeves's presence. "Pardon me, ma'am," he muttered. "Doc. I gotta take your horse."

"Try and I'll shoot you down." The doctor didn't even look up.

"Ah, come on, Doc. I gotta go after that thief."

"Patients could die while I'm stranded here. Besides, I believe the deputy already took off after the thief."

"The deputy took my horse! That's the darned thief I'm going after!"

"I got a mule," the farmer offered again.

"What about the blond boy's horse? I'll take it."

"It's lame. That's why he stopped here. He was going to take my money *and* my mule, I reckon."

The sheriff opened his mouth, caught the look of disapproval on Mrs. Reeves's face and closed it again. He looked at Doc's uncompromising frown, then at Reeves's hopeful smile. "Ah, hell, a mule."

Emily awoke slowly as the first rays of light crept through the window. She felt more at peace than she had since she was a child. She smiled dreamily. "Jake," she murmured.

She rolled over to snuggle against him and discovered she was alone in the bed.

She sat up, looking around the room. His clothes, which he had scattered on the floor with her petticoats, were gone. She fell back against the bed. Perhaps he had gone down for breakfast. The mere thought made her stomach lurch. Being married hadn't ended her morning sickness.

But she was probably right. He knew she couldn't stand food this early, and he had let her sleep while he went down to the dining room.

She sat up again, swinging her legs slowly over the side of the bed, anticipating the brief dizzy spell. She would get dressed and gather her things so she would be ready to go when he returned. She didn't know if Jake would want to ride home or take the longer but easier train trip.

She found her drawers and shift, smiling as she remembered how they had been removed the night before. She was in the process of folding the borrowed petticoats when her eyes fell on the chair by the door. The gun belt was gone. Jake might have decided to wear it, even down to breakfast. But the coat was also gone.

She tried to tell herself that he was out buying train tickets or on some other errand. She shook her head. The gun and coat weren't all that was missing. The saddlebags were gone. She was positive she had seen them on the floor, under the chair.

Perhaps he had moved them when he got dressed. She quickly searched the room, but the bags were gone. In fact, Jake had taken everything of his with him.

She stood for several long minutes in complete bewilderment. "He's done it again. How could he do this? After last night, how could he just abandon me?"

The hurt finally gave way to anger, and she hurriedly gathered up the rest of the borrowed garments, leaving them on the bed. She jerked the riding skirt out of the carpetbag along with a blouse, muttering all the while. "Does he think he can just leave me here? Hasn't he learned anything yet?"

She threw the last of her things together and tied her reticule at her waist. She was down to just a few coins, but Jake didn't know that. She half expected to find a train ticket waiting for her downstairs.

After checking at the desk and finding no messages, she hurried past the doors to the dining room, then retraced her steps. She needed to check, just in case. Holding her breath, she peered inside. There were only a few early diners. None was Jake.

She withdrew, muttering. "When I catch him this time—well, I don't know what I'll do, but he'll wish he hadn't abandoned me again." She had to hold on to her anger or she would cry of disappointment.

She was outside, crossing the frozen street to the livery stable, before she thought about going to the sheriff. She considered it only a moment. She was a little afraid of the sheriff even if neither Jake nor Hannah seemed to be.

The stable was dark, but she found a lantern and a box of matches and soon had a light. Technically she was trespassing, she reminded herself. She walked cautiously down the length of the barn, checking all the stalls. Her gelding was there, but Jake's mare was not.

"Darn that man anyway," she muttered.

"You talkin' 'bout me?"

Emily jumped, nearly dropping the lantern. A short, potbellied man stood watching her, rubbing his whiskered face. The red legs of his union suit were visible beneath the hem of his long coat.

"Do you work here?" she asked.

"I own the place," he corrected indignantly. "I live next door and seen the light. You wantin' your horse? It's the bay gelding, right?"

Emily ignored the question. "When did Jake Rawlins come get his white mare?"

The man moved past her to an empty stall. After a moment he turned back to her. "Sometime in the night, I reckon."

Emily sighed in exasperation. "Did you talk to him, or see him go?"

"Nope."

"Great. Yes, I'll need my gelding."

He had the nerve to smile. "I'll have him saddled in just a minute."

Emily was too impatient to stand and watch. She stepped back to the door and looked over the town. There were only a few people moving about, shuffling their feet through the snow on the boardwalk.

On sudden inspiration, Emily turned to look back at the door to the livery stable. There were her prints, two sets now, the liveryman's, and possibly others, all mixed together. But there was only one set of horse's prints. She stepped away from the building and looked up and down the street. Only one path had been made through the snow. She wasn't a tracker, but she knew enough to follow that path.

When the horse was finally saddled and her bag tied on behind, the liveryman helped her aboard. She eagerly kicked the horse into motion.

"The boarding's on the house," the man called after her.

"Thank you," she called back, more grateful than he could know. She had forgotten that she might owe the man money.

Out of town, she found herself following two parallel trails. Was someone with Jake? Or following him?

Perhaps the sheriff had seen him leave town and was in pursuit. She smiled to herself. It would serve Jake right to tangle with the sheriff again.

Her enjoyment didn't last long. The sheriff might actually harm Jake. She kicked her horse to greater speed. She had to catch up with them.

Emily stopped once to study the tracks; they told her next to nothing. She couldn't tell how fast Jake and the second rider had been going. But she could see the trail clearly in the snow to where it dipped below a rise. Looking beyond it, she thought she caught a glimpse of a white horse on the next hill.

"Jake?" she breathed.

When she crested the rise, she realized the horse was coming toward her at a run. Alarm cut through her. What would make Jake push his mount that way? She drew up, looking around for someplace for her and Jake to take a stand against whatever hounds of hell were after him.

It wasn't until the horse was almost upon her that she studied the rider. She had been so sure she recognized the horse that she hadn't noticed that the coat and hat were too pale to be Jake's. She recognized the rider only a moment before he pulled up beside her.

"Emily." He was breathing hard and it took him a moment to say anything more. "This is quite a surprise."

To be confronted with Anson now when she was expecting Jake nearly knocked the wind out of her lungs. Truth to tell, he was the last person she wanted to meet. And he was riding Jake's horse! Terror washed over her. Where was Jake?

She tried to get the question past her clogged throat. Anson's presence was of course the reason Jake had left her. How could she have thought he had abandoned her? Jake had *always* been there for her, even when she was a little girl. And now he might be dead!

Anson glanced over his shoulder, and Emily realized the drumming she had taken to be her pounding heart was really an approaching horse. Anson grabbed Emily's reins out of her hands. He drew her horse close to his and wrapped the reins around his saddle horn.

"Do exactly what I tell you," he said, closing his fingers tightly around her arm. "You can explain how you got here, later."

Jake came to an earth-plowing halt several feet away.

"Damned if it isn't the deputy from the train." Emily could see Anson had a pistol drawn, half-concealed in his coat.

"Let her go, Berkeley."

Berkeley laughed. "You don't understand. She may be an old friend of yours, but she's my woman. I left her behind to delay you. Not that I think much of the job she did."

She wanted to warn Jake that Berkeley had a gun. The warning might be enough to make Berkeley fire it, though. Not knowing what would be the best thing to do, she sat still, nearly frozen in terror as Anson's fingers dug into her arm.

"Get off the horse, Deputy," Anson said. When Jake hesitated, he brought the gun up into view. Jake dismounted. "Now show me how far you can throw your gun."

Emily saw Jake hesitate again. Slowly he withdrew his pistol and tossed it aside.

"Emily," Anson said, releasing her arm to return her reins. "Ride over and bring his horse back."

Emily kneed the gelding forward, wondering if there was some way she could help Jake, something she wasn't seeing. Her eyes met Jake's, but if he gave her any kind of signal, she didn't understand it. *Please God, don't let Anson shoot him.*

She rode back to Anson, the horse in tow, and he motioned her to keep going. She didn't want to leave Jake, but anything she might do could make matters worse. She didn't go but a few feet before she turned in the saddle. "Come on, Anson," she called. "Just leave him out here."

Anson glanced toward her, grinning. He wheeled his horse, his pistol still in hand, and rode toward her. She kicked her mount forward, hoping he would fall in beside her. To her relief, he did. After a few yards, she let the reins to Jake's mount slip from her grasp.

Anson saw it immediately and turned back, catching the horse easily. Foolish animal should have run back the way it had come, she thought.

It was probably better that Anson thought she was glad to be with him again, though that would take considerable acting. She couldn't even remember what she had ever seen in him.

She was afraid to turn and look back at Jake for fear she'd give herself away to Anson. Leaving Jake afoot, in the cold, in the middle of nowhere was horrible. But not so horrible as leaving him dead.

Jake watched them ride away, frustration nearly overwhelming him. In spite of what she had said, he knew Emily didn't want to go with Berkeley. It didn't matter if she did, he realized. He would go after them anyway. She was his wife, and he felt a surprising wave of possessiveness.

They had started off in the general direction of Council Grove, though he doubted if that was where they were actually headed. After he retrieved his pistol from the ground and wiped it carefully with his handkerchief, he started after them.

He had gone only a short ways when he heard pounding hooves behind him. In a moment the sheriff pulled a huge mule to a halt beside him.

"Where in the hell's my horse?" the sheriff demanded.

"Berkeley took it."

"You let him have my horse?" The sheriff threw himself off the mule and stepped toward Jake, one fist raised.

Jake took an involuntary step backward. "He had Emily," he said.

The sheriff let his fist drop. "Ah, hell," he muttered. After a deep sigh, he suggested, "Let me give you a lift back to town, and we can raise a posse."

Jake shook his head. "I'll accept the ride but no posse. I'm going after them alone."

Emily and Anson rode for several minutes before Anson veered to the north. In the shelter of a few trees along a creek, he dismounted. "You gotta give me a hand," he said, tying the mare and Jake's borrowed horse to a tree branch. He sat down near the bank of the little stream.

Emily dismounted and tied the gelding. "What's wrong?" she asked as she joined him.

Anson opened his coat to reveal his bloodied shirt beneath.

Emily took one look and felt the bile rise to her throat.

"Tie this up a little better," he said.

His voice sounded as if it came from a great distance. Emily turned and staggered away a few steps and retched. She stood, doubled over, waiting for her head to stop spinning.

"Damn it, baby. I need your help!"

"Yes," she managed to say. "Yes, I'm sorry. Give me a minute."

She heard his muttered curse and slowly straightened. She tossed the hood off her cloak, letting the cold air hit her clammy brow. Her head seemed to have cleared, but her stomach still churned. She tried to imagine touching Anson's bloody shirt and doubled over, retching again.

"Oh, for God's sake," grumbled Anson. "You're useless."

She heard him return to the horses. She wondered if he would leave her if she simply remained standing where she was.

"Get on your horse," he demanded. "We'll find someone who can help me."

Emily stumbled toward the gelding, casting Anson the quickest of glances. She was glad to see that he had closed his coat. In a moment they were riding off across the prairie again.

Emily wasn't usually squeamish about blood. Of course she had never been confronted with so much of it. She felt faint just thinking about it. She tried to turn her thoughts to other things. Like worry over Jake.

"The old lady put a bandage on me while her husband held me at gunpoint," Anson said. "Crazy old fools. I was bleeding like a fountain, and they told the boy to get the sheriff. Sheriff! Hell, you'd think they'd be going after a doctor.''

Emily felt her head spin. She doubted if there was anything left in her stomach to lose. She wanted to tell him to talk about something else, but she didn't want to talk to him at all.

"A man would think his woman would ask how he came to be bleeding like this."

"Please, Anson." There was a real danger of her fainting and falling off her horse. She put her head down to the gelding's mane and closed her eyes.

He laughed. "It really bothers you, doesn't it?"

She turned her head enough to glare at him.

"I'm sorry, baby." He didn't sound sorry at all. "It's not really that bad. I'll pull through. The old lady did wrap me up, and I think it's mostly stopped bleeding. Here, see?"

She turned her head away, fighting nausea.

He laughed then turned his attention elsewhere, in a lighthearted mood now that he had ridiculed her weakness. She didn't care. Just as long as he left her alone.

The day was warming considerably, and Emily realized that the snow that had made tracking so easy for her was in danger of melting. Jake might be afoot now, but he wouldn't stay that way for long. As soon as he could, he would come after her. But first he would have to get a horse, and by then, the trail through the snow would be gone.

She hung back as much as she felt was safe without rousing Anson's suspicions and, remaining hunched over the horse's neck, she tugged at the hem of her riding skirt. The darned thing wouldn't tear.

There were no petticoats under it. Her drawers were short enough she couldn't reach them. Her blouse would surely tear easily, but she might have trouble explaining how it came to be torn. Deciding on her reticule, she reached inside her cloak and untied it from her waist.

"What's keeping you?"

Anson was turned in the saddle, glaring at her. She hadn't realized how far she had lagged behind. She sneezed noisily, then quickly searched her bag for her handkerchief. He turned away in disgust.

Keeping the handkerchief handy in case he turned again, Emily fingered the items in her bag. What should be the first to mark the trail?

Her choice had barely left her fingers before Anson reined in beside her. "You should be in Denver by now," he said. "Tell me why you're out here instead."

"Well," she began, thinking fast. "I couldn't keep Jake on the train."

"Yes. Jake, your old friend."

She ignored the sarcasm in his tone. "He got the engineer to stop the train and walked back to Americus. Well, *we* walked back. I got off, too."

"And why did you do that?" There was a definite ring of suspicion in his voice.

"He was going after you, Anson. I went along to slow him down."

"And how did you accomplish this?"

"Let's see. I got a blister on my foot. But that wasn't intentional. He kept trying to send me back, but I always went after him." She hoped a note of fondness hadn't slipped into her voice at the last. It was going to be hard to deceive Anson when her love for Jake was so new.

But her life and Jake's might depend on Anson trusting her. She had to make it real. "It's been a horrible few days, Anson. I don't know why he took off this morning. I thought he had finally given me the slip. I was afraid of what would happen if he found you." The last was true, at least, though not the way she wanted Anson to think.

Anson was quiet for several minutes, during which time Emily wanted to drop something else on the trail but didn't dare.

Finally Anson spoke. "I appreciate you keeping the deputy busy." She tried to ignore the insinuation in his voice. The bastard actually thought she had slept with Jake to save *him*. "But it occurs to me. Now, you're slowing *me* down."

He kicked the mare to a faster pace, drawing a snort of protest from the horse he was leading. Emily dropped a coin before catching up.

The sheriff arranged for a horse while Jake bought a few supplies. Before noon, he rode out, heading somewhat west of the southwest route to Reeveses' farm. On their way into town, Jake and the sheriff had seen where the three horses had turned north. Now, he hoped to find Anson's trail without backtracking all the way to where the two trails diverged.

By the time he had been two hours on the open prairie, he began to wonder if it had been a poor gamble. The snow, which had left such a clear trail earlier, was gone and the ground, though soft now, might still have been frozen when the pair passed.

Jake was considering the possibility of heading back toward familiar ground to pick up their trail where they had parted, when he saw the sun glint off something in the distance. He rode toward it, losing it for a moment when the sun went behind a cloud.

He dismounted at the spot and picked up the picture of Anson Berkeley. He nearly laughed aloud as he tucked the picture into a pocket.

"Thanks, Emily," he said, searching the ground for other indications that they had passed. When he was sure of their direction, he swung into the saddle, following confidently behind.

Chapter Fifteen

By noon Emily was longing to stop. She had had only water from the canteen since her wedding dinner the evening before. She knew in another couple hours fatigue would make it difficult to stay in the saddle even if she weren't starving.

She wished, besides, that she had spread her coins a little more thinly. Soon she might have to drop the reticule itself. If she could have a moment of privacy, she could tear some undergarment to ribbons and hide the pieces in her reticule for future distribution.

Perhaps she could simply stop. Would he leave her? Or come looking for her at an inopportune time? It was worth a try. She pulled the gelding to a stop and dismounted. She wished she had food in the bag but knew there wasn't so much as a crumb.

She watched Anson, hoping he would drop out of sight over the next hill. Instead, he glanced over his shoulder and turned the mare back.

"What is the problem now?"

"I need to stop," she said, searching for an excuse.

"There's nothing here. Why would we want to stop?"

"I have to…take care of nature."

"I should leave you behind. Let you slow that deputy down if he's following."

She watched him for a moment, wondering if he was serious. She didn't want him to know how much she would welcome the prospect.

After a moment, he dismounted. "Well, get on with it. I'll hold your horse."

The tops of a couple of straggly bushes were just visible where the ground dropped away a little to her left. She hoped the ravine itself would offer more protection than the bushes promised. With a determined stride, she walked toward it.

It wasn't as deep as she had hoped. She removed her cloak and hung it on a bush, enhancing her screen. Working quickly in the cold, she ripped the ruffles off her drawers, and tore away the hem of her blouse. When she had them in six-inch lengths she stuffed them into her reticule. Deciding that Anson wouldn't let her stop again, she quickly emptied her bladder.

As soon as possible, she threw her cloak around her shoulders and climbed out of the ravine, shivering inside. She was now cold, and hungry and tired.

Anson had been busy while she was gone. He had lowered the stirrups on her bay gelding to fit his longer legs and shortened them on the black he had taken from Jake. "Mount up," he ordered, handing the black's reins to her.

"That's my horse," she said, pointing to the bay as he swung into the saddle.

"Yeah? Well, I'm riding him." He started away, leading the white mare.

Emily struggled to mount the taller horse. She was forced to run him to catch up with Anson. There was no question about being left behind, now. She wanted her horse.

"When are we stopping to eat?" she asked.

"When we find some place to stop. How should I know when that'll be?"

"There." She pointed to the right toward the horizon. "Smoke."

"So it is." He reined his horse—*her* horse toward the column of smoke.

As soon as he was well ahead of her, she drew one of the ruffle pieces from her reticule and let it flutter to the ground.

As they came over the hill and got their first view of the ranch house below, Emily was struck by its familiarity. This was the Kinney ranch where Jake had gotten the map. The ranch with the four big sons.

And Anson hadn't been there.

"I hope we're not too late for dinner," she said brightly. "I'm starved."

Anson pulled his horse to a stop and watched the house.

"What are we waiting for?" she asked.

He spared her barely a glance, his attention on the yard. The figure of a man left the house and walked toward the barn. He was followed in a moment by a second, then a third.

As Emily watched Anson's profile her heart sank. He was being too cautious. When he turned his mount away from the ranch, she pretended not to understand.

"Why aren't we stopping? We need to eat and someone should look at your...wound."

She wished she hadn't mentioned it. It brought the bloody image to her mind. She felt a little dizzy.

"It's because of the wound, I can't stop. They could get too curious."

"But we have to stop someplace."

"Yeah. But not here. They've got a whole army working for them."

The "army" didn't work there, they lived there. And most of them were only boys. But she wasn't about to correct him. If he knew she had been there and was eager to return, he would be even more inclined to distrust her.

It was midafternoon when the trail of coins and ruffles led Jake to the hill above the Kinney ranch. He could see where the horses stopped for a time and turned away, bypassing the ranch. After a moment of hesitation, Jake rode down the hill to talk to Kinney.

Twenty minutes later he was back on the hillside, picking up their trail. He had a small sack of food tied to the saddle horn but little new information. Kinney and two of his boys had seen riders on the hilltop, but they hadn't come in. The Kinneys had thought it seemed odd at the time, but had soon forgotten about them.

The Kinneys had placed the sighting at shortly after the family had finished their noon meal. That put them about two hours ahead of Jake. He was definitely gaining on them.

Berkeley was wounded, and Emily was no doubt exhausted by now. They were traveling more slowly than he was. But they also had a spare horse. His own was in danger of being pushed beyond its limits.

But his worry for Emily made it difficult to pace the animal. He knew how tired she became in the afternoon. He remembered holding her in front of him while he rode, letting her sleep. Would Berkeley do the same for her? He didn't know whether to be more upset at the thought that he would, or that he wouldn't.

And had Berkeley found anything for her to eat? He was sure they hadn't stopped any place up to this point and had passed up Kinney's ranch. There had been no food in his saddlebags when Berkeley stole his horse. There was probably nothing in the sheriff's, either. Emily, almost certainly, hadn't eaten before she rode out to find him.

It was his fault that she had fallen into Berkeley's hands. He should have made sure she was awake and understood that he would be back. She must have awakened to find him gone and believed he had abandoned her again.

He prayed he would get a chance to make it up to her. He didn't trust Berkeley to take care of her the way he would.

Emily let another piece of ruffle slip from her fingers.

"What the hell was that?"

He had turned at precisely the wrong time. "What was what?" But was there really any use pretending?

Anson swung around and grabbed her horse's halter so there would be no escape. "Get down," he demanded.

She did as she was told. He dismounted, gathering the reins to all three horses, then walked to the tiny white flag. "I don't think this accidentally tore off your riding skirt," he commented as he tied the horses to the tough stalk of a dried sunflower.

"No," she said, sounding more courageous than she felt. What would it take to spook the horses? The stalk wouldn't hold a frightened horse. But stranded with Anson afoot didn't seem like much of an improvement over the current situation.

"You've been leaving a trail for that deputy friend of yours, haven't you?"

"If the wind didn't blow it away, yes."

He stormed toward her, and she thought for a moment he might strike her. He seemed to make an effort to control himself. "You know, Emily," he said, exuding the dangerous charm she had once found so attractive, "I've wondered if that deputy got to you. I know women aren't particularly faithful creatures. But you see, it doesn't matter. You work just as well as a hostage as you do a partner."

Emily forced herself to hold her ground. She watched him pick up the bit of ruffle. He considered it, considered her and even looked back the way they had come as if he expected to see more flags every few feet. He needed to make a decision.

And so did she. If she could get one of the horses, preferably her own gelding, she would ride back the way they had come. Perhaps she would be lucky enough to reach Jake before Anson caught up with her. And if she didn't?

Anson turned to her with a cold smile. "Give me the rest of these," he said, waving the bit of cloth.

"That was the last."

He started toward her. "I don't believe you. But if it is, we can just make some more."

She turned to run, but he caught her, spinning her around. He tossed aside her cloak, leaving her gasping at the shock of cold air. One hand closed around the front of her blouse. "Are there any more?"

"Yes. In my reticule."

He snatched it away from her waist, breaking the strings. She hated herself for giving in so quickly, but she couldn't stand out in the cold for long. The moment he let her go, she snatched up her cloak and drew it around herself.

"My, my," he said, withdrawing a handful of ruffle. "You were prepared. Now, how to use this to lead the deputy astray." He tossed her another grin.

She knew the moment he came to a decision. She only hoped he would brag about his plan so she might have a chance of spoiling it.

"You, my dear, will wait here. With your horse."

Her surprise and pleasure must have shown on her face because he laughed. "Don't get excited. You won't be going anywhere."

He grabbed her again, forcing her hands behind her back. He tied them quickly with his handkerchief. "Please, have a seat," he said, giving her a shove.

Emily regained her balance and carefully sat down on the ground. It was cold and damp. "What are you going to do?" she asked. She had little confidence that he would answer her.

"You know, I haven't taken the time to see what our friends were carrying." He found a length of rope in Jake's saddlebags. He used it to tie her ankles together. In the other saddlebags, he found some bread and cheese.

"Imagine," he said, unwrapping it. "This has been here all along." He took a bite, brushing away several crumbs.

Emily's stomach rumbled noisily, but she wouldn't beg for food. She gave him a level glare.

With a muffled chuckle, he turned back to the horses, leaving her gelding and leading the other two away. "I'll be back in a few minutes," he said, mounting the black and leading the mare.

She watched him ride away at a canter. Before he dropped into the next valley, she saw a bit of ruffle drift to the ground. A false trail, she thought. He would drop markers for a ways then double back and change direction. And she wouldn't be able to drop anything else; he would watch her too closely.

She strained against the knots that bound her, succeeding only in knocking herself off balance. She lay on her side, fighting tears.

"Well, I was wanting a rest," she said aloud. The sound of her voice calmed her a little. Jake would find her, she told herself. Anson's plan wouldn't fool him. She tried to believe it.

Emily wasn't sure how much time had passed before Anson rode back to her. He returned without the black and offered no explanation for its whereabouts. He merely dismounted, untied the rope that held her ankles and helped her to her feet. He untied her hands and, with an awkward shove, helped her into the gelding's saddle. He used the rope to retie her hands to the saddle horn. "We'll be moving a little faster now," he told her.

As he mounted the mare, the strain of his wound was finally beginning to show. Or perhaps he had injured himself further when he was pushing her around. She watched him closely for more signs of exhaustion, forgetting her own.

In spite of what he had said, he walked the horses for nearly a quarter of a mile, before setting them at a canter. They would leave more shallow tracks, she supposed, thus insuring that Jake followed his fake trail. She wanted to cry in desperation, but the job of keeping her balance left her no time.

Anson kept them moving, walking the horses only occasionally, until nearly dark. He spotted a farmhouse beside a creek and pulled up. When Emily was alongside he untied her hands. "I don't imagine you'll try to run off now," he said. "That—" he pointed toward the house "—is the nearest food."

Emily tried to glare at him but was too exhausted. She rubbed her wrists instead.

"You are my wife, by the way. My wound was an accident. We need food and shelter and will be on our way in the morning."

"With any money they might have in the house." It was out before she thought, but she wouldn't regret it.

"So you know about that, huh? If you had come through a little better with your brother's money, I wouldn't have had to do it."

"You could be halfway to Denver by now, Anson. You've been going from house to house taking everyone's savings. The house we passed up at noon, you could have been there three days ago."

He gave her an odd look as if he thought she had gone crazy.

She explained. "You spent Saturday night with the Garveys, the folks with the obnoxious son. They gave you directions to the Kinneys. You could have made it by Sunday noon, but you decided to roam all over the territory robbing everyone instead."

"So you were right behind me, were you? That's what I suspected. *That's* why I changed direction. Now, shut up. You give me away to these people, I'll kill them *and* you."

He started forward, jerking the gelding's reins.

A grandmotherly woman met them at the door. She hollered to her husband who came to see to the horses. "You poor children, you must be freezing."

She ushered them inside where they both collapsed into chairs near the fire.

"Ma'am," began Anson, his voice quivering with exaggerated fatigue. "My wife and I would be pleased to accept your hospitality for the night. And some food if you have any to spare."

"Of course," the woman said. "I'll bring you some bread to hold you while I make some soup from what's left from supper."

The woman went through a doorway into the back of the house. From where she sat, Emily could watch Anson as he scanned the room, looking for hiding places, no doubt. She vowed not to let him out of her sight.

In a moment the woman returned with a plate of sliced bread and a crock of butter. She set it on a table across the room, and Emily moved to take a seat there.

"My name's Bertha," the woman said. "My husband's Alfred Hoover."

"Emily—"

"Wilson," interrupted Anson. "Andy and Emily Wilson, that's us." He rose but took his time walking toward the table.

"Good to meet you," Bertha said. As soon as she returned to the kitchen, he did an aboutface, gliding quickly to a set of shelves near the fireplace.

Emily was torn between her hunger and her need to protect this innocent couple. She lifted a slice of bread from the plate, her eyes on Anson. As long as he didn't find anything, she needn't interfere, she reasoned. Still, how was she to stop him if he did find something?

The immediacy of that worry ended when Mr. Hoover came inside. At the sound of the door latch, both Anson and Emily spun toward it. The man eyed Anson curiously, perhaps wondering why he was standing near the shelves instead of sitting at the table. He glanced at Emily, and she was afraid he read guilt in her eyes.

Anson let out a loud groan and, holding his side, staggered to the nearest chair. "Perhaps you or your wife would be willing to take a look at this wound," he said.

"Good God, man, what's wrong?" Alfred was quickly at his side, helping him out of his coat.

"I had a little accident," Anson said, his breathing labored. Emily turned away, more disgusted by his act than the sight of his bloody shirt.

"I was trying to show the missus how to fire a gun, and the fool girl shot me."

Emily glanced back to find Alfred turning to look at her. She supposed she should have *tried* to look guilty now, but it was too much to muster on the spur of the moment. She averted her eyes and raised the bread to her mouth.

"She tried to wrap it up a little," Anson continued. "That was early this morning."

"You just sit still," the man said. "It looks like the bullet passed through the flesh on your side. I don't think there's any more damage than a nasty gash. I'll get some bandages and fix you right up."

"Much obliged," Anson murmured.

Hearing the description of the wound made Emily feel close to fainting. She fought it. She had to eat. For her own sake and for her baby's.

Alfred returned in a few minutes with bandages and a bottle of whiskey. Emily didn't watch, but it sounded like more whiskey was going inside Anson than on the wound. The man probably thought Anson was in terrible pain. If he was, he had hidden it well all day.

Emily ignored the men's conversation and concentrated on eating the bread very slowly. She had finished two slices and was wishing for a glass of milk when the woman returned with two bowls of soup. She hurried back to the kitchen for coffee and Alfred helped Anson to the table. Emily was grateful that Alfred had provided him with a clean shirt.

Anson brought the bottle along and took several pulls on it as he ate. He entertained the Hoovers with extravagant lies about himself. Emily was reminded of evenings out with Anson and his friends. It seemed incredible that she had found his boisterousness so amusing then.

When they had finished eating, Anson and Alfred seemed content to remain at the table and continue their conversation. As long as Alfred was present, Emily deemed it safe to leave Anson. She gathered up a stack of dishes and followed Bertha to the kitchen, easily interpreting Anson's warning glare.

In the kitchen she helped Bertha wash the dishes, wondering all the while if she should tell her about Anson. But what could the woman do? Anson had threatened to kill these kind people if she gave him away. The best thing for them would be for her and Anson to move on in the morning, leaving them none the wiser and, preferably, none the poorer.

But that wasn't the best thing for Emily. She wanted to find Jake and tell him she was a fool to have ever thought she loved Anson. She hadn't known what love really was until she had fallen in love with Jake. She longed to tell him how much she wanted him to be her baby's father.

"You look so tired, dear," Bertha said, interrupting Emily's thoughts.

She nodded. "It's been a long day. But I feel so much better for having eaten."

"You and your husband can have our bed, if you would like."

"The floor by the fire is fine for us," Emily protested, not liking the thought of the old couple on the hard floor.

"There's still a bed in the loft, if you think your husband can make it up the ladder."

If he couldn't, it wouldn't be the wound that

stopped him; it would be the whiskey. Somehow being alone with him in the loft seemed more revolting than in the spacious room below. Still, in the loft he wouldn't be able to search through the couple's belongings.

With a sigh, she realized it wasn't up to her. Regardless of what she might decide and tell her hostess, Anson would make the choice.

By the time they rejoined the men, Anson had made considerable progress toward the bottom of the bottle. She found herself wishing he would pass out. She had never seen it happen, but suspected that in the past he had been on his best behavior most of the time she was around. The better to fool her, she supposed.

Mrs. Hoover made the same offers to Anson that she had made to Emily. Anson, choosing personal comfort, pleaded pain from his wound and accepted the bedroom.

Emily smiled an apology at Bertha. Anson saw it and answered with a smirk. Emily followed Bertha out of the room, intending to help her make the bed that the old couple would share.

In the bedroom, Bertha tossed a rug off a battered trunk and opened it. "I sure hope your husband's injury doesn't become infected," she said.

"Yes," Emily answered. The door between this room and the next stood open. The men's conversation seemed to have waned. Was it safe to try to warn Bertha of the danger? She was about to speak when her eye caught sight of Anson's reflection in the mirror across the room. He was watching her intently.

Bertha lifted two blankets from the trunk and

straightened. She gave Emily a searching look. Perhaps she was already suspecting something was wrong. If so, it would be disastrous if she spoke of it now.

"Let me help you," Emily said, taking the blankets from the woman. "Did you want these in the loft or by the fire?"

"By the fire, I think," Bertha answered, gathering sheets from the trunk. "I never liked the ladder much, especially as I've gotten older."

Emily forced herself to smile and left the bedroom, avoiding any glance in Anson's direction. Alfred, it seemed, had had a few drinks from the bottle and chortled at nothing. Bertha set her stack of bedding down on a chair and turned toward the table.

"I think it's time I rescue the bottle from you fellas," she said.

"Put her away, Bertha," Alfred said. "Or I won't want to do chores in the morning."

Emily heard the cork squeak into place and Anson's unhappy grunt. She kept her eyes on the small fire in the grate. Bertha's footsteps tapped toward the kitchen door and were gone.

Alfred gave a heavy sigh. "Do you need help to bed, son?"

"You propose to help me?" Anson asked with a laugh.

The old man laughed, too. "I was offering outa politeness."

"I'll endeavor to make it on my own." Chair legs scraped against the wood floor. "It was a pleasure sharing your company, Mr.—"

Anson had evidently forgotten their host's name. Mr. Hoover didn't seem to notice.

"And a bigger pleasure sharing my bottle," commented the old man.

Anson laughed and made it to his feet. Emily heard him come up behind her. "Let's go to bed, wife," he said.

Emily closed her eyes for a moment. The last thing she wanted to do was go to bed with Anson. No, she realized, the last thing she wanted was something to happen to Bertha or her slightly inebriated husband. They were not her protectors, as she had hoped, but she theirs.

She turned toward Anson and let him throw an arm across her shoulders. With her own arm around his waist, she helped him into the bedroom. He turned her loose and closed the door behind him. The room was thrown in darkness except for pale moonlight from a lone window.

"God, I'm tired," Anson muttered, crossing the room to sit heavily on the bed. "Be a good little wife and help me off with my boots."

"Take them off yourself," she hissed. "I won't help you with anything."

Anson chuckled. "We'll see. I think come morning, you'll help me find the old coot's stash." He bent and took off his boots.

Emily sat on the far side of the bed and removed her own shoes. She unpinned her hair and braided it quickly. She hadn't thought to bring in her carpetbag and neither had Alfred when he took care of their horses. She wouldn't have changed clothes anyway. She crawled under the covers fully dressed.

Anson stripped down to his underwear before climbing in beside her. "You've got a soft spot for these old people, haven't you?"

"They're nice folks. They fed us, and they're giving up their bed for us. They don't deserve to be robbed."

Anson laughed. "The bed is lumpy and so was the soup."

"That's not the point."

They were both quiet for several minutes before Anson spoke again. "You know what's funny." Emily could easily imagine his grin. "The way the old lady watched you. She knew something wasn't right between us, and you didn't do or say anything to ease her mind. Here's the funny part. My guess is she suspects you shot me on purpose."

His soft chuckle seemed to fill the room.

Emily lay still, staring at the moonlight outside the window. If Anson was right, any warning she might try to make tomorrow would be misunderstood.

Chapter Sixteen

Emily didn't think she would sleep, but the ordeal of the day caught up with her as soon as the house grew quiet.

Small rustling and scraping sounds brought her awake. The first light of dawn was streaming through the window, revealing a sparsely furnished bedroom. And Anson going through a chest of drawers.

She groaned aloud. For a second as she was awakening, she had expected to find herself with Jake.

Anson clapped a hand over her mouth. "Quiet," he muttered. "Granny's in fixing breakfast, and the old man's gone out to do the chores. You gonna be quiet?"

She nodded and he lifted his hand. His grin was unpleasant as he turned back to the drawers.

"Anson, please," she whispered, tossing off the covers and sitting up. She held her head in her hands as the wave of dizziness passed. She found her shoes and put them on before joining Anson where he continued his thorough search.

"Forget it. These folks don't have anything," she pleaded.

"Oh, you'd be surprised. Even the poorest-looking folks keep a few dollars tucked away."

Emily stared at him. "A few dollars! Your father's rich, Anson. Why are you doing this?"

Anson closed a drawer and turned to glare at her. "He cut me off, the bastard. I've got nothing."

He took a breath, visibly trying to regain control. He continued with exaggerated patience. "I need a stake to make a new start in Denver. It was supposed to be a new start for us." He turned away and slowly pulled open the next drawer.

Emily shook her head. There was no reasoning with him. She had started toward the door when a soft, elated cry brought her around. Anson held a huge roll of bills and was fairly dancing as he waved it at her.

"Old coot must not believe in banks," he whispered.

Emily felt dizzy again.

Anson tucked the money into his pants pocket. "You give me away, and I'll kill them both," he warned, stepping closer. "I think I killed an old farmer yesterday. It was easy."

Emily backed away from him, finding the doorknob behind her. She hoped he was lying. "I'm going to go help with breakfast." His eyes narrowed and she added, "They'll expect it."

He nodded, motioning her through the door. "I'm wounded," he whispered close to her ear, "so I'm going to go sit by the fire. They'll expect it."

She was glad to leave him and slip through the door

into the kitchen even though she knew the smell of brewing coffee would be even stronger there. Brewing coffee and other cooking smells. She used to love these smells, she reminded herself as she fought down a wave of nausea.

"Morning," Bertha said cheerfully, turning around. "My, you look pale, dear."

"I'm fine," Emily said, looking for a chair. There was a small bench near the outside door, and she hurried toward it.

"Well, you don't look fine." Bertha left the stove and pressed a hand to Emily's forehead.

Emily tried to take tiny shallow breaths. She had thought of a way to stop Anson, but she needed this woman's help. And to get that, she needed to be able to tolerate the kitchen. She would fight down the nausea by force of will.

No, she wouldn't. She jumped to her feet and threw open the door in one motion. Doubling over, she lost the contents of her stomach.

By the time she decided it was safe to turn back into the kitchen, Bertha was waiting for her with a damp cloth and a glass of water. And a smile. Lord, did every woman in the world know morning nausea meant a baby?

"Does your husband know?" Bertha whispered, tipping her head toward the other room.

"He's not my husband," Emily murmured, accepting the glass.

Bertha raised an eyebrow. Emily sighed. Now the woman thought she had left her husband and was having her lover's baby.

She opened her mouth and closed it again. She had

been about to explain that Anson, or Andy as he had
introduced himself, wasn't the father, either. But he
was. Somehow she had actually forgotten that. She
felt a smile tug at her lips. She had already begun to
think of Jake as her baby's father.

The smile faded quickly. She had more immediate
problems. Like gaining Bertha's help. She heard
voices in the next room. Alfred was inside now. There
wasn't much time.

Bertha gave her a disapproving scowl and returned
to the stove. "Ma'am," Emily began, following her.
"Do you have any laudanum?"

"You can't take it in your condition!"

"No. It's for Andy."

Bertha frowned. "If he's in that much pain Alfred
better have another look at that wound."

Emily wanted to scream in frustration. Her stomach
was churning, making it hard to think. "I've already
checked the wound," she said, hoping she was convincing. "It looks fine, but he doesn't tolerate pain.
City boy, you know."

Bertha seemed reluctant, but after a moment she
brought down a bottle from the top shelf of a nearby
cupboard. She handed it over along with a spoon.
"You can take it in to him if you think he needs a
dose before breakfast."

Bertha evidently wanted the runaway wife out of
her kitchen. But Emily knew how to be persistent.
"He likes it in his coffee," she said.

This got an even deeper scowl from Bertha. Emily
realized she had made it sound as if Anson were de-
pendant on the drug. She caught herself before she

smiled. Now Bertha's opinion of Anson was almost as low as her opinion of the runaway wife.

Bertha turned her back on Emily and continued with the breakfast preparations. Emily found a cup and, trying to stay out of Bertha's way, poured it three-fourths full of coffee.

She set the cup down on a worktable and, with her back to Bertha, poured a small dose into the coffee. She wanted to put him to sleep, not kill him, but she didn't know how much to use. She sniffed the coffee, and her stomach turned over. The coffee smell alone could do that. She wasn't sure if she smelled the drug or not.

She was putting the lid back on the bottle when the door burst open, startling her. She tried to hide the bottle behind her back but was too late. Anson bore down on her.

"Whatcha hiding, baby?" The voice was far more menacing than the words.

He didn't wait for her reply but jerked her around and snatched the bottle away. He smiled a cruel smile, one hand still gripping Emily's arm. "Tell me what you were planning, little girl."

"Nothing. It was for me. I have a headache." She could just imagine what Bertha was thinking now. The runaway wife had planned to poison her lover.

Anson set the bottle down on the table with measured movements. "I see. Well then, go ahead and drink your doctored coffee."

Emily was afraid to breathe. Anson could surely read terror in her eyes. When she didn't move, he lifted the cup with his free hand and held it out to her. She waited until it was in front of her face, then jerked up her hands, knocking the cup away. The contents flew into his face.

He swore, releasing her arm. She backed away, looking around the room for a weapon, noticing the Hoovers staring at them in shock.

Anson recovered more quickly than she expected. His hand flew out, hitting her on the side of her head. She was flung to the floor, one hand extending to break her fall, the other wrapping around her stomach.

"Don't! The baby!" she heard Bertha scream.

She recovered as quickly as she could, needing to see what Anson would do next. The door to the main room stood open. Alfred had probably gone to get a gun. But Anson was already armed. He stood glaring down at her.

"Baby?" he scoffed.

The outside door burst open. Emily turned, expecting to see Alfred. "Jake." She wasn't sure if she spoke the beloved name aloud.

"That's right," Jake said, advancing on Anson, his gun drawn. "My baby. My wife."

Anson was too stunned to move. Jake disarmed him and left Alfred, who had returned with a double-barreled shotgun, in charge of him.

A moment later, Jake was at Emily's side, lifting her into his arms. "How did you find me?" she asked.

He reached into his pocket and pulled out a handful of coins. "You left quite a trail."

"But Anson found out and—"

"I know. That confused me for a time, and the trail was harder to follow without your help, but I never lost it, Emily."

Bertha approached with another damp cloth. Jake thanked her as he took it and held it to Emily's bruised cheek.

"I reckon we oughta eat," she said. The woman's face was a picture of curiosity.

Jake helped Emily to her feet. "Do you want breakfast?" he asked softly.

"You know, I think I might," she said, laughing.

She realized Anson was glaring at her, his hands raised, and the Hoovers both looked mystified.

"Let me make some introductions," she said. "Bertha and Alfred Hoover. This is Deputy Jake Rawlins. That—" she pointed "—is Anson Berkeley. I'm Emily...Rawlins." She couldn't resist launching herself into Jake's arms as she said the last.

She would have been content to stay wrapped in his arms forever, but the sound of horses and a shout made Jake set her gently aside.

"Now what?" Mr. Hoover muttered.

Jake went through the house and peered cautiously out the front window. Emily followed him into the main room and watched him open the front door to admit the sheriff.

"Did you catch him this time?" boomed the sheriff.

"He's in the kitchen," Jake answered.

The sheriff stuck his head outside and called to two of the men. Jake officially turned Anson over to them.

When they were leading him toward the door, Emily stepped forward. "Wait! He's got the Hoovers' money in his right pants pocket."

The sheriff searched him roughly, handing the roll of bills over to a grateful Alfred.

''Now, there's the small matter of my horse,'' he said to Anson. ''I understand you took it from the deputy here.''

''I turned him loose,'' Anson replied with a smile. ''Sorry.''

''Ah, hell. Beg your pardon, ma'am. I liked that horse.''

Anson shrugged.

''Get him back to town,'' barked the sheriff.

''My mare and Emily's gelding are both in the barn,'' Jake cut in. ''You can put Berkeley on the horse I rented. He's tied behind the barn.''

The deputies nodded and led Anson out the door.

''Sheriff, he turned your horse loose when he laid the false trail,'' Emily offered. ''I might be able to find the place.''

''The false trail?'' The sheriff nodded. ''I know the place. I split the posse up when the side trail only showed two horses, besides Jake's. I reckon the rest of the posse might find my horse.''

Bertha again suggested breakfast. The sheriff stayed and ate with them, assuring Bertha that his deputies had food along and would feed Anson. Emily wasn't sure that anybody else had thought to worry about that. She certainly hadn't.

An hour later the three of them were on their way back to Council Grove. Bertha had packed a lunch, and they stopped at noon and had a picnic. It would have been quite romantic, Emily thought, except the sheriff was along. He dominated the conversation most of the day, offering advice on anything from marriage to tracking. Jake listened intently, or seemed to.

By early afternoon, Emily didn't care if the sheriff knew she was bored. She was so tired she didn't think she could stay in the saddle. She wondered how she had managed the day before. Surely she had survived simply out of necessity. Why did it seem next to impossible to do it again?

"Hold up a second," Jake said. "Come over here, before you fall asleep."

Jake helped her climb onto his lap. This was definitely where she belonged. When she was settled, he kicked the mare into motion again.

"You gonna just trust that gelding to follow?"

Jake glanced toward the sheriff and back at the gelding, trailing a ways behind. "It worked once before."

The sheriff muttered something about foolish boys and rode back to gather the gelding's reins. In a moment he was riding alongside again. He opened his mouth once to say something, glanced down at Emily's sleeping face, and closed it again.

Jake tried not to smile. He wished he had thought of this sooner.

Emily closed her eyes and let Jake's strong shoulder cushion her head against the jolting of the train. They were on their way home at last.

By the time they had ridden into Council Grove they had long since missed the train and had spent another night at the Hays House. The room was the same one they had shared before, producing instant memories as soon as they had walked through its door. Neither of them had gotten much sleep.

Emily laughed softly, thinking of the fun they had had most of the night and half the morning.

"What?" Jake whispered close to her ear.

"Just thinking," she answered.

"Come on, share. I could use a laugh."

"All right," she said, feeling her cheeks warm. "I was just thinking about…being tickled."

"Yeah? Was I the one doing the…tickling?"

"Of course."

He snuggled her a little closer, but when he spoke again, his voice was serious. "Emily, we haven't talked about what we're going to do. I have a job but the pay's not real good. I could go back to working for your brother—"

She turned to place her fingers on his lips and shifted so she could watch his face. "What do you want to do?"

"I want to make you happy."

"I know, sweetheart," she whispered seductively, "but we can't do that all the time."

He laughed. "All right. I want to become a lawyer."

Emily couldn't hide her surprise. "Since when?"

"I don't know. Since being a deputy didn't turn out to be exactly what I expected. I've tried to put money away for school, but it isn't accumulating very fast."

"Jake, I know some wealthy folks who might consider investing in our future. In fact, for taking me off their hands, they'd probably be happy to."

"You think so? I hate asking your family for favors."

"Really? I'm used to it."

Cassandra Austin   293

Jake laughed. "We can work all this out later. Come back here where you belong."

When she was snuggled in his arms again, she said, "I'm glad we're going to be home for Christmas, but to be honest, Jake, I'm a little worried about facing my family after acting like such a fool. I must have worried them sick."

"I sent a few telegrams. They knew you were with me. They even know we're on our way home." He toyed with her fingers as he talked.

"Do they know we're married?"

Jake was silent long enough for Emily to guess his answer.

"Emily, I'm not sure how your parents will feel about all this, but I know your brother. He's going to figure I've got a lot to answer for."

"You? I'm the one that ran off, taking some of Christian's money with me."

"I don't think your brother is going to care as much about that as he will about what I've done. I married you without your family's consent. I dragged you all over the countryside, hungry and cold most of the time. I let you fall into Anson's hands."

Emily struggled to sit up. "But you didn't," she protested. "I ran off with Anson. I—"

"I even got his little sister in the family way."

"Jake. *You* didn't."

He settled her back into his arms. "They don't need to know that," he whispered against her ear.

Snow started falling shortly before they reached the ranch. Emily watched it settle on Jake's hat and shoulders and hoped he was feeling as warm as she.

When they had left the train in Strong, Jake had taken one look at the heavy clouds and insisted she put on every stitch of clothing she had with her.

Jake had sold the mare in Council Grove and picked up his own horse in Cottonwood Falls where the sheriff had been looking after it. The gelding had come with them in the livestock car and Emily rode it now. She planned to give it to Christian. It wouldn't really make up for the horse Anson had sold or the money she had stolen but it was a start.

Jake turned to look at her and she smiled. Riding beside him, even in the snow, seemed more like home than the ranch did. She wouldn't be in any hurry to get there at all if she knew for sure that Jake had at least put on extra socks.

As they rode past the front of the big stone house, Emily lifted her head to gaze at the imposing structure. She blinked snowflakes off her lashes and shaded her eyes with a hand. "Lynnette?"

The figure on the balcony jumped. "Emily!"

Emily laughed as her sister-in-law turned and ran back into the house.

"What was she doing out there?" Jake asked.

Emily shrugged. "I bet she's sent her characters out in the snow and wanted to know how to describe it."

"We could help her there."

Christian was on his way from the barn by the time they rounded the house. He caught Emily's horse and lifted her down. Instead of spinning her around as she expected, he wrapped her in his arms and held her.

After a long moment he pulled away and gazed into her face. His blue eyes looked suspiciously bright.

"There were times when I wasn't sure I'd see you again, muffin," he said.

"You got my telegrams, didn't you?" Jake broke in.

Christian seemed reluctant to take his eyes off Emily, but finally he turned to Jake. "Yes, I got them." With one arm wrapped firmly around Emily he held the other out to Jake. "Thank you for bringing her back to me."

"I'm not exactly bringing her back," Jake said, shaking the offered hand.

Lynnette had joined them, and Emily caught her knowing smile as Christian asked, "What do you mean?"

"I've decided to keep her."

Emily beamed at Jake. After all his talk on the train, he faced her brother without flinching. She wanted to be at his side, but Christian had other ideas.

"Lynn, get her inside where it's warm. Jake and I'll take care of the horses."

"Oh, no you don't," Emily protested. "I'm going to the barn with you."

"I agree," said Lynnette. "I wouldn't miss this for the world."

Christian scowled down at Emily. "Bring the horses, Jake," he said without looking up. He turned Emily toward the barn. "I just want to talk to him about where you've been the last several days," he said in a low voice.

"I know Jake," Emily said quietly, glancing back to see that they were well ahead of him. "He's going to take the blame for everything, and you'll believe him like you always did."

Christian chuckled as they entered the barn. "Em, I never believed him."

Emily groaned. "Then don't give him a hard time."

Jake entered the barn, leading the two horses.

Lynnette walked beside him, looking quite pleased. She smiled up at her husband. "Why don't you and I take care of the horses and let Jake and his bride go inside?"

"Bride?"

"Bride," Emily confirmed, grinning up at her incredulous brother.

"Bride," Jake echoed, apology evident in his voice.

"Bride," Christian repeated in defeat.

Lynnette laughed, drawing Emily away from Christian and toward Jake. "You two get inside where it's warm." Her voice dropped to a whisper as she added, "Don't expect us in anytime soon."

Emily and Jake hurried through the falling snow. At the door, Jake drew her into his arms. He planted a tender kiss on her lips before he said, "I can't blame Christian for being upset."

"He's not upset, just surprised," Emily said, pretending to be cold as an excuse to snuggle closer.

"He wants the best for his sister, and an almost-broke deputy is hardly the best."

Emily shook her head. "I know the best when I find it." She drew him toward her for another kiss. "And I've found it."

* * * * *

Take 2 bestselling love stories FREE

Plus get a FREE surprise gift!

Special Limited-Time Offer

Mail to Harlequin Reader Service®

3010 Walden Avenue
P.O. Box 1867
Buffalo, N.Y. 14240-1867

YES! Please send me 2 free Harlequin Historical™ novels and my free surprise gift. Then send me 4 brand-new novels every month, which I will receive before they appear in bookstores. Bill me at the low price of $3.94 each plus 25¢ delivery and applicable sales tax, if any.* That's the complete price, and a saving of over 10% off the cover prices—quite a bargain! I understand that accepting the books and gift places me under no obligation ever to buy any books. I can always return a shipment and cancel at any time. Even if I never buy another book from Harlequin, the 2 free books and the surprise gift are mine to keep forever.

247 HEN CH7L

Name	(PLEASE PRINT)
Address	Apt. No.
City	State	Zip

This offer is limited to one order per household and not valid to present Harlequin Historical™ subscribers. *Terms and prices are subject to change without notice. Sales tax applicable in N.Y.

UHIS-98

©1990 Harlequin Enterprises Limited

Not The Same Old Story!

 Exciting, glamorous romance stories that take readers around the world.

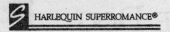 Sparkling, fresh and tender love stories that bring you pure romance.

 Bold and adventurous—Temptation is strong women, bad boys, great sex!

HARLEQUIN SUPERROMANCE® Provocative and realistic stories that celebrate life and love.

 Contemporary fairy tales—where anything is possible and where dreams come true.

HARLEQUIN® INTRIGUE® Heart-stopping, suspenseful adventures that combine the best of romance and mystery.

LOVE & LAUGHTER™ Humorous and romantic stories that capture the lighter side of love.

Look us up on-line at: http://www.romance.net   HGENERIC